D1135643

SUFFRAGETTE CITY

By the same author

Arms and the Woman

Kate Muir

SUFFRAGETTE CITY

MACMILLAN

First published 1999 by Macmillan

an imprint of Macmillan Publishers Ltd
25 Eccleston Place, London SW1W 9NF
and Basingstoke

Associated companies throughout the world

ISBN 0 333 74167 6

1 3 5 7 9 8 6 4 2

A CIP catalogue record for this book is available from
the British Library.

Typeset by SetSystems Ltd, Saffron Walden, Essex
Printed and bound in Great Britain by
Mackays of Chatham plc, Chatham, Kent

FOR BEN

Chapter One

You would think when someone makes the effort to haunt you that they might be more professional about it. Like they might have read a few guidebooks, dipped into some Victorian melodramatic literature, organized an acceptable ghost costume and stuff. But instead she snuck in without announcing herself properly and it was downhill from there. We're talking tainted advice, questionable decisions, interference on a big scale. I mean, I'm not complaining, but I should have known: just because she was dead didn't mean she was dead right.

I didn't really notice him either at first. Well, he wasn't an obvious suspect, was he? I remember that Tuesday when they both turned up – I believe the technical term is that fateful Tuesday – and I was feeling lousy. I was so foulmouthed and antsy that Nosmo said, 'Better out than in, Albertine,' and threw me out of the apartment.

I went down to the Cafe Babylon on Macdougal. The season of sweat and great sluggishness had been upon New York for days, it was ninety-five degrees outside and the cafe fans weren't working properly. My coffee stayed unnaturally hot and time slid by like mucus. I glanced up, saw my face in the mirror on the wall and it looked like thunder. Sort of purple. Not surprising, because that August I felt my life had truly bottomed out. I was right in the U-bend: my work stank, my room-mates stank, and I hadn't had sex for 187 days.

I sat there damply drinking coffee and glowering indiscriminately at the other customers. The heat had an equally unpleasant effect on the rest of Manhattan: the city roiled and swore, the murder rate tripled, and the garbage moved queasily as rats bulged the bags. Rich people had already taken the precaution of getting out of town to the beach, leaving behind a stew of the poor, the mad and the weird. I felt I rated in all three catgories.

Particularly the weird. In that last year I had noticed my behaviour becoming curiouser and curiouser, but I suspected this was merely part of a national if not worldwide trend. After all, I was not alone in floating about the city in eccentric getups looking for salvation or at least revelations. Everyone was cracking up that summer. A man wearing a placard wandered by the Cafe Babylon window, picking his nose and talking to himself. 'The End of the World is Nigh,' said his sign in front. 'Hell is Hot,' added the back informatively. Guys like that screaming damnation on street corners had become daily sights, and the heat only encouraged them to multiply like bacteria in the last few months of nineteen-ninety-fucking-nine. God, I was sick of the millennium by then. The whole business transfixed me with boredom. But I firmly believed that the world was on its way out – the sandwich-board man's only error, I felt, was to assume the apocalypse would be a one-day surgical strike on New Year's Eve rather than the slow putrefaction already evident all around. Life was hell already, and it was definitely hot.

With sandwiches on my mind, I ordered the Cafe Babylon special – roasted red peppers with melted Manchego cheese on semolina bread, the latest lettuce on the side. Bathed by the ceiling fans, I let my belly unfurl in the space between the chair and the marble table. I looked like a snake that had swallowed a basketball. I stared at my stomach for a while, felt it for kicks in a motherly manner, and got out my book by way of a prop. The waitress, wearing little more than a bra, arrived with the food. I asked her for Rolling Rock too.

'Are you sure you wouldn't prefer our homemade pink lemonade?' she said, looking righteously at the swelling beneath my Empire-line mini-dress, and then over at the sign on the wall which said, 'Health Department Warning: Consumption of alcohol by pregnant women has been shown to cause birth defects.'

'Quite sure. Just get me the beer,' I said.

Irritated, I braved the wall of heat, moved out to a sidewalk table and burrowed into my fake Hermès bag. I found some Camel Lights, seen so rarely that the very packaging induced nostalgia. Since smoking had been banned inside all public places throughout the New World, the home of tobacco, I had a duty to set an example by smoking whenever possible, as much as possible. I lit up, and checked in the window to watch the disgust sliding down the waitress's face. Two previously funky women at the next table suddenly acquired their mothers' looks of disapproval, whispered and eyed my belly in its cloud of smoke. I perked up. The scene was going according to plan. The beer battered down on the table, with a lipstick-smudged glass. I ignored it, slurped straight from the bottle, and got back into my paperback, *Birth And Your Baby – A Practical Yet Down-to-Earth Look At Parenting.* I looked up drugs and alcohol in the index, and it advised: 'alcohol enters the fetal bloodstream in high concentrations. Each drink a pregnant mother takes is shared with her baby.' I grinned and thought, Why drink alone?

It was fascinating the way that an oversized belly brought out the sanctimonious expert in everyone. It made strangers feel they could advise me, touch me, and ask personal questions of a veterinary nature. Fortunately, I was fond then of making a public spectacle of myself and willing to discuss the miracle of birth with almost anyone. Approval and disapproval were equally interesting reactions for me, and I stored them all for future use. I ordered another beer and the waitress gave me a death-ray stare.

Although the cafe clientele remained stagnant, the sun had moved west of MacDougal Street and lurked behind low yellow clouds. Though I never wore a watch then – well, I had no reason to – I knew it was time to go when the briefcases started to march past. Leaving the tip entirely in nickels and cents, I adopted the ponderous stride of a third-trimester elderly primagravida, and marveled once again at the dinosaurish sound of the title. August was a wicked month for anyone resembling a Zeppelin, and I could feel my blood start to simmer. I stopped at the King Kong Korean wash 'n' fold for my laundry, and the extra fifteen pounds brought me to boiling point as I lumbered home. On Broadway, I felt alternate vibes of sympathy and guilt from sweating people as they watched me struggle under the load. But, true to form, not one single New Yorker offered to help a pregnant woman in distress. Even the panhandlers kept their paper cups away.

Then something sniffed at my feet. I peered round the belly-and-bag mountain and saw a piebald mongrel with a cute black patch of fur around one eye. The dog was accompanied by a thirtysomething man with a matching pirate-style eyepatch. What is this? I thought. The Captain Hook fan club or what? The guy was not necessarily ugly, but he certainly looked sinister with the patch. I should have paid him more attention, because he was due to take the male lead in this story. Not a big part, admittedly, but an important one.

'Looks heavy. Wanna hand?' asked the dark stranger (what else could he be?), holding out his arms. Oddly, I remember my throat tightening when he fixed me with the one eye. He also smelled good – of fresh sweat rather than aftershave. I hate aftershave. Anyway, I gave him a slight smile and shook my head to ward him off. I was worried that he might be crazy – I certainly was at that time. I also thought he might be a pervert with a fetish for incredibly clean folded underwear.

'I'll manage. I'm nearly there, thanks,' I said.

The man and the dog took rejection well, and settled back to wait beside the lamp-post outside my apartment building at 666 Broadway. The man lit a cigarette, and the dog sat on its haunches and hung out its tongue. Their three eyes followed me as I pressed the buzzer on the armored door. Safely behind it, my step lightened and I ran into the rattling lift up to the tenth floor, the laundry bag hoisted high on my shoulder. The rent was oddly cheap for downtown, which just showed how religious most New Yorkers secretly were. The 666 number was, in fact, a godsend, so to speak, because everyone remembered the address. Postcards were abundant, but the downside was that various Swedes or Italians I had picked up on European holidays years ago kept turning up expecting bedding of either sort, and had to be disposed of mercilessly.

'Welcome, Madonna of Macdougal Street. You in a better mood now?' said Nosmo, undoing the locks. He eyed my belly. 'Thought you'd put a stop to that during the hot weather?'

'Well, people are more peculiar when it's sweltering, I didn't have anything better to do, and there's nothing like really suffering for your art.'

'Snapple?' said Nosmo, raising an eyebrow as though he had said something very sexy.

'Oh, peach iced tea, if we have it, please.'

His curly cherub head came back round the door. 'By the way, Albertine, your grandmother rang. Not the Michigan one, the crazy one from New Jersey. She's coming round at seven.'

As Nosmo headed for the kitchen I lifted up my dress, took the round orange cushion from my bodysuit and returned it to its correct place on the purple chaise-longue. There was a ring of sweat on my stomach.

I stared in fresh horror round the living room, which had been redecorated the week before and not by me. That's the problem with sharing an apartment with the lower echelons of the fashion glitterati. I flopped onto the mauve crushed-velvet platform and tried to avert my eyes from the candy-shaded mockette stools by the mini-bar at the other end of the loft. Eight long windows gave a fine view up Broadway and of the checkerboard of homeless mattresses on a roof opposite. The lemon walls made the room light and airy. It was not an ugly space. It was just that I felt I was trapped in a bowl of mixed sorbet.

'How come I have to live with these colors anyway?' I yelled out.

'Because, sweetheart,' said Nosmo, skipping in with the Snapples, 'your sort of artist doesn't earn a decent living. In fact, you don't earn anything at all. Now, if you did installations of decaying food or body parts, or miniatures of people's Schnauzers on request, instead of painting great pink whales of women, then you, too, could have your home featured in *Architectural Digest* and you would not have to submit to the admittedly curious tastes of Wanda Wong.' (Wanda was my other roommate. She designs clothes. She had the money we lacked for home decoration. Money is power.)

'You hate it too. Why didn't you say something to her? Why didn't you do something about it?' I moaned.

'I don't do, I am,' said Nosmo, who read too much Oscar Wilde to let an attempt at an epigram pass him by. But, in his case, the statement was true since he did little other than be a figure of import about town and write the Nosmo King column in a society magazine containing pull-out samples of hormone extracts for ladies with lines.

'Appearances, apart from my own, mean nothing to me,' he added, looking fondly at his muscle definition, helped by an unnecessarily tight purple V-neck T-shirt. (Nosmo was always trying to look hard and cool, and whatever he did, he still came out blond and mushy.)

He sat on the pink bar stool, sipped his Snapple and

7

stared at me for a while. 'You sort of suit that ripe pregnant look. Maybe you should actually get pregnant one day. I mean the simplest Freudian analysis would tell you—'

'Oh, fuck off. This stuff is, you know, sort of performance art or – I dunno – maybe trawling the psyches of the sort of women I paint. It's serious.'

Nosmo snorted, but he was interested despite himself. 'How d'you get into all that anyway?' he asked. (Amazing that you could wander around with a fake pregnancy for two months before your room-mates bothered to ask you why. That's how normal we were at 666.)

I lit a cigarette. 'Well, I started seeing how altering one part of my body affected people in the street, and painting the results. I started with fake breasts before the fake pregnancy. I was in the middle of doing a full-length painting of one of those big, flabby, trailerparky women. She was naked, but for red welts left on her skin by a too-tight bra and panties. I suddenly realized that I needed to really *know* as a skinny person what it was like to have enormous breasts – big hooters, gazunkas, snack-trays, bristols, bazooms – so I borrowed one of Wanda's bras—'

'One of those Olga 38DDs?' said Nosmo, with relish.

'As it happens, yes. I stuffed it with socks – of course the weight was wrong. The pull of a full can of Campbell's soup in each cup would have been more like it, but it gave me the idea. Out in the Village, I was pneumatic. New Men reverted to old, and old men reverted to dirty. Women went to buy Wonderbras.

Not one single person looked at my face. So I came back home, and cut the head off the canvas of the trailerpark woman. Much better painting.'

Nosmo started spinning round and round on his bar stool. 'So the fake pregnancy's the same thing?'

'Yeah, I'm collecting information for a new series of paintings called Confinement.'

'What?'

'That's the ancient term for labor and birth.'

'Uh,' said Nosmo. 'Do you think I could do that?'

'What, go round the city pregnant?'

'Naah. Get, like, an enormous codpiece and go around wearing it, or maybe wear skirts for a few weeks – Wanda's been designing these fabulous silk wrap-around skirts for men, you know – and then write it up for my column. The reactions and all that.'

I left him musing and went off to work in my room. I can only take Nosmo for so long.

My studio was enormous, with good light, and that's why I stayed there for so long despite my general incompatibility with Wanda and Nosmo, but over the years my bed had become barely visible among the detritus of paint-pots, wood, canvases and moldering gym gear. That evening the heat was still thick as the air-conditioning gasped under old grease and dust. I felt too lazy to lift a paintbrush (somehow that meant a final decision, something I was increasingly incapable of) so I sat down at the old door on trestles I used as a desk. I looked through the Polaroids I'd taken of myself in various pregnancy outfits, with bellies large and small. I took out my sketchpad and went back to a *Gray's Anatomy*-style drawing of a side view of the fetus in a

9

woman proudly thrusting out her huge belly. I dusted the charcoal baby away, and replaced it with a neat copy of Joe Camel from my Camel Lights packet, wearing his sunglasses but curled up in a fetal ball. He had his tiny thumb in his tiny mouth just like one of those Pro-Life posters.

I was sitting staring at the sketch when the buzzer went on the intercom. Rose, my grandmother, wanted me to help her get a trunk upstairs.

'What *is* that?' I said, when I saw her with the trunk on a baggage trolley. 'I have enough crap in my room already.'

'Ah, but you need this, Albertine. Dead interesting. Anyway I don't have the room for it.' Rose began shoving the enormous brown leather thing towards the elevator. She was wearing white shorts, which showed her wrinkly brown legs and baggy knees, a pink T-shirt with a lacy collar and matching pink Reeboks: an outfit I considered unseemly for someone of seventy-six. She'd also re-hennaed her hair an unrealistic orange.

We got the trunk upstairs into my room. (Of course, mysterious trunks play a significant role in your typical ghost story and I know now I should never have let the thing into the apartment in the first place.) Rose demanded a beer. We sat on the trunk and shared my last Camel.

'So?' I asked.

'Well, this is a wee bit of your heritage, so to speak, and you'll be glad of it one day,' said Rose, who retains an impenetrable Glasgow accent, although she has lived in New Jersey since she arrived in 1946 as a (pregnant) war bride. 'I brought this with me on the boat. I'm no' wasting it now. I gave it to your mother, but she'd no use for it. Don't think she ever opened the lid. She dropped it by me on her road to Florida last year, and I've been meaning to bring it over ever since.'

(Relative-wise, I infinitely prefer Rose to my parents, Carole and Albert Andrews, who have retired early to a condo on a swamp near Palm Beach, following their joint conversion to rabid Christianity. They drive in a half-timbered Bronco to worship at their local ChurchMall, and have such confidence in their spiritual future they have shed all trace of the past.)

But for Rose, I think, this trunk of history must have been a sort of security blanket for her when she left her home after the war and crossed the ocean with an American soldier she hardly knew. She proceeded to unlock it. Instead of the musty, mothbally smell I'd been expecting, there was a fresh, well, *human* scent. Rose pulled out a pile of Edwardian-looking clothes. 'These were my grandma's. Let me see what would Agnes be, now? Your great-great-grandmother's.' There were neatly ironed white blouses, velvet and bombazine skirts and dresses, and button-up shoes, all, I realize now, oddly well preserved. 'You could still wear some of these, you know. She was all skin and bone like you.'

'Who?' I said. 'What are you talking about?'

'Agnes McPhail. Don't tell me your mother never told you about her?'

'Nope.'

Exasperated, Rose stubbed out the cigarette and dumped three piles of letters on my lap, all tied neatly with black ribbon. The ink was dark blue, the paper white and crisp, the writing large and confident. 'There are nearly five hundred there. See? Your mother hasn't touched them. Och, well, her loss.' Rose put on her fake Chanel bifocals. 'Now, these are Agnes's letters from Glasgow to her sister in India, oh, from, let's see, 1899 to 1912. They start almost exactly a hundred years ago . . .'

I swallowed away a yawn. 'But why would I be interested in the letters of some woman who—'

'She's no' "some woman". She's your own flesh and blood, Albertine. Wait and I'll show you.'

From under the clothes and the Be-Ro Flour cookbook from the 1920s, Rose pulled a framed wedding photograph of my great-great-grandmother. Pretty shocking, because the face in the photo was, of course, mine. I didn't say anything to Rose, but I suspect she'd noticed too. And although the picture was black and white, the woman seemed to have the same long frizzy red hair as me, except hers was in a bun. 'The Rev. and Mrs D. McPhail, Blythswood Studios', it said on the back. Agnes must have been in her late teens or twenties, in a high-necked blouse closed with a cameo, a dark suit with a nipped waist, and a direct stare. At least a foot taller, her husband was mustached and old, his hair graying above dark beetling brows. He was wearing a minister's collar. His stance and his lips were both poker straight, while Agnes held a half-ironic smile. Behind them, a clumsily painted Scottish hillside faded into the distance.

I found my great-great-grandmother's knowing stare oddly compelling. I took the photo out and propped it on the shelf. Agnes was so like me it looked like I'd stuck my head through one of those Old Timers' cardboard costume cutouts you get at Coney Island. Nosmo would love it. To humor Rose, I said I'd look at the letters later, and chucked them back in the trunk, which I shoved in a corner, planning to use it as a seat – it wasn't exactly Vuitton, but it was pretty cool. Then I persuaded Rose to take me out for a Chinese on her sizeable widow's pension.

I got back at midnight a bit drunk, and crashed out on the bed. About three a.m. I was startled awake with that guilty, hangoverish feeling. A smell of perfume in the room made me feel nauseous. I reached out for the bottle of Evian by my bed, drank it all, and lay back down feeling like shit. Then it happened. I could hear breathing. Someone was breathing lightly at the end of the room. Waves of ice flowed up my spine, and the usual 'Woman Burgled, Raped, Tortured and Shot at 666' headlines went through my head. I could see no one, even though the room was only in half-darkness because of the street-lights outside. I stayed motionless for about five minutes, hoping the murderer would not spot that the bed was occupied among the canvases. But the breaths continued, slow and calm.

'When he comes to my bed at night,' started a barely audible voice with a Scottish accent much softer than Rose's, 'I want to be a true wife to him – God help me I do – but sometimes I feel the cold body of his first wife lies between us . . . I thought maybe that it would not matter with Duncan being fifty, and me nineteen . . .'

I shot out of bed and slammed on the light. There was a sudden silence and emptiness.

'Fucking trunk,' I said. I believe in confronting the

13

worst, so I walked up to it. It was still shut. I was about to lift the lid, when I realized the trunk was long enough to be a coffin. Close to throwing up, I forced my hands down on to the metal clasp and pulled. Inside, nothing had moved. The letters lay in their neatly tied piles, the cookbook, the clothes, the shoes, the photographs. 'Everything there for the afterlife,' I said to myself, or perhaps to her.

Back in bed, the sheets were hot and soggy with my own sweat. Of course, I couldn't get back to sleep, particularly since I had no intention of switching off the light. I was extremely annoyed, not just about being haunted, but being haunted in such a clichéd and traditional manner. There's no originality in my family, no wit. And the ghost-in-the-trunk device – well, it's just so obvious. I felt like ringing Rose to complain, but then I realized she'd probably deny it all and cast doubt on my sanity and sobriety. Still, after an hour's paranoid insomnia, I surrendered to the inevitable. 'Better the devil you know,' I said, and untied the black ribbon on the first pile of letters.

Chapter Two

Dowanhill Road, Glasgow

20 July 1899

Dearest Ishbel,

The town is awfully quiet just now with all the
yards and factories out for the Fair, and everyone has
gone 'doon the watter' and I am left behind. Even
Duncan has taken the steamer down to Rothesay and
Dunoon to hold Temperance meetings in the tents
again – he is not a man who likes his flock to stray too
far even when they are on their holidays, although I
think myself that they probably want a wee bit of time
off from the fire and brimstone and I have my doubts
that anybody will be wanting to join the Temperance
movement on their only fortnight off. Anyway these
next couple of days I will get a bit of peace and quiet
to myself for the first time since the wedding, because
Duncan says he thinks that in my condition and in this
heat I should not be travelling long distances and that
suits me fine.

Oh, Ishbel, I wish I had minded what you said
about marriage – I know I went into this with my eyes
open, and I feel it is my duty and my rightful place
helping this man of God, being at his side in the
ministry, but I feel I have lost part of myself, a part of
my strength or my soul. There is a weight pressing

15

upon me and I do not know what it is, and I think I would not be feeling this heaviness in my heart if I had gone off to the missionary school in Dundee. Mind you, I am sure I will get used to it, and Duncan will get used to addressing me as his wife and not thundering at me as though I was the whole congregation of Colquhoun church! My compensation is the parish work, and strangely enough, Duncan says my condition – I am three months gone now – precludes me from taking a steamer trip but it need not prevent me from doing that, and even if I can help in one or two cases of hardship or write to the Presbytery charities on behalf of a family, then I feel that my time is well spent.

Yesterday I went to visit a woman who had a room and kitchen in Partick, and her situation made a great impression on me about how uncharitable our charity can be. Her husband died last year of pneumonia, and she was left with two daughters and a baby to keep. One of her lassies, who would be about fourteen years old, has just started working at Porter's upholstery factory in Buchanan Street, but on a pittance, and the other is still at school. I wrote a month ago for Parish Relief for the woman, and she told me the inspector had come round to her home – she is very respectable; the linoleum is polished, and she had put a few flowers from the railway bank in a bottle – and he told her she had to sell most of her furniture before she qualified for the Poor Law. The poor woman was incensed, and she said to me, 'That means if I had been a spendthrift, a ne'er-do-weel, and dragged my family down, I would get help?' I did not know what to say to her. In the end we arranged for a wee 'loan' of her sideboard and table and settee to the neighbours across the close, and left her with a mattress in the bed recess for her and the baby, and another on the floor for the girls, and when the parish authorities come again next month, they will see she is needy, all right.

I like those days, being out and about in the town meeting people. It has opened a whole new world to me, just as India opened one to you. (Please tell Mr Dalyell how very delighted we are here about his promotion to chief engineer for the southern railways.) I was awfully shocked by what you said in your last letter about this village Mr Dalyell visited where dozens and dozens of children seemed to be boys, and he saw only two girls. I cannot believe what they said about keeping them inside – not in that weather, or the tales about being 'lucky' to have sons. I am sure you are right in saying that they must be letting those wee girls starve to death as if they were the runts of the litter, but I can hardly believe any mother could be so cruel to her own child, particularly not now as I await my own. Yet it seems that even here, sons are worth more than daughters – with Duncan it is 'my son this, my boy that', as though there were no chance of a female child being born. That sort of talk makes my spine shiver when I think of the terrible way his poor first wife died...

You know this wean, girl or boy, will be born, God willing, in the twentieth century, and it is a peculiar thought. I worry sometimes about Duncan being so much older; whether he will be here to be a father until the child is fully grown. There is a sadness about him that touches me, perhaps with him being a widower for

17

so long. When he comes to my bed at night I want to
be a true wife to him – God help me, I do – but
sometimes I feel the cold body of his first wife lies
between us. I thought maybe that it would not matter
that Duncan is fifty, and me nineteen, but I think it will
take a while before he sees me more as a wife than a
daughter. (He has three daughters, you know. The
younger ones, Margaret and Lily, will barely speak to
me and live with their aunt on the South Side, and have
done for the last ten years since their mother Effie died;
I understand that they do not approve of a step-mother
only three or four years older. Duncan rarely sees them.
Then there is the eldest, Kirsty, who is awfully kind and
a year older than me – imagine! She is learning nursing
in Edinburgh and has come over a few times to stay.
We have got on very well, odd as the situation is.)

I am sitting writing to you from the new tea-room
on Argyle Street, Miss Cranston's, having crumpets and
butter. It was not here when you left, and it is a sight to
behold: the walls are whitewashed and there are light
wooden chairs with backs like ladders, made by the
same Mr Macintosh who is doing the art school, and
purple designs in the plaster and wall hangings. The
result is a feeling of lightness *and* they do a good scone.
You can sit on your own here, and nobody will bother
you at all. I take the tram up here quite often, because
sometimes it helps to get out of the house and think. It
is not that there is anything wrong with the Manse – it
is perfectly comfortable, but (and please keep all this to
yourself) the presence of the first Mrs McPhail seems
to be in the old air and it is strangely oppressive.
Duncan will not have a thing changed from the way his

wife had it. When I took up the blinds in the sitting room, pulled back the heavy red velvet curtains and washed the antimacassars and cleared away a slew of china ornaments, souvenirs from Blackpool, dogs, shepherdesses and whatnot, he was beside himself. He said, 'Leave it as it is, woman. If it was good enough for Effie, it's good enough for you.' The walls must have been a greenery-yallery colour once but everything is browned by twenty years of tobacco smoke, and you need the gas on to see to read in most of the daytime. I hope I have murdered the aspidistra by neglect, but they are sturdy plants and hard to do away with.

Send me news of Jennie and wee Allan and the baby. Tell me how you are all doing, and will you also put in the address of where you are going in the hills for the rest of the summer, because the post is terrible and I might as well send my letters ahead of you this year. My best to Mr Dalyell,

Your affectionate sister,

Agnes

Chapter Three

' "Fashion," ' I said reading from one of Agnes McPhail's letters, ' "is a sort of shuttlecock for the weak-minded of both sexes to make rise and fall." There we have it, I think, Wanda.'

'Just die,' said Wanda, continuing to draw.

We were sitting in the kitchen. Wanda was trying to sketch designs, and I was still reading the complete works of my great-great-grandmother Agnes, which went on and on. I'd been up half the night with them, though fortunately not with her. The correspondence varied, irritatingly, from dull to gripping, because you never knew when some juicy little chunk about her relationship with grumpy Duncan was going to pop up in the pious prose. Besides, if someone starts haunting you, you want to find out why, or at least who you're dealing with.

The breakfast table was covered that day with bits of Wanda's fat-free sugar-free salt-free bran muffin and swatches of hairy fabric. 'Do we have to have the mohair actually on the table so I get little furballs in my granola, or could you put it somewhere else like the floor?' I asked.

Wanda ignored me. 'She's right about the shuttle-cock. I feel like I've been battered to pieces and I've got three more weeks of this,' she said.

'I don't think that's quite what Agnes meant,' I answered, squeamishly poking the mohair samples away with a knife. Wanda can be a bit obtuse sometimes. 'I think it was a reference to the ephemeral nature of your trade.'

Wanda was designing her spring collection for next year and she looked terrible. Hanks of dirty hair were held back by two brown rubber bands. Her nails were ragged. Her skin had broken out in sympathy and she had retreated for the last few days into graying sweats and sneakers. You would not clock her as 'Best New-comer' from last year's Council of Fashion awards. In fact, were she on a street-corner, you might give her a quarter.

'What's wrong with all those?' I asked, looking at the garbage can, which was overflowing with scrunched-up drawings of ill-dressed stick-women. (I like Wanda's clothes designs as much as I like her taste in interior decoration, but I can't say that.)

'I can't do this shit any more. I mean, everyone else is doing this oh-so-postmodern streamlined stuff in metallics and polyplastics and neoprene and 2000 AD T-shirts. How obvious can you get? If I hear the word millennium again, I'm gonna bite whoever's used it.'

'You could go retro like before,' I said, sniffing the milk cautiously to determine its age – my room-mates were not big on hygiene. The year before, Wanda had based her collection on Vita Sackville-West's gardening clothes and hats redone in Dayglo colors – Bloomsbury on acid. The Bloominescent collection, as it was unfor-tunately labeled, enabled her to open Wanda Wong

21

Soho, and, much to my regret, redecorate *my* living room.

'Don't have any ideas . . .' she wailed.

'What about my new guru in all matters?' I said, waving the letters, suddenly pleased that we might get something useful out of Agnes McPhail.

'Thought she'd just expressed deep contempt for all fashion and frippery?' said Wanda.

'On paper, yes, but in real life she appeared to be hip in the late Victorian sense of the term. Well, maybe it's not all her stuff in the trunk, but there are some exceptionally weird items in there. Come rip them off.' I had told Wanda about the trunk and the letters, but I had not mentioned the late-night phantasmic visitation.

Granola in hand and humming 'Soldier, soldier, won't you marry me?' with particular emphasis on the lines 'And *up* she went to her grandfather's chest / And brought him a coat of the very, very best / And the soldier put it on,' I led the search for inspiration down the corridor to my room. I pulled out a dress of velvet and gabardine with curious underskirts and handed it to Wanda, who laid it flat on the floor to make sense of the silhouette. There were also some hats squashed out of shape bearing the remains of ribbons and cockades, button-up gloves for seemingly child-size hands and a yellow parasol. A fox-fur stole squinted from one glass eye. Wrapped carefully in tissue paper, there was a silk Votes For Women sash, in purple, green and white. Wanda grunted with excitement at the sight.

'What's that?' she asked.

'Suffragette sash. The colors represent Give Women Votes or something: green, white and violet,' I said. Wanda knows even less history than I do, thanks to our quality schooling by the state of New Jersey. She can barely remember the name of the last President. 'Hey, look at this. Seems like they were into selling themselves with souvenirs and logos way ahead of their time. Look. They even did matching carrier-bags.'

'Never knew that,' said Wanda yawning. 'Suffragettes were never what you might call a big thing for me.'

Wanda may have been bored with the background, but she knew when an idea was worth stealing. She went back clutching a pile of clothing and began scribbling a calf-length circular skirt made of about a dozen vertical Votes-for-Women sashes, fluttering into strips from just above the knee, the words giddily repeating. Then she did a short, flippy skirt in the same pattern with violet and green pencils. She added an early motoring hat held on with a chiffon scarf to balance the figure. 'Fab,' I said, over her shoulder. 'You owe me ten per cent of the profits.' Wanda grinned cheesily and continued to draw lime green and lilac fake-fur stoles, with snouts and little button eyes.

I dug in behind the *New York Times*. We drank more Amaretto-flavored coffee. 'Says here that you can adopt a Chinese baby for six thousand dollars plus airfare, Wanda.' (Wanda is half Chinese herself. She was thirty-six then, and her biological clock was ticking on loud-speakers.) 'They've got lots of spares in orphanages. Would solve your present insemination crisis. And it would match as an accessory.'

23

'Ooh, cute,' said Wanda, breaking off from her drawing to look at the photograph of a chubby-cheeked baby, tiny dark eyes peering from a red silk padded jacket. 'I'd love one of them.'

'They only have girls available, but you won't mind that.' I read aloud from the paper: ' "The ratio of male to female births is a hundred and twenty to a hundred, showing more disparity each year. By the year 2000 there will be eighteen million more males than females in China." Ooh, lucky them. "Much of this is blamed on the illegal practice of doctors telling women the sex of their children after ultrasound examinations. For a bribe equivalent to twenty-five dollars, the family can discover sex, and thereafter thousands, perhaps millions, of female children are aborted. The Chinese single child per family policy also results in many of the girls born being abandoned outside orphanages." That's funny. This is just what I was reading in one of those letters about India a hundred years ago. Probably hasn't changed at all there either.'

'Let me see,' said Wanda, grabbing the newspaper (a small act that changed her life). The second picture showed forty or so cots in one dingy room with a bored woman sitting at a table nursing a cup of tea instead of the babies. 'Wouldn't it be much better to save one of these little things from a horrible orphanage than go to a sperm bank and reproduce some generic nineteen-year-old jock of a medical student?'

Wanda had long ago given up on finding a living, breathing man to father her possible child. She had not had a steady boyfriend in four years. All that was on offer were emotional offcuts from unhappily married men. As a second generation half-'n'-half, as she referred to herself, Wanda had little interest in the traditional types in the Chinese community, and they had less in her. She claimed most white men suffered from 'geisha psychosis' but never quite explained what that entailed. 'Imagine the girl shortage when all these Chinese kids grow up. It'll be the opposite of New York. They'll all have to take at least two husbands. Dee-lightful,' she said.

The ratio of single women to single men in New York was at least two to one, three to one if you figured in homosexuality. The ratio of single women to single men with faintly human characteristics was more like fifty to one. Both Wanda and I could testify personally to this fact. After all, by then I hadn't had sex for 188 days.

Of course, Wanda wasn't really interested in plain old sex. She wanted reproductive sex. She asked me if I wanted a baby too.

'No way,' I said. 'I can't look after myself never mind someone who isn't old enough to order pizza by phone. And I'm so absentminded I might leave a baby behind in a bar or a park, like I do with my sketchbook all the time.'

'You're just too young,' said Wanda. (I was thirty.) 'Once you're my age you get so desperate you want to wear an "I Am Ovulating – Donors Welcome" sign in the middle of each month. Mind if I keep that?' I handed over the paper and Wanda cut out the article with her sewing scissors, folded it carefully three times and tucked it in her portfolio. She began drawing more purple and green figures.

25

As usual, when someone else shows any signs of being creative, it immediately stymies me. It brings out jealousy, guilt and laziness in equal proportions and reminds me of those long days in the back row at Parsons art school, when I was paralyzed with fear. I decided to leave Wanda to it, gathered up a small rucksack of sketchbooks and smelly gym clothes, and headed out for the park.

Park was an over-hopeful term for Washington Square that August, since there was nothing green about it. The leaves were pale beige with layers of dust and pollution, and the grass was worn down to grim patches of yellow stubble. I waded through the glutinous air towards a shady bench by the dog run, got out my newspaper and tossed the Business and Sports sections aside. A bunch of mangy squirrels were behaving very oddly, running round the base of a tree, biting each other, and making loud chattering noises. I consider city squirrels to be little more than rats with fat tails, and usually ignore them. But these ones were being particularly aggressive. Two benches down, a large polyester-clad woman, clearly a tourist, was feeding them bread from a paper bag and making annoying cootchie-cootchie sounds. The squirrels were fighting over the bread in a most unnatural manner. Then one approached the woman's bloated ankle, and sank its teeth right in. She screamed and leaped up, shouting hysterically about rabies, and ran towards a taxi. I watched this with some delight, and then looked at the ground around the tree. There were discarded plastic crack vials scattered everywhere, with tiny traces of the drug left on the stoppers. The squirrels were crackheads.

Good action so far this morning, I thought. I often selected this particular bench by the dog run for observation, not of the dogs, but of the behavior of the human owners. Next to the West Side dog run by the Natural History Museum, Washington Square was the hottest, safest pick-up joint in Manhattan. A single man with a dog has to be someone who *cares*, went the reasoning of those on maternity hunt. If he can pooperscoop with a plastic bag in public, it's only a short step to baby wipes and Pampers. Last year Wanda had even bought a Shar Pei of exquisite ugliness in order to hobnob with suitably sensitive male pet parents. For some reason Maud, her dog, was constantly sexually harassed by larger dogs, and Wanda became an object of mirth for other owners. She resold the Shar Pei three weeks later after it pissed on her lap in public.

I was content to remain as audience outside the fence and watch the dogs run in circles, incomprehensibly impervious to the heat. I thought if I opened my mouth wide, hung my tongue out and panted canine-style, it might be cooler. I was trying this out when a voice behind said, 'D'you mind if I take a look at your Sports section?'

'No. Go right ahead,' I said automatically, wondering if I'd been noticed in mid dog-pant.

The man was maybe thirty-five and wore sunglasses, a white shirt and chinos. He had a big Roman nose and dark hair slicked back by sweat or some kind of Brylcream. He sat lankily down on the bench, separated for decency by a wrought-iron arm, and took up the Sports section. Then a small dog settled beneath his feet. I snuck another look from behind the Living section. The dog had a black patch of fur round one eye, one ear up and the other down. No question, it was the dog from last night, and its master had replaced his pirate patch by aviator sunglasses with leather flaps at the sides. Ohmigod, I'm being stalked, I thought. He's obviously a serial killer and, worse still, he knows where I live. Maybe he followed me. Or else I'm being picked up. Or possibly this is a coincidence – he just lives near me. The guy – and he could, after all, have been a sensitive pet parent – smiled at me, picked up his dog and dropped it over the fence where it joined the circling pack of larger dogs and exuded a great deal of attitude considering its size. Generally, I find dogs – particularly small, sly dogs – offensive, but not when accompanied by a man with slim hips and good bone structure. (My taste has been heavily influenced by too much life drawing.) I decided to be forward.

'What's it called?'

'Spot.' The man sat back down, grinning.

'S'pose it had to be that,' I said.

'Yeah, well, all the dogs in this run, they have proper dog names like Jack, Rover, and Shep. This is what you might call your biker dog run. Dogs have to be big, like Labradors or Alsatians, or small and tough, else they don't make it socially.'

'You're right. I've never seen any poodles or Pekes.'

'Nah. No rat-sized designer dogs with French names here. They go down to the private dog run on Mercer.' He took out a packet of Marlboro Lights and offered me one. So rarely do two smokers meet in New York that I nearly shouted, 'Hallelujah.' Instead we lit up conspiratorially and I asked, 'It's a private dog run like private school?'

'Oh, yeah, fee-paying and all. It's two hundred seventy-five dollars a year, I think now, and there's a waiting list and they check out you and your dog for compatibility, i.e. wealth, and you have to supply a vet's certificate.' He nodded over at the run. 'See that woman with a spaniel there? She was rejected. She's been traumatized for weeks.'

'So's her dog,' I said, pleased. The spaniel cowered behind a tree, and rolled over pathetically when other dogs came to sniff it.

We talked for about half an hour. I quite liked him on the whole, because he took a suitably dark view of the world, bit like myself, but I found it uncomfortable not seeing his eye(s). It was sort of like watching television with the sound turned down – it felt wrong. He told me his name was Leonardo Ianucci, almost as stupid as my own. We reckoned neither Leonardo nor Albertine were appropriate names for the biker dog run.

'My father's was Albert and he added the ending,' I told him. 'In fact, it's my middle name. My first name, which I hate, is Senga. They invented it in the forties after too many people were called Agnes, so they reversed the letters.' (Probably another reason why I'm a prime target for hassling by dead relatives.)

Anyway, by then this Leonardo guy was staring at me strangely. 'I hope you don't mind me asking, but do you have a sister or someone who is the reverse, or rather the same as you, except very pregnant indeed? I thought I saw someone with long red hair like you yesterday on Broadway.' He stretched out, in the way large felines do when playing with their prey.

I was hoping he'd forgotten, or not connected. I considered lying, but then I realized I was blushing. (Blushing is an ability most people sensibly lose in their teens. Not me.) So I confessed. 'No, that was me. It's an experiment I'm conducting this summer.' I thought I'd blown it, but he didn't even seem surprised.

'Uh-huh?' he said, awaiting a better explanation, his mouth in an ironic twist. 'You got some kind of fake belly? I've seen them in a magazine once. They had these things called 'empathy bellies' for fathers: heavy, made of rubber, guaranteed to bring on a sore back and make you piss every ten minutes.'

'Mine's a cushion,' I said, and explained my painting project in an overflow of words in case he stopped me before it made at least some sense. I did not mention the giant breast experiments for reasons of propriety.

'I get what you mean. I've been in Rikers for six months,' he said casually.

I nearly screamed. He was, as suspected, a psychopath fresh from prison. The dog was merely bait. Behind the sunglasses were the eyes of a killer.

'You have to experience that kind of thing as though it really was you before you can begin to represent it,' Leonardo continued cheerfully. I remained in rictus. *He may have a gun*, I thought.

'I've been doing this film on Rikers Island, and until I spent a whole week, day and night, on the cell block, I had no idea whatsofucking-ever of how awful it was. Everyone's HIV positive, apart from the little guys who are about to become HIV positive if they're not careful. I've got four hundred hours of tape to cut down to two hours, and it really should go out in real time – all four hundred tedious hours – to show how foul the place truly is. That's why I'm here at the dog run, avoiding dealing with it. And the air-conditioner's gone in the cutting room, so what's the point?' He looked sweetly dejected, almost sulky, although it was hard to tell without seeing his eyes. I had taken off my own sunglasses, a ridiculous winged fifties' pair, in hope of encouraging him, but there was no parallel reaction.

'So what sort of guys do you meet in Rikers? Don't they hate being filmed?'

'Not if they think they can use it to their advantage, or they just plain don't care. Some kind of live there. I mean, they don't seem to mind. There's this guy who came in twice while I was there, and says it was his sixteenth sentence. What he does is he stays out for about a month, but then he gets sick of homeless shelters and stuff.' Leonardo slid closer along the bench. 'So he dresses up in this smart jacket and tie he keeps in his bag, and goes to some real fancy restaurant. Last one was Smith and Wollensky's steak house. He has a huge meal – he likes shrimp cocktail and rare sirloin and claret and a vintage brandy to finish – and then he tells the waiter, real polite, that he can't pay and waits quietly at the table until the police come to arrest him. Then it's a quick hearing and back to Rikers for thirty days. He says the food in prison's pretty good. He likes the French fries and the cherryade.'

'Is he fat?'

'Enormous.'

'What are your prisoner's other recommended restaurants?'

'Well, he likes a classy joint, but not too fancy. He thinks the end of the world is coming . . .' I raised my eyes skywards in irritation. '. . . and he wants to eat in all of New York's great old restaurants before it does. He goes to Sparks in Manhattan, or Peter Luger's in Brooklyn – he actually books sometimes. He thought Le Cirque was a bit "chi chi", his own words. Then he likes the Sea Grill at the Rockefeller Center, and he will make an exception and go slightly downmarket for a good rib joint.'

There was silence. I smiled at him. 'You hungry?'

'Yeah. Haven't eaten anything yet. You want to get something?'

Leonardo whistled and Spot ran panting to the fence. He put him back on the lead, and we walked off to a coffee-shop.

'Can we sit outside for the dog?' Leonardo asked, but I wondered if it was so he could keep on his sunglasses. There was reddish skin in the socket just under the glasses. Maybe he had been in a fight. What else was under there? Glass eye? No eye? Yellow wolf eye? It would have been more comfortable to know, but I couldn't ask outright.

We positioned ourselves among the exhaust fumes under a Pellegrino umbrella. The dog got a saucer of water. Leonardo ordered two eggs over easy, hash browns, sausage and a beer in the way that men do, and I ordered a Caesar salad and the fruit plate and white wine in the way that women do. But apart from menu selection, we were not behaving as a typical man and woman on a first date. In fact, I didn't feel this was a date at all. I detected no tension, no fear, and no desire to run to the bathroom to check that my dirty bra strap wasn't poking out from my sundress. There was something curiously reserved and non-threatening about this guy (should have paid more attention to that, too) – perhaps it was the lack of eye-contact. He was more like – how can I explain? – an *ex*-boyfriend than a future candidate. I was attracted to him, but it also seemed like we'd fallen back into the middle of a comfortable conversation we'd started years ago, and we might, or might not, finish it that day. It didn't matter.

Our talk was stalled by an overwhelming joint desire to check out the scene at the next table, where a full-scale first date was occurring among members of the younger generation. A man and a women, both exquisitely beautiful, both in their early twenties, were holding hands and staring at each other in rapture. She was still wearing, at noon, a black strappy beaded evening dress, vast earrings and last night's makeup.

'They've obviously been to his place last night because he's got a clean shirt,' said Leonardo in my ear. The newly bedded couple pushed aside their breakfast, barely touched, and began to consume one another instead. Clearly, it had been a long night, but not long enough.

'So what do you do for a living, then?' said the young woman to the young man when they extracted their tongues.

We tried to suppress any signs of laughter.

'Awesome,' I said. 'Imagine not asking that for twenty-four hours. Myself, I prefer a full interview, two references and their mother's home phone number before I even consider the sex question nowadays.'

'So you want my resumé?' said Leonardo, raising his eyebrows.

I started to smile, but then I saw my double reflection in his sunglasses, and it gave me the creeps. I decided to say nothing.

In the uncomfortable silence, the dog started whining and snapping. I looked round, but I couldn't see anything – just the silvery heat haze across Union Square. Then, out of the shimmer in the middle of the tarmac, a woman emerged in full Victorian or Edwardian gear or whatever, with a long skirt, a high-necked white blouse and a straw boater. It was either Mary Poppins or, more likely, Agnes McPhail, desert-mirage style, out to ruin my attempt at a date. I couldn't believe it. I put it down to the wine and the beginnings of sunstroke. But then Agnes walked over and had the audacity to sit down at one of the empty chairs at our table. She didn't even bother to introduce herself.

'Wouldn't trust him,' she began abruptly, pointing at Leonardo and shaking her head. 'I would steer clear of that one, if I were you, dear. More complicated than he looks.'

My mouth hung open. Leonardo appeared to have noticed nothing, but the dog was going berserk.

'What's with you, Spot?' He pulled the lead. 'I'll just take him round the block for a piss. Back in a minute,' he said, and went off.

'Jesus,' I said, hiding my mouth behind my hand,

because it was clear to me that no one else could see Agnes, and I was a crazy person talking to thin air. 'What do you mean by doing that? I'm busy here. I'm in the middle of what I'll have you know is a rare lunch with a man.' I stopped. What was I doing even talking to this person? 'Who are you anyway?'

She smiled smugly. 'You know quite well who I am,' she said. I stared at her. She seemed much the same age as me – not the gauche nineteen-year-old of the first letters I'd read. She was skinny, too, same rusty hair, but in reality (whatever that was), her teeth were smaller and her features finer than mine, being undiluted by New Jersey DNA. 'Just felt it was my duty to warn you,' she continued. 'God knows, someone's got to keep an eye on you . . .'

'Oh, come off it. Nobody does this sort of corny thing any more. You're raving. Or I'm raving. Or—'

'You need to get yourself sorted out. I want to talk to you,' said Agnes, folding her arms. 'Here you are, with all the opportunities in the world and you're wasting time with men like that, sitting around doing nothing all day.'

I jumped up, threw twenty dollars on the table, and stormed off. I took one look back, and Agnes seemed to be fading into the heat haze behind me. Like the Cheshire Cat out of *Alice in Wonderland*, all that remained was the shadow of her stupid boater.

Leonardo was coming back with the dog. 'Sorry, I've got to go. I'm late for a meeting with someone,' I said, panicking.

'Oh.' He looked insulted. The dog cocked its leg unpleasantly close to my feet.

35

'So I'll see you around, then? Your phone . . .?' he asked uneasily.

'Um, yes,' I cut in. 'You know where I live.'

There was a bodyshaped shimmer in the air beside us.

'Gotta go,' I said, starting to run.

Chapter Four

Dowanhill Road, Glasgow

17 November 1899

Dearest Ishbel,

You may moan about your monsoon season and your roasting winds, but there is a great brown fog shrouding Glasgow today that would make you eat your words about missing home. There is a stench of rot and mildew in every room of the Manse, and a long damp patch has begun to grow down the sitting-room wall. Oh, I know I have nothing to complain of compared to the poor folk in the tenements across the way with half the slates missing, but this seems to soak right into my bones. The place is so dreech, one day fog, the next rain coming down like stair rods, and it has clung on for over a week, and last Sunday you could barely make Duncan out – and his voice is plenty loud – over the coughing and wheezing in the congregation. I wish you could hear Duncan give a sermon, for it is his way with words that drew me to him.

He is no ha'penny Revivalist, like the dozens of chancers who have descended on the town in the last few years demanding donations and raising tents and false hopes, and he does not bring his flock to the point of hysteria or flatter them with sops and promises of 'the beautiful blue vaults of heaven and hosts of angels'.

As for the singing, it is proper, with solid psalms and hymns and none of that catchy self-satisfied dross from the Moody and Sankey hymnbook. No, the church of the Reverend McPhail is one of thundering denunciations of wickedness and worldliness, the real Gospel of Christ — I often think he would make a fine actor when he seems to become the Prophet in the pulpit, and when he re-creates Biblical scenes, they are like photographs in my head.

His theme in the last weeks has been the second advent of Christ. He has been reading passages from Revelations, but the problem is that the congregation has probably been reading those penny dreadfuls about Nostradamus and the apocalypse that are everywhere suddenly like some kind of madness. Duncan preaches salvation, his black brows raised and his eyes flashing: 'For without are dogs and sorcerers, and whoremongers, and murderers and whosoever loveth and maketh a lie,' he shouts, and we shiver in the darkened pews.

Strange as it may seem to be drawn to a man through his sermons — although he is handsome with it — Duncan told me something even stranger when we were sitting in front of the fire the other night. He said he got the notion to propose to me after I organised a petition to have a lead factory shut down which was on church property. You would not credit it, yet he said he came to admire me for my efforts and thought I would make him 'a fine wife and companion'.

I do not think I told you about this at the time, but a church down from Colquhoun, although in the same parish, was renting out its old hall to a lead processor. I have no idea exactly what went on in that factory, but the fumes and pollution from the lead meant that plants on the window-sills withered from the poison, budgies and parakeets all died at once and it was said that even the rats feeding off the middens were dying. I thought if it was doing that to animals it must have been doing equally terrible things to people, and the local doctor had been dealing with all sorts of curious complaints – all this on Church property too, with the Presbytery making a profit from the suffering. Despite the petition from a couple of hundred parishioners, they allowed the factory to stay for another year, not the most Christian of decisions. Anyway, it was that which started Duncan pleading his cause with me, until eventually I gave him the answer he wanted.

The first months together were not easy, as you know since we have settled down. Somehow, with knowing him first as the minister, I felt I should be calling him Reverend or Mr McPhail as though he were a stranger, yet there I was sharing his home. Since he had been a widower for these past ten years, and his girls only disturbed his peace when their aunt and uncle were away on holiday, he had become set in his ways. Dinner at half past twelve, tea at six o'clock, reading in his study from seven every evening, bed at ten, fish on Friday, roast on Sunday, bath once a week: those were the immovable pillars of his life, strongly supported by Mrs Minto, his housekeeper and cook for all that time. They treated me like an invading army at first and, of course, the way *we* ran our house bore no relation to the ancient traditions here so I was at a complete loss. Mrs Minto was quite frosty to begin with until one day she caught me crying when she came back from doing the messages, and relations have been easier since, particularly with the baby coming.

All that makes it sound as if I am not fond of Duncan, but of course I am, and there is nobody but you, Ishbel, that I can confide in so honestly. He is a good-hearted man, and he cares desperately about his vocation and I respect that. Yet you married a man much your own age and went about building a life and family together, while I feel I have to knock part of this household down before there is space for me, and only now, almost a year into our marriage do I feel there is room to stretch just a wee bit. Well, Duncan can be all bluster, but underneath there is a pliability about him which I never expected.

Take the matter of reading novels: Duncan considered this, as do many still in the church, to be frivolous if not blasphemous and told me I was polluting my mind with rubbish. Yet for me reading is one pleasure, one need that I could not give up, and I vowed not to be forced into reading in secret as though it were some sin. So I defied him. He would sit reading his tracts and lives and the *Christian Herald* (which, by the way, sometimes provides much entertainment with an extraordinary page of prophecies by a Reverend Dr Baxter where he calculates the date of the millennium by comparing texts from Scripture) and I would sit with my wicked novels. Then one night, when I was reading this terrifying new book by H. G. Wells called *The War of the Worlds* about brutal creatures from the planet Mars trying to destroy the earth – I must send you it – I felt strange and went up to bed. I came down for some milk an hour later, and Duncan was completely engrossed in my book. He jumped guiltily when I came in. 'I was just seeing what sort of foolishness people are reading nowadays,' he said. Often, I find my bookmark has mysteriously moved a few pages back or forward in the night.

Talking of foolishness, you were asking me about the latest fashions here, but I am sorry to say that news of the latest thing in London probably reaches Scotland about the same time it reaches India. And you know what I have always said about fashion being a shuttlecock for the weak-minded of both sexes to make rise and fall. Still, I am enclosing the *Ladies' Magazine* from last month in hope that it meets your requirements. I have discovered there is one distinct advantage in being heavy with child: I have discarded corsets and stays and those high-boned collars, which used to rub raw places on our necks. How I am going to reach down to button my boots soon, I just do not know. But I can be as unfashionable as I like, and nobody blinks an eye, so I have taken to a large brown velvet jacket, a man's, I think, which one of Duncan's family left behind, and I wear it nearly every day about the house.

I am still awaiting the photograph you promised of the weans, and I would not mind one of yourself in your new muslin that you were so keen on. The Christmas parcel should be with you soon – I sent it last month.

Your affectionate sister,
Agnes.

Chapter Five

25 August 1999

So you tell me. What the hell was this uptight religious zealot doing making unasked and unwanted visits to my life, which had been going perfectly badly without her anyway? What on earth had I to do with a rainy grim Glasgow filled with sermons and apocalypses and husbands who think dull novels are dirty? More to the point, what was she doing walking into New York coffee-shops in broad daylight? You're not even hearing the half of it. I mean, I was having to read *all* her bizarre letters, never mind just the ones I'm sandwiching here for you. And, let's face it, there was enough weird in my average day already without this inconvenient addition.

Take what I was doing a week later. I was deep in the pre-Raphaelite section of the Metropolitan Museum of Art, lurking casually by a Rossetti. I was wearing a substantial black straw hat to set off my long red hair and pale skin, just like those of the woman in the painting conveniently nearby. I have to admit I couldn't keep my hands off those clothes in the trunk either, due mostly to my extreme poverty. So I was wearing one of Agnes's dresses, a flowing peach lounging gown, maybe it was a nightgown – whatever, it was not in the least Presbyterian and it fitted perfectly, of course. I only just managed to squeeze the pregnancy cushion underneath.

Don't ask me why I was doing this stuff – maybe it was more a Prozac placebo than research – but I used to spend hours hanging round the pre-Raphaelite section in full costume just talking to people. Some of them thought I was a guide, and tourists will speak to anyone because they don't know any better. That day, a pug-faced German asked me if I was related to the model in the Rossetti painting. I said yes. He took a photo of me.

The Impressionist and pre-Raphaelite sections were pretty good places to look fecund and the same costume served for both, but I drew the line at the Flemish masters: the white corrugated doily collar and the black barrel dress were not my scene. In general, fecundity-wise, the Met had plenty of Madonna and Child, but a major shortage of Madonna-with-Child, which was curious, I thought, since women had been pregnant on almost a full-time basis for the last nineteen centuries. (I'll tell you who does good pregnancies: Vermeer. Lots of fertile bulges in his paintings but then he had eleven children.) Anyway, I resolved to fill the historical gap by painting a graphic Virgin Birth Without Epidural, so the day's work was done – inspiration had occurred.

After that, I moved down the stairs from the gallery with what I like to think was a ship-like dignity, belly out ahead, enjoying my last voyage as a gestating woman since by then I had plenty of material for the Confinement project. I was basically at the Met for the air-conditioning and some time off – well deserved since I had spent the morning painting *trompe l'oeil* Victorian toys on the bedroom wall of some over-nurtured Park

Avenue two-year-old. (Back then, I painted murals-to-order in order to eat.) So I had time to wander around. By the Temple of Dendur, an item cadged from the Egyptians during the building of the Aswan Dam, I found a lunch-time concert about to begin. Under the glass pyramid, which gave the audience the views but fortunately not the late-summer heat of Central Park, was a string quartet. I took a seat in the audience, noting that it consisted of the chronic long-term unemployed rich – my typical mural clientele. I identified Oscar de la Renta, Gucci and Chanel among the casual little outfits on Upper East Side ladies in my row. Right next to me was a fey young man in what appeared to be a cricketer's garb and tortoiseshell glasses. 'Overdressed, overeducated and underworked,' I observed of the crowd.

'Excuse me?' said the fey man politely.

'I was just saying how much I adore Mahler,' I told him. 'I'm here to expose my unborn child to culture. Apparently they can hear music in the womb.'

'Fascinating. I didn't know that. Are there composers who work particularly well?' His pebbly eyes fixed upon me.

I clamped my teeth together to keep my face straight and then drew a deep breath. 'Well, I find the baby seems to move around inside to Chopin, Debussy, Satie, you know, anything quite light.' I noticed the man's eyes were now following a red wine stain (deposited the night before) down my – well, Agnes's – gown. I kept going: 'The baby's not so good on Wagner or Bach. Perhaps babies have high-frequency hearing like dogs?'

'Mmmn. Fascinating. I wouldn't know,' said the man, opening his program to avoid further conversation with me, this stained madwoman. He sat twitching edgily until the music started up.

He looked at me even more peculiarly when, after the concert, I started picking Met visitors' identity buttons off the floor and stuffing them in my bag.

Outside the museum, New York was still a putrid swamp, as it had been since July. I had taken to coming uptown for my jaunts, partly because of Central Park, and partly because I was avoiding Washington Square with its proximity to the film-cutting studio and Leonardo Ianucci. I didn't want to be caught hanging around looking hopeful on park benches, an activity I hadn't indulged in since I was in knee-high socks, and I was embarrassed by the way I'd behaved last time. So I tried to get my quota of chlorophyll in Central Park instead, because if you only see Tarmac and concrete all summer, it makes you kill close relatives. That's why they invented the Hamptons. In the park that day, a lamentable number of overweight people of both sexes had taken their tops off, which almost put me off plans for a Nathan's hot dog. Hot dogs were not a regular part of my diet, but I figured looking pregnant allowed me strange cravings and went for it. I squeezed the plastic mustard bottle and the tomato-shaped ketchup along the sausage in dozens of red and yellow Ben Day dots (you know, like in Lichtenstein paintings), holding up everyone behind in the line. A couple of workmen stared at me and then pushed past. 'Gotta problem, lady?' said one.

'Many,' I answered.

I lay on the grass, after first checking for syringes, and ate the hot dog along with a beer. Then alcohol

45

made my brain slop to one side of my head and then the other, so I shut my eyes under the trees and looked at the bright orange and mauve patterns the sun made inside my eyelids until I fell asleep. Obviously my defences were down, because Agnes was in there like a rat up a drainpipe. The dream went like this: I was sitting at my table in front of that fifties' shell-framed mirror I found at the Sixth Avenue fleamarket, and my hair was down all around my sholders like your prover-bial burning bush. (I thought I looked pretty OK – not too freckly.) I could see a pair of disembodied hands brushing it from above. A sneering woman's voice spoke: 'I have been thinking about this hair. How it would feel. How red it is. How old-fashioned it looks.' The metal bristles of the brush become tangled in my hair, and the disembodied hand kept pulling roughly, until I yelped with pain.

I pushed the hands away and they melted, as things tend to in dreams. Then I noticed I could see the back of my head and the front reflected into infinity, dozens of Albertines, because there was a mirror behind as well. Then I realized they were not me, but other red-haired women. Reflected behind me was my mom, with the long sixties' hair she once had. In front was my grand-mother, Rose, as she used to be in her wedding photo-graph. Behind again was Rose's mother, Isabel, I think, and in front, two mirrors away, was Agnes, auburn hair up like the photograph in the trunk, but this time in living, breathing color. They all seemed to be about the same age as me and oblivious to each other, just staring. There were more women, unrecognizable, stretching off into a red-haired genetic distance.

46

Someone tried to snatch my bag from under my head, but I'd hooked the strap round my shoulder, so I felt an enormous wrench and woke up swearing as the guy ran off empty-handed. I don't give up my real-leather fake Hermès that easily. It was only when I was walking to the subway at 77th and Lex that I started wondering about the dream. So we've all got auburn DNA, what does that prove? I grouched. But I kept remembering staring Rose and Agnes in the face, and wondering what they wanted of me. I felt guilty, some-how, but I'd no idea what crime I had committed in their eyes.

Down in the piss-polluted oven of 77th Street station, the present immediately wiped out the past. Two black men in baggy jeans were slugging each other, and drew a slight gasp from the crowd when one rolled towards the edge of the platform. Otherwise everyone regarded them indifferently, as though they were just more old chewing gum on the station floor. No one thought to interfere. Perhaps they were even glad to see an old-fashioned fist fight, without a knife or gun in sight. One of the fighters jostled my bag as he reeled backwards. 'Oh, I'm sorry,' I said politely, as I slid away. It always paid, I had discovered, to apologize to people who bumped into you in New York, especially if they were completely in the wrong. Earlier that year I'd read in the *Daily News* of the arrest of a serial killer nicknamed Mr Manners who had stabbed four passers-by to death on various occasions after *he* jostled *them* and they failed to apologize. 'People have got to learn some manners,' he said to the reporters, as the police led him away. From then, on I'd always taken his advice.

47

The 6 train arrived at last, and the two men immediately stopped fighting to board, and then continued. I avoided their door, ending up in the packed last car where every seat was taken. I was reduced to strap-hanging and lurched into a small Hispanic-looking woman wearing blood-black lipstick. The woman showed no signs of stabbing me, which was a relief, but then said, 'You know strap-hanging sometimes causes the umbilical cord to ride up and strangle the baby?'

Bullshit, I thought. 'Thanks for the advice,' I said. 'But you've probably noticed no one has got up to give me a seat, so that's not particularly helpful.'

'Yeah. What's new?' shrugged the woman.

We lapsed into silence and I watched beads of sweat form on her moustache about four inches from my face.

'For without are dogs and sorcerers, and whore-mongers, and murderers and whosoever loveth and maketh a lie,' came the boom of a megaphone from the platform as we drew into 42nd Street. Heard that before somewhere, I thought, but a posse of EvangelAngels raided the train before I could remember where. It was my second EvangelAngel experience that week, and I was mightily pissed off. An offshoot of the Guardian Angels subway vigilantes of the late eighties, the EvangelAngels were sullen, heavily muscled guys wearing light blue berets – more heavenly, I suppose – and matching T-shirts with the words 'God Squad' and 'Armed for Armageddon' on them. The EvangelAngels combined their crusade against crime with a crusade for God. They had multiplied a hundredfold recently.

'I was lost, but now I am found. I sinned, but now I am saved. Come to Jesus. Come to Jesus. He is the

Light, the Truth, the Way. Take Jesus into your life. Take Him into your heart,' chanted a spotty boy over a portable megaphone as his comrades forced leaflets into our hands.

'I hope they're not going to sing,' I said to the Hispanic woman.

'Christ is Right! Christ is Right!'

'I always felt He was more a Christian socialist, but there you go,' I added, but the woman had turned away to receive her leaflet. At the end of the car, four other crusaders accompanied by a huge boom box broke into a rap version of 'Onward EvangelAngels, Marching As To War', their battle song. There was also a buzzing sound as subway riders turned up their Walkmans to full volume to block them out.

'Repent! Repent! Come with us and be saved!' exhorted the boy, his zits erupting right in my face.

'Hare Krishna,' I said, pointing to the peachy-orange gown, proving itself doubly useful. The boy pulled his beret lower down his bullock brow and moved on. Another marched by, wearing a 'Slug a Mugger for Christ' T-shirt with the sleeves cut off. This made it easy to see he had a three-inch cross branded high up on each arm. Branding – previously favored by cattle and medieval criminals – had recently replaced tattoos and tongue-piercing as a status symbol. People edged closer to the walls as he passed. 'Be not afraid, for the Lamb of God is with you, even in this city of sin,' he informed the car.

City of sin, definitely, I thought as I grabbed a seat at last and opened the *Daily News* at a page that featured a shoot-out in a Madison Avenue lingerie store by an aggrieved flat-chested woman, which would probably soon make a 32A chest a mitigating circumstance. Anyway, this Lamb of God crap, I continued in my head, how come they don't find a more urban metaphor? Lamb just makes city people think of medallions of, rack of and possibly a delicious daube. A few pages further on there was a double-spread advertisement. 'By public demand, Jesus Lopes will preach for an unprecedented tenth night at Madison Square Garden. The Messiah has come. Call Teleticket.' The city was in evangelical overload. There were fifty-seven religious channels now on television, including one program called *Cooking with the Saints* but Jesus Lopes outdid them all. I'd seen previous articles about Lopes, who was no mere Billy Graham, but considered himself really to be the Saviour and dressed in silver lamé suits. As thousands came forward on their knees to be saved every night, Lopes slicked back his hair, crooned religious oldies into the microphone and reminded people they had four months until the Day of Judgement. There was a school of thought that suggested he was Elvis resurrected. Thirty thousand people – at forty dollars apiece, over a million dollars in all, I reckoned – were going to see him every night at stadiums on his national tour: 'The Second Coming'.

I had a hammering headache and was having very unChristian thoughts by the time I surfaced from the subway at Astor Place and Broadway. Nosmo was mooching around at home as usual. He told me Wanda had gone to her sweatshop in the garment district to 'exploit the immigrant underclass', i.e. to supervise her cutters. Although it was late afternoon, Nosmo was still wearing his neatly ironed Japanese cotton pajamas. The pale blue cloth with his blond curls made him look like a Botticelli baby who had lived too hard.

'Up late or going to bed early?' I asked.

'This has been a Slough of Despond day. I've been unable to do anything except watch the Designer Shopping Channel, although I did happen to see a divine Paul Smith vest.'

'What's the problem?' I said, taking off my hat, removing the cushion, and then lighting a cigarette.

'Well, I was down at the Riveters late last night – I know I shouldn't but I couldn't help it. A few Martinis and I lost all grasp on taste and sensibility and ended up bringing home a piano mover, of all things.' He rolled his eyes.

'Particularly muscly, was he?' I blew a slow smoke ring, feeling a touch jealous.

'Enormous. We're talking rough trade, strong meat, the lot. Anyway Amadeus was so scared – perhaps it was the pheromones coming off this guy – he hid in the closet all night and wouldn't come out until I coaxed him with chicken liver Pussy Snax the next day. Of course, his instincts were absolutely right. The man was a brute, he left at four a.m., and I feel distinctly used. I've been in the bath twice.'

'You do smell quite delicious. At least you still have sex. This is now my – hold on – hundred and ninety-sixth day without it. Anyway, stuff that. I bring you good news – the new Met visitors' button: pea green with the M in white.'

'Excellent. Don't think I have that one. I'll just have a look.'

I followed Nosmo into his room where he had (and has) the largest and possibly the only serious collection of the little metal buttons museum-goers get to prove they have paid. The Metropolitan had issued the buttons since the early seventies. For those of you who care, at first the logo was the initials MMA, but later the design improved to a black curlicued M on different-colored backgrounds, and in recent years, it has changed to white on colors. Not many people know that the source for the M logo was Luca Pacioli's *De Divina Proporzione*, a fifteenth-century mathematical treatise. Nosmo was a connoisseur of these subtleties, and carefully curated his hundred or so buttons on a white velvet background in a glass-fronted polished wooden case, the sort once used for pinning butterfly specimens. He referred to the Metropolitan buttons as his 'high-art *objets trouvés*' and had a parallel 'low-art *objets trouvés*' collection of used crack vials, also exquisitely displayed on his wall in a butterfly case. The increasingly rare vials were found in their natural habitat on the streets of the East Village, and there were over fifty different models, largely differentiated by their colored stoppers, each carefully cleaned of all traces of the drug with a tiny test-tube brush. Nosmo was particularly fond of two unusual rocket-shaped vials with gold and silver plastic stoppers. He took his curation seriously: 'You may laugh,' he said, and people did, often, 'but one day the importance of these collections will be recognized, not as detritus but as fine examples of the postmodern flora and fauna of New York.'

The two butterfly cases were the only flashes of color in Nosmo's tennis-court-sized room, the rest being decorated in black and white with photographs on the walls, Nosmo's homage to Cecil Beaton. I plonked myself on the black velvet chaise-longue since the checkerboard floor was making me dizzy. Meanwhile the new button was carefully preserved behind glass. Nosmo poured us some wine as a reward.

A glass or so down, I started moaning to Nosmo about my problems – my normal, rather than paranormal ones. Even he wouldn't stomach those. 'You know I caught myself today holding up the whole line at a hot dog stand because I was covering the sausage in alternating Ben Day dots in mustard and ketchup. Then I stood staring at the pattern of red and yellow on tan for about five minutes, and everything around seemed to stop. Do you think I'm beginning to go crazy? Maybe I spend too much time alone.'

'My dear, we all spend too much time alone. For instance, some people might say the business with the big breasts and the pregnancy is a bit peculiar too, but I think if you come home and actually paint something, then it's worth it.' He refilled our glasses and got into his philosophical stride. 'Being single and semi-jobless, which we both are up to a point, means we are doomed to spending too much time with ourselves. We are a generation destined for loneliness and copulation instead of coupling and vegetation. Look at me – I can spend three whole days hunting for a perfect pair of Oxford brogues and write a column about it. Wish I had the same dedication when it comes to maintaining a relationship.'

I took off my shoes and curled up on the chaise-longue with another cigarette. 'I dunno. I'm beginning to feel sort of edgy about being so self-indulgent. I haven't done anything disciplined, or possibly even worthwhile, for years. I think it's making me eccentric.'

'But I like that,' said Nosmo.

I told him about the scary build-up of Doomsday activists, EvangelAngels, Jesus Lopes, and little old dribbling men with signs saying: 'Hell is Hot.'

'Everyone's so tense and peculiar,' I said, emptying my glass again.

'So? That's normal in New York.'

'I mean, more so than usual.'

'Might be a good sign. I think when a nation's tired of messiahs, it's tired of life.'

'But don't you ever think, even just for entertainment, about the millennium or Doomsday or whatever? Or is it just people like me with nothing better to do?' Nosmo assured me that if possible he never let it cross his mind.

'But say the guys with the Armageddon sandwich boards are right – and let's face it, I won't be on the A-list for salvation – we've only four months before the world, and the two of us, are discontinued. Doesn't that bother you at all?'

'Nope. But, then, I'm still on the edge of sanity. Also, I'm still slightly sober.'

But I rolled on, slurred and oblivious. I told him about the mirror dream. Agnes was starting to get to me (and she'd barely opened her mouth). I felt her presence somehow, although she had yet to reappear, like some radar shivering on the back of my (her) collar. 'Sometimes I think: Do I and the Andrews dynasty, of which I may be the final representative, mind much if we die out now? Here I am, the end product: taller, more streamlined, better educated and built from Breakfast of Champions and vitamins and greens.' I started feeling all tearful and cheesy-poetic: 'Here I am, brought in generations of sacrifice and struggle from Europe, contained in genes stretching back to Dublin and Glasgow, of immigrants funneled through the docks of Boston and raised up by the Colgate factory in New Jersey.' Nosmo was staring at me in amazement. 'And along the way, a whole slew of women dying in childbirth, red-knuckled doing the washing, in prison for the vote, fighting all those battles so there are none left for me to fight. Now I've ended up a waste of space in New York, all that hope of generations boiled down to a few dregs of cynicism. I don't know what to do, and I don't even have a proper job,' I wailed, draining my wine in a suitably *fin-de-siècle* gesture, and looking round in vain for a fireplace in which to smash my empty glass.

Nosmo took it from my hand. 'You're wasted, in both senses. Has someone been getting to you or something? You usually talk garbage but not this sort of garbage. Anyway, some use may come of you, sweetheart.' He tried to think of something, and snickered. 'For instance, you may yet change this world's perception of big hooters.' I felt he hadn't quite got the point. He rubbed my back in much the same way he soothed that over-strung, over-fluffy cat. 'Look, Albertine, look at it this way – even if you're not worth it, the previous generation can't get their money back now.' I looked worried, because the previous generation appeared to be pursuing me from the afterlife, perhaps for that very reason. The whole business was ridiculous and unbelievable. We fell into silence.

'What you need is some sushi,' said Nosmo.

'What I need is a man,' I said, almost tearful.

'Don't we all?' said Nosmo. 'On that front, may I suggest you check the mail on the table which you ignored when you arrived? Far be it from me to pry, but I did notice a postcard. Who's Leonardo?'

The postcard showed the State Penitentiary, Starke, Florida. 'Trapped in the appropriately named Starke for month filming on Death Row. Am torn nitely, as they say here, between taking dinner at the Big Boy, McDonald's or Hardee's, the three best establishments in town. Fresh vegetables illegal. Send care package, or alternatively dine with me on return early Oct.'

'Forward, isn't he?' said Nosmo, blatantly rereading over my shoulder at the same time as dialing the Japanese restaurant. 'That's why you never want to leave the coast. Inner America is full of gastronomic retards. No, not you,' he said, as he got through. 'This is a delivery for six six six Broadway, top bell. Four tuna, four yellowtail, two eel, two urchin roe, two shrimp, two salmon and one California roll and one yellowtail and scallion roll. Seaweed salad on the side,' said Nosmo into the phone. 'And skip the miso.'

Chapter Six

Dowanhill Road, Glasgow

4 January 1900

Dearest Ishbel,

Thank you so much for our presents – there were far too many, and please pass our heartfelt thanks on to Mr Dalyell. Duncan is very pleased with his tea – enough for a whole year, it looks like – and the bolt of pale orange silk is even now on its way to the dressmakers to make nightdresses and blouses for myself and Kirsty, since there is plenty enough for two. Kirsty came to us from Edinburgh for a fortnight over Christmas and New Year – I cannot tell you how fond of her I am. She is tall, and wise beyond her years (and mine) and she has grey eyes that pierce to the heart of everything. I would fear getting on her wrong side, she has that of Duncan in her, but somehow it is tempered with a tenderness, I suppose with her being a nurse. The idea that I am her 'stepmother' is laughable, since she is looking after me.

She has been a Godsend to her father too, but more to myself, since being about the size of a Clydesdale nowadays, I am having a bit of trouble getting out and about. This is the busiest time of the year in the parish, and Kirsty took my place on the seasonal visits to the sick and the elderly, and when I could not manage to

get to services. My mind is going too – I keep
forgetting things and Duncan says I am as daft as a
ha'penny watch. I have become very keen on just
putting my feet up and reading, and Kirsty has been
bringing me all of Thomas Hardy and George Eliot
from the library. I am praying that it will all be over
soon, since I cannot bear this waiting for my
confinement any more.

I am saddened to hear how lonely you have been
with Mr Dalyell away for the month and only the
children and the house servants for company. Your
afternoon teas with the English ladies sound as dry as
the dust you complain of outside, and all that dressing
up for a sandwich! As for your accent being 'quaint',
well, that would make me give them the rough edge of
my tongue – my particular Scots tongue. Your India
sometimes sounds like an awfully small world in an
awfully big country.

Let me tell you instead what we are just after
talking about here. Aside from the war in South Africa,
and the claims of success for this year's enormous
Evangelical Campaign, the great debate in the
newspapers was started by Lord Kelvin, who said at a
public meeting just before Christmas that the world was
within nine days and three hours of the Twentieth
Century. This started a great palaver, with a whole body
of men claiming that it was still a year before the
Twentieth Century commenced, and saying the century
does not end until the close of the last day in the 100th
year, that is the end of 1900. Well, the pages of the
Glasgow Herald were filled with people who had nothing
better to do than speculate. There were angry citations

of the *Funk and Wagnall's Standard Dictionary*, and all sorts of shenanigans. The *Herald* said the subject was 'a guid gangin' plea' and it should not be ruthlessly nipped in the bud since arguing is good exercise in cold weather. Myself, I like to think this is the next century here and now. It gives me hope for this child.

Still, whatever the great men were saying in their newspapers and halls, the reality in the streets was that ordinary folk were not going to let 1900 come in quietly. All Hogmanay, half-mad evangelists marched up and down Sauchiehall Street wearing placards predicting all sorts of doom and despondency, which by midnight had not occurred. As the new century began, every ship's horn on the river sounded, every factory whistle went off, and you could barely hear the church bells over the din. Even up here, a mile or two from the Clyde, it was deafening. The streets were filled with people celebrating and singing, most of them the worse for the drink. Funny enough, it made me want to cry, sitting at home listening to all these sounds in the dark. I felt so much part of this city, in the centre of this great machine churning out iron and steel and ships, part of the folk that do the smelting and forging and casting and creating in this crater surrounded by green hills. I thought about 'Let Glasgow Flourish' and that it now means letting the salmon die in the poisoned Clyde so that ships can be born, and I felt a certain odd pride in that.

On Ne'erday, the revelling went on. From the front window I saw two working men on the road, reeling drunk and fairly expanding my vocabulary with their insults. Then they got down to giving each other a right battering and shouting their heads off. A few seconds later, Mrs Minto burst out of our front door with a bucket of icy water which she threw over them, her normal remedy for cat fights. 'Get back to your homes and your wives this instant or I'll skelp you rotten,' she said, and they meekly did. Duncan took an equally strong line with the swaying back row at his Ne'erday service, which I managed to waddle down to. He made several pithy remarks about sobriety, which were thoroughly ignored by the gentlemen at the rear with a few flasks in their coat pockets, insurance against the cold. Anyway, they showed great enthusiasm if not skill for the hymns, and it was fine to see a congregation of three hundred in a church that usually has half that – and who can deny them a wee tipple on their one day off?

22 January 1900

Oh, Ishbel, I have given birth to a wee girl. I can hardly believe it, and only now a couple of weeks later have I found the strength to get out of my bed and post this to you. She is perfect in every way – she weighed seven pounds on the kitchen scale and I have decided to call her Isabel, after you. She has a few wisps of red-gold hair and a voice like a drill sergeant. I had just put down my pen as I was writing the first part of this letter to you and had gone down to make a cup of tea when the pains started coming, and I shouted for Kirsty, who was fortunately still with us, and with her midwifery training, she knew exactly what to do – sit and wait, as it turns out – although Duncan insisted on calling Dr Menzies, more for his own reassurance than mine. I was hoping secretly that he would bring some chloroform, which has been taken up by many since the Queen used it all those years ago for her eighth child, but the doctor's main role seemed to be smoking cigars in Duncan's study.

Thank Heaven for Kirsty. I need not explain, because you of all people know what childbirth is like, Ishbel. She did not leave my side for a minute, held me, stroked my hair, and above all talked calmly as the terror of the pain threatened to engulf me. Duncan could not bear to hear me, and went down into the kitchen in the basement. Still, he must find it so hard after his wife died after having her fourth girl, the life drained out of her. The experience must bring back terrible memories. It was strange, because when Mrs Minto went out the bedroom door and said, 'You have a fine wee daughter, sir,' I am sure I heard him just saying, 'Oh, I see,' in a blank empty way, but maybe I was still half deranged from the pain and excitement. He so wanted a son, I know that. Sometimes in the last few days I have been just sitting on the bed in my dressing gown and crying, thinking about the first and second Mrs McPhails and their fates. Duncan takes little interest in Isabel – to him she is just a squalling bundle, but perhaps matters will improve when she is older. He spends hours locked up in his study attending to various church correspondences. I spend hours unable to do anything, unable to lift a book or a duster or have a rational thought. I cannot seem to pull myself out of this gloom, except when I am with little Isabel, and I remember that I must hold myself together because she needs me for ever.

How I wish I could talk to Duncan about all this, it would give me some peace of mind, but somehow I cannot broach the subject. The previous Mrs McPhail is only mentioned nowadays when her better housekeeping or parish work is compared to mine, which fails in a great many ways. I do try my best, but I cannot get awfully interested in the varieties of mutton stew, and Mrs Minto would resent it if I did. As to the parish, my ways are considered 'too interfering' by some of the church elders, who assume that all solutions are held in the Good Book, and not in complaining to landlords or writing to charities. I seem to be at odds with this age, thinking that perhaps the problem is that I am part of this next century, and others like Duncan are part of the one already gone.

Holding Isabel, my hope, I feel everyone around me is older and stiffer, trapped in the past. At night, a few gentlemen or some of the elders come round to Duncan's study and boil up a fine fug of pipe smoke and conversation by the fire. When I take them in the tea, they are always talking about great philosophies and religious debates, the circumstances of the poor and whatnot, but their words are empty, and any suggestion from me about the connections between Christianity and Socialism, any mention of the practical worth of the Independent Labour Party (in which I have been taking a great interest) are met with roars of laughter. 'Learn some sense, woman, before you dip into matters of the Church,' says Duncan. While they were discoursing away the other night about 'the true Way', a beggar rang the bell, a shrivelled man with a clapped-in face, but friendly, and I was about to give him a dripping sandwich and a few pennies when Duncan came into the hallway and shut the door on his face, saying I should not encourage them, and they should get themselves some honest work. It is then that I wondered if my God is a very diffeernt one from his.

I was just rereading this (I must stop whenever the wean opens her fine lungs to bawl, so everything gets half done) and I do not mean to sound so dismal, Ishbel, when here I am announcing the birth of our first child. I will send you a photograph in a few months as soon as she is fit to present in public and has a bit of hair under her bonnet.

I miss your sensible, calming words at times like this, and I wish every day you were here to explain how on earth to look after this baby. Write soon,

All my love,
Agnes.

Chapter Seven

17 September 1999

Beneath the pillars of the octagonal entrance hall there was a marble table piled two feet high with pomegranates, oranges, pink grapefruits, lemons, limes and waxy yellow passionfruit. Grapes and leaves trailed the edges. The display, though low cholesterol, had a certain Roman obscenity to it. Dotted round the table were stainless steel Ogetti juice extractors, and guests were creating their own fresh fruit cocktails. The chemically dependent, such as myself, added iced Stolichnaya while the rest wallowed in their own healthiness.

'Wish I'd brought a six-pack of Brooklyn lager,' I snorted in Wanda's ear.

'You can only stay if you pretend not to be a Philistine,' she said, squeezing my arm hard.

We were in trend central – the TriBeCa loft of John Outlaw, the fashion designer, and his model girlfriend Dellaria, who like many models, lacked a second name. The party was to celebrate the launch of Outlaw's spring collection for next year, which was made entirely from recycled rubber and plastic soda bottles. Wanda was often invited to such events and took me as chaperone-cum-analyst. We both agreed, as thirtysomethings, that the best part of going to a party nowadays was dressing for it. After all, the party itself would be unlikely to produce any surprises or, indeed, sexual encounters, and you always knew you would be going home, alone, in a taxi. A. N&P, a network and plumage party, was our code name for such barren social events, and with that in mind we had spent an hour at home selecting outfits. I decided that since it was after Labor Day I could return, like every other woman in New York, to my natural habit of black and dug out a long bias-cut dress. Although selecting a black, somewhat papal costume for herself – she liked to cover up her curves – Wanda forced me to test out one of her new pseudo-Victorian creations, a tight, peplum jacket in pink damask with a vague cabbage rose pattern.

'This is upholstery material, right?' I said, squeezing a pomegranate in the machine.

'So? You look like a very sexy late eighteen-nineties sofa.'

'You might have told me that before we left,' I said, discomfited into doubling the dose of vodka.

'Wandaaaa! How *are* you?' A man with red hair and what appeared to be a rubber wetsuit wrapped himself round Wanda and began to gush. Immediately, I recognized Outlaw's signature insincere smile from magazines. Fashionable society's affection towards Wanda rose or fell in direct proportion to the number of times her clothes appeared in *Vogue* or *Women's Wear Daily*. This was obviously a good week.

'And have you met my friend Albertine Andrews?' asked Wanda.

'Hi.' Outlaw peered at me like I was shit stuck inconveniently to his shoe, and then found something of much more interest. 'Is this jacket one of yours? For next season?' Wanda nodded shyly. 'Ooh, I love the cut. I knew it was yours straightaway.' Without asking me, he turned up a corner to look at the darts and seaming inside. 'Lined properly.' I might as well have been a dummy. I thought about slapping him, but I valued Wanda's career too much, so I slid away from his slimy hands. Not that he even noticed. 'What's your source for that great upholstery fabric?' he was asking Wanda. 'I'm bored to death with this recycled plastic crap. I want to return to decadence.'

Treated like a sofa, I thought I might as well behave like one, and parked myself against the wall in a dark corner of the living room. A CD-ROM magazine was being projected on the opposite wall, a triple-split screen changing images at triple-quick time, enough to make a person who had just drunk a double vodka rather queasy. One section appeared to be of banned MTV videos with the sound on full, and in the box beside that, an Outlaw catwalk show. At the bottom there was a question and answer session with the designer's words running like ticker-tape in six-inch letters: 'Fashion-is-the-recycling-of-ideas-so-it-must-be-constructed-from-recycled-materials – Conservation-is-Consumerism.' Silhouetted heads bobbed in the way of the projection.

I finished my pomegranate-passion vodka cocktail and headed for the bathroom, mainly because it had four walls with no one else between them. Unfortunately, one of said walls was taken up with a cascade of blue-lighted water, and it was not clear whether this was a urinal or a fountain.

Then I noticed someone had left behind a bloody tourniquet from shooting up on top of the toilet, a rare sight these days. I moved away from it quickly, and went to the mirrors above the washbasin-object. By tapping the corners, I located the hidden bathroom cabinet. I love the revelations of other people's bathroom cabinets, and they're always useful when you're nervous at parties. There was anti-aging cream with placenta extract for men (whose placenta? I wondered), uppers and downers, Xanax, Prozac and a megapack of Nurofen. I selected Dellaria's Nars lipstick in Red Lizard, painted my lips and then found my hand moving across the wall mirror. I hadn't even thought about it, but I watched huge words appear in the blue gloom: 'Fashion is a shuttlecock for the weak-minded to make rise and fall'. I shivered involuntarily, but no one was there except me. The blood-red copperplate handwriting, however, belonged to Agnes McPhail.

No sign of her, though. I sat on the edge of the bath and regrouped. There was no doubt: I was losing it. Then in the cabinet I noticed three little brown dripper bottles of homeopathic remedies. Containing extracts of arnica, arrowroot, eye of newt and suchlike, they were titled: 'Weepy Needs Support', 'Stressed and Exhausted', and 'Tense and Nervous: Use Appropriately'. I qualified for all these descriptions. I put a drop of each on my tongue, and immediately felt able to face the outside world.

I stood once again in front of the CD-ROM projection, where Outlaw was now opining full face, and found my edginess replaced by a growing irritation and a desire to punch my host. Who in their right mind promotes themselves at their own party? I muttered, 'self-aggrandizing, rubber-coated git. Makes me wanna throw up.'

'I couldn't have put it better myself,' said Agnes, a disembodied Scots voice from nowhere. I jumped, and looked around shiftily, but there was nothing. Then I saw the projection on the wall: a black silhouette of a head, like one of those Victorian shadow cut-outs, except its lips were moving. I slumped on a chair and took a slug straight from someone's bottle of vodka lying nearby.

'What now?' I said wearily to the shadow on the wall, which, of course, no one else had noticed. Still, at least in the uproar of the party, no one could hear me.

'Well, what sort of shenanigans is this, Albertine?'

'What we in the very late nineteen nineties call a party.' Agnes clearly hadn't been much of a happening chick in Glasgow, what with all that Presbyterianism.

'Are these the sort of people you respect, that you think are important? Are these your friends?' snapped the silhouette.

'Christ, you're worse than my mother.' I couldn't quite connect this bossy, aggressive Agnes pursuing me with the softer version in the letters. 'Why're you doing this? What's your problem?'

'You. You're my problem. I'm trying to prevent—'

'I can look after myself, thanks.'

'Look, dear, have you stopped to think why you were put on this earth?'

'I don't need any religious zeal, thanks. I get enough of that on the subway.' I groaned and got out a cigarette.

'This has nothing to do with religion, you know,' said the shadow, leaving a silence between us.

I had been prepared to be sympathetic to whatever Agnes wanted because I'd been quite moved by the last letter about the baby and all that – I also come from a family where sons are valued more than daughters – but she seemed angry and brittle now, her voice anyway, because I couldn't see her face. I stuck my head in my hands.

'Agnes. I presume you are Agnes. Could you just—'

'Excuse me?' said a tall, short-haired woman in a black Mao suit. 'You OK, or was it just the home movie?' she said, gesturing at the wall and screwing her nose up.

'I, um . . .' I tried to think of something to say about Outlaw, and turned my back on the silhouette. 'I'm not exactly convinced that the save and recycle stuff is genuine, but it's convenient for Outlaw for a year, particularly this year.' I took a sideways glance at the screen, but Agnes had gone and I was jerked back into what passes for reality in New York.

The Mao-suited woman grinned and continued, 'Wish you could see the real home movie . . . Johnny Law – he lacked the Out then – and his five brothers growing up on a chicken farm in Toad Suck, Arkansas.'

'Toad Suck?' I smiled, reaching for more iced vodka, skipping the juice.

'It's a real place, I kid you not. There's also a Greasy Corner just down the road. The guy is white trash, recycling trash, but he doesn't want to admit it. Unlike our president, he denies his roots entirely.'

The woman had clear grey eyes, and fine, angular features. She was rather beautiful in her minimalist, unadorned way. She became my best friend. Her name, she said, was Nancy Klinger, and she confessed she had recently been pressganged by her employers at *Vague* magazine to write a smarmy profile of Outlaw. It was suggested by the editor that she did not mention the words 'Toad Suck', or use 'Law' without the 'Out' prefix, and so the designer's early, less glamorous history mutated to 'Born in Arkansas comma'. Outlaw, after vetoing photographs unless they showed his best side, was delighted with the piece, and doubled his advertising in the glossy magazine. Nancy was put permanently on his party guest list.

'That's a bit like this guy Nosmo King who I share an apartment with.'

'Yeah, I've read his stuff.'

'He was born in New Jersey like me, and was called Norman King then, but at least he admits it. He says the choice was changing his first name to Nosmo or his surname to Bates.' I lit a cigarette and exhaled in relief. 'So why bother coming here if you want to annihilate this Outlaw guy?' I asked.

'It's my job. Need to eat. Have to stay in touch with this lot or I'm in trouble,' she said, gesturing round at the models, designers, minor Kennedys, lesser Rothschilds, photographers, bimbettes, and worse. 'Sometimes I just listen. It's a little tapestry of pretension. Here, I'll give you a tour.' She led me by the hand behind a group of perfect abs and buns.

We began eavesdropping on a beauty-writer-cum-novelist also from *Vague*. '. . . so I was so short of money last month that I had to give up my facial, my pedicure, my manicure, my massage, and my personal trainer was furious, and let me tell you, girls, painting your own toenails is no joke. They kept sticking together. I was in tears, literally. At least I kept my cleaning lady – that just would have been too traumatic. Rubber gloves . . .' She shuddered.

Next to her was an up-and-coming stylist: 'Then we just took over Sixth Avenue – well, it was three in the morning – from 23rd to 26th Streets and put the boom box on the sidewalk and hung out and rollerbladed. They'd just resurfaced it. It was kinda cool . . .'

The beauty writer kept going: 'I only recovered after I checked into the New Age Spa upstate for a week.'

We moved over to a group of performance artists – 'I define myself as a bisexual fag-hag, but nobody appreciates . . .' said one in a purple catsuit – and finished with Dellaria, Outlaw's very own Barbie: 'I'm still absolutely exhausted from last night. I wore McQueen and danced for hours with some film director who wanted to show me his collection of "restraints".'

I could hear Agnes repeating in my head: 'Do you hear the drivel they talk?' The fact was, I kind of aspired to being trendy or rich enough to talk that sort of drivel.

The men were no better. They took a grander tone, but the same stench of total self-interest rose from them. There was no conversation in the traditional sense: promotional soliloquy followed soliloquy. Nancy and I didn't get a word in, despite introductions. We were just there to be impressed.

'. . . and have my card. This is the fifth restaurant I've opened so I should know. It's the models that bring 'em in. Get those long legs and the suits will follow,' a Hugo Boss informed us.

An Armani answered, 'I know. Everybody told me a

private restaurant – we're unlisted, of course – would never work, but they underestimated the pull of exclusivity.'

In the corner, some self-proclaimed intellectuals were proving themselves with long words and longer drinks.

'I've been up all night crashing a piece,' said an artsy man from the *New Mocker* with dark shadows under his eyes. 'I get it in, then can you believe one of the fact-checkers asks me who Foucault is?' Everyone looked sympathetic.

'. . . for me, it was Auden that changed everything,' said a man who had failed to do the same with his shirt for some time.

Nearby, a banker had two black turtlenecks glazing over with boredom: '. . . at Warburg's, I was at Goldman Sachs, but I wanted more of a challenge.'

The turtlenecks turned away from him toward the drinks table. 'I told you I went back to my astrologer and had a full chart done for my guinea pig?' began one.

'Outta here,' I said, feeling like I'd zapped too many channels. We went into the kitchen, which was all stainless steel with a stuffed long-tusked marlin swaying above the center counter. Nancy told me more about her sufferings in the name of fashion. If you ask me, she was (and is) in the wrong job. The Mao suits, for instance, she had adopted as her uniform after being unable to acquire ten new outfits per season in order to keep up with the rest of the office. 'Got five. Twenty dollars each in Chinatown. They think it's a statement at work.'

This decision, she said, had come just after a testy

memo from *Vague*'s editor arrived on her desk saying: 'If there is *any* problem with bills from hairdressers or manicurists, please add them to your expenses. Appearance is important in our work here.' At that, Nancy had gone to the barber's for a crew-cut (which fortunately she suited) and had presented them with the fashionably incorrect bill for ten dollars.

Wanda reappeared, looking sweaty and flustered. She was wobbling on her purple heels, and there was a russet and a plum lipstick mark on her cheek. 'I can't remember any of their bloody names and they all know mine,' she said, reaching for the bottle.

The three of us escaped in a taxi to the Sunoco Bar on the West Side Highway. I reckoned that Agnes had probably done her bit for the night and would not follow us there. Do ghosts take taxis to get around or what? Our driver had a gilt-framed photograph of Jesus Lopes dangling from his mirror. 'No fender-bender since I get this,' he told us with joy, as we drew up at the Sunoco. The bar was a delightful, ill-lit place, converted out of an old gas station and serving essential Brooklyn lager, great shrimp in batter, and all-night breakfast. There was also the added pleasure of watching cars draw up for gas, only to discover that the pumps were antique and the whole place was a fake.

I shrugged off my sofa-jacket and stretched. I'm particularly fond of New York at three in the morning, the hour of screaming arguments and screaming tires. That night the smell of fresh bread came from the bakery in the next building, and the air was clear and warm with the last dregs of the summer. We sat at the open window and watched the lighted riverboats on the glutinous Hudson and for once felt we were nestled in the belly of the city rather than crawling through its entrails. It occurred to me that New York now and Glasgow back then were not far apart: each a dirty, heaving, decadent megalopolis on a poisoned river.

We drank beer. 'For five years I've yearned to go to parties like that, the sort you read about in the papers the next day. I wanted desperately to meet these people and when even one reached out their hand to draw me into their shining circle, I felt blessed,' said Wanda. 'Now, on closer acquaintance, I think they're all assholes.'

Nancy gurgled happily. 'All you have to do now is separate the assholes from the asses-you-have-to-kiss to stay in business, and you won't have to see most of those guys ever again.'

'No, it's more than that,' said Wanda. 'The more I see of the inner world of the great designer, the less I want to be part of it. I don't want to live in a vacuum of self-obsession.'

'You want to give up your business now that it's just all coming together?' I asked.

'Nah. I like designing the clothes. I just don't want to have to spend my life promoting myself in order to sell a few shirts. Maybe I could be the Thomas Pynchon or J. D. Salinger of the fashion world and never, ever do interviews. You see, now that I know I can do my job, now that I've got a workshop, an accountant, a manager, a shop, a label, all those things that make it real, I realize it's not enough.' She paused and looked at once embarrassed and ebullient. 'Which is why you can expect a home visit from the Manhattan social-work department in the next few weeks to check me out. I've been meaning to tell you.'

'They're checking out your asylum entry qualifications? For that nice White Plains place upstate?' I guessed.

'No, child-care services. A home study. Checking out my qualifications to become a parent.'

'They check you out nowadays when you're pregnant?' said Nancy, astounded.

'No. Adopting,' said Wanda.

'Oh, God,' I said, turning to Nancy. 'She means it.'

I was kind of insulted that she hadn't discussed it with me first. I mean, I'm as near as she's got to a best friend apart from Nosmo. But Wanda is never a slow operator and she'd taken immediate action on the newspaper article about the adoption of Chinese babies. That day, it seemed, she had contacted an overseas adoption agency and found a support group of New York parents who had adopted orphaned Chinese girls. She was, she said, already deep in the dump-truck of paperwork required by the Chinese authorities.

'Everything has to be certificated, authenticated, notarized, something called exemplified, sent to the immigration service and then translated into Chinese. It's probably less bother to set up an illegal arms deal.' Wanda kept talking in the void of disbelief she had created. I was still dealing with the facts that (a) Wanda was a closet mother and (b) there was soon going to be a baby roaring in Mandarin in the room next door to me. You would think we room-mates would at least have been consulted.

Wanda continued to detail her hassles rather than

her emotions. She had police clearance to say she was not a wanted criminal, a set of fingerprints, a health certificate, and was waiting for the home study from the social worker – endless forms and questions and a visit to the loft to check out cleanliness, space and the suitability(!) of the other occupants.

'Will we have to hide Nosmo, or will he pretend to be a suitable father figure?' I asked.

'They're quite happy in China for me to adopt as a single mother, so none of that matters. We just have to clean the fridge, and I'll turn my office into the baby's room. They visit during the day, so you probably won't be drunk.' I scowled at her. 'As for me, I just have to be appropriately nurturing.'

'I can't believe you haven't told me for so long,' I said.

'Well, I wasn't sure I'd be eligible. Thought I'd be too old, so I waited until it was confirmed.'

'How could you know there and then that you wanted to adopt? It's such a big thing.'

'Well, once I thought about it at all, I could see no reason *not* to. I've got enough money, I've got a flexible job and, above all, I don't have a man and I see little chance of finding a suitable one. And if I do, he'll just have to fit in.'

'Why not?' said Nancy. 'Why assume the love of your life will also be the father of your child? As, I think, Clare Boothe Luce said, "It's ridiculous to think you can spend your entire life with just one person. Three is about the right number."' (Later, I realized Nancy always has an appropriate quote for the occasion. She's far too well-read to be working for *Vague*.)

We drank on, although inside I was incredibly freaked out by the adultness of Wanda's decision. She continued, her face round and moony. 'Then I thought, the baby girls are orphans, half of them die in the first year in China, and even after that their prospects aren't great. How could life with me be any worse? And once I came that close to deciding, I suddenly felt as if in a way I was pregnant. It knocked me sideways, the hugeness of it, and then I wanted to keep it secret while the idea gestated.'

'Oh, my God, I still can't believe you've done this,' I said, the drink making me even less tactful than usual.

Nancy, who looked a little morose, suddenly spoke up and touched Wanda's shoulder. 'I understand completely. I think you're doing a wonderful thing. I wish I had the courage to do that.'

'Don't tell me you want to collect a Chinese orphan too?' I said, aggressively. 'This is getting too much. I thought the Mao suit was a career move.'

They both looked at me like I had a problem. Which I did. But when Nancy explained precisely why she understood about Wanda, I wanted to crawl under the table and die: like half the thirtyish people I seemed to meet then, Nancy was infertile. Her husband, she said, (and she did not look like the marrying sort), had become desperate for a child as soon as they discovered it was almost impossible. Her fallopian tubes were scarred from chlamydia which had gone undetected way back. For four years, they had tried to conceive. Each attempt at artificial insemination was $10,000, and each time her period came a little late, maybe bordering on miscarriage. Each time they felt a child had died, a terrible

77

sense of loss. Each time, their marriage took another pounding.

'Then we gave up, and suddenly there didn't seem any reason to be together anymore. It seemed unnatural, and every time I saw him, I knew he could go on to another life, a family life and I couldn't. He didn't want to adopt, so we separated this summer. I still bear the scars,' said Nancy, now laughing and showing her left hand. There was a narrow white band on her suntanned finger where a wedding ring once had been.

I sipped a second beer in silence, not sure what to say. You would think I might know someone somewhere who could make children by merely having sex, rather than buying them on American Express from laboratories or foreign orphanages. But artificial had become natural, at least for the people I hung around with. It's almost enough, I thought to myself, to make you long for an old-fashioned marriage with a Victorian Presbyterian minister.

The next morning I awoke with a godawful hangover. I crawled downstairs to Tony's Bagel Shop and he prescribed toasted sesame and cream cheese, a pint of brackish coffee, and three Advil, which he supplied from behind the counter. Tony is the sort of understanding man I would marry if only he wasn't five foot three inches tall and sixty-five years old.

I sat there tarring my lungs and thinking. I was depressed. I was manless, childless and penniless. Perhaps I should marry Tony, a happy widower, because no one else was going to have me. As for my other Italian

interest, well, things were looking lousy. Leonardo Ianucci seemed to have melted away after his postcard, and
I had no idea where he lived or how many eyes he had.
Annoying, because Agnes's warning me off him had
made me all the more keen. Anyway, it seemed to me
that she had been no great judge of men herself, considering her rotten marriage.

My other irritation was that all my friends were
having babies, or purchasing them in foreign lands, and
when people breed, I knew from experience, they sort
of move on to European time, go to bed when I'm just
getting up, book tables at seven p.m. for dinner, and
don't drink sufficiently. Eventually, they fall into a
forgotten corner of your address book.

Added to this, there was the increasingly worrying
question of my sanity. Either I was imagining Agnes, or
else I needed a priest and an exorcism, but since the
hauntings were occurring all round the city and not
merely at number 666 Broadway, this might prove
tricky. If I knew exactly *why* I was being harassed by my
undead great-great-grandmother, I could perhaps do
something about it. I decided to ring Rose and skirt
round the subject a bit, see what she knew. I took out
Nosmo's mobile, which he'd left behind while he was
on holiday with one of the President's spin-doctors in
Martha's Vineyard, and called Rose in New Jersey.

'Hello, dear. You sound terrible. Sound like you're
on twenty a day, and at your age too.' I could hear Rose
puffing away herself. 'I've just seen a nice wee red suit
on the Home Shopping Channel just now, forty-nine
dollars, not bad, eh?'

Rose overdid the home-shopping thing. 'Don't do

it,' I warned her. 'Everything they sell is highly flammable, made of Crimplene and plastic. Smoke, the suit'll melt and you'll fry, I guarantee you. Anyway, I was ringing to ask you a question. Have you read all those Agnes McPhail letters?'

Rose sounded like she was either laughing or coughing. 'Uh-huh, I have. Took a while, but they sort of got to me in the end.' She paused, something she never does. Rose likes conversation seamless.

'Did they, um, sort of bother you?'

'Yes, you could say that. Quite an influence, ye might say.' If Rose had been more honest at this point, it would have saved a lot of needless trouble. But she was cagey. 'Why are you asking all this anyway?'

I told her I was just interested. 'You met Agnes. What was she like then?'

'Granny? We didn't see her that often, because my Da had something against her, I think. But I used to be a bit feart of her when we went down for the day to Largs where she lived. She would take us to Nardini's cafe and buy us a chocolate éclair, but on top of that she'd ask difficult questions about what we were doing at school, and what we thought of things in the newspaper, which we'd never read. She sort of had a bone to pick, I think, after all she'd been through in jail with the suffragettes and everything. She expected a lot of us weans.'

'She was a suffragette? She went to jail?'

'Oh, yes, hunger strikes, the lot.' I could hear Rose lighting another cigarette.

'But I thought she was married to this stuffy old minister. She doesn't sound like that from what I've read so far,' I said, not mentioning what I'd seen.

'Ah, well, she doesn't stay the same in those letters. Well, you'll see. Doesn't take her long to know her own mind. She's a tough cookie, you know.'

'Umph,' I said, wondering why Rose was talking about Agnes in the present tense.

'Oh, hold on,' said Rose. 'They've reduced that wee suit to thirty-nine dollars now. I have to go before stocks run out. Give us a call later, dear.'

She rang off. Tony left the counter and came over to sit opposite me with his coffee. He was all smiling, embarrassed and confessional. 'Hey, Albertine, I gotta tell you the good news. I'm getting married. Better late than never again, eh? She's my next-door neighbor in Queens.'

Chapter Eight

Dowanhill Road, Glasgow

8 November 1900

Dearest Ishbel,

Here I am sitting at the kitchen table eating a piece and jam, an act which oddly makes me long for our old conversations in the afternoon at home over endless cups of tea, and sends me looking for pen and writing paper. Little Isabel is with me, right into a jar of wooden spoons on the floor and, by the way, looks much the same as your Jennie did at nearly a year. She has lost that puddin' face now, and has soft hair the colour of apricots. I pay her far too much attention, and I talk to her a great deal more than I talk to Duncan, telling her my innermost thoughts which I hope she is too young to remember.

Having Isabel has suddenly given me a purpose, a feeling of worth, but it also has set me off in a different direction from Duncan and his world, into a conspiracy of women and their children where much can be left unsaid because it is already understood. No longer am I braving the smoke in his study to poke my nose into parish affairs, which is probably a great relief to everyone concerned. Duncan has been a bit ill-tempered and peely-wally recently, complaining constantly about unidentified pains and a knot in the pit of his stomach.

Dr Menzies says it can be cured by eating bland foods, which seems to mean anything white or greyish brown, recipes, incidentally, at which Mrs Minto excels. Duncan himself favours a more direct attack, and has been sending out to the pharmacist for every indigestion remedy on this earth, drinking Andrews's Patented Stomach Medicine by the pint, and taking Beecham's Pills for, as they say, 'all bilious and nervous disorders, impaired digestion, constipation, liver complaints, sick headache, wind and pain in stomach', which surely covers whatever he has got, poor soul.

Myself, I think he is exhausted from working too hard. I have been trying to persuade him to get away from Glasgow for a week — it is so dank here — and go for one of those rest cures everybody has been taking at Peebles Hydro. You know, Duncan has not taken a holiday since I married him, and it surely was no better before, and I keep saying to him that he may have a mission, but God surely wants him hale and hearty to carry it out properly. Anyway, the air is clear there at Peebles, away above sea level, and there are all the home comforts, as well as Turkish baths and the most extraordinary cures, according to Kirsty, who is up on all these curious things like 'electric light baths', whatever they may be, and Russian needle treatment.

I do not know what comes into me sometimes, but I worry about what I would do if Duncan passed away, particularly when his skin looks grey and he stoops at the end of the day. I have no other home, and what would I do? I was thinking about what you said about the laws in India against those women committing suttee on their husband's funeral pyres, and I was horrified, but I also wondered what there is for us in this world other than being a wife. A few months ago I remember Duncan reading me this quotation, I am sure to bedevil me, from some Rabbinical text that was cited in one of his theology books and it said: 'A woman before marriage is a shapeless lump, and concludes a covenant only with him who transforms her into a useful vessel.' Yet it is strange that before marrying I did not consider myself a shapeless lump, yet after it I might tend that way.

Anyway, it was about the time I was having these dark thoughts that Duncan put me on to something which has, unexpectedly, given me a whole new lease of life, or perhaps a real life: running the weekly ladies' Colquhoun church social, since Mrs Potts said it was too much for her. Mrs Potts is a terrifying woman with a wrinkled, baggy neck, a booming voice and a prodigious chest, and I am sure people came out of fear more than anything else. I took a bit of a scunner to her – she likes humiliating people – and had not (thankfully) been to that many meetings, what with my confinement and now Isabel. I found the meetings awfully boring, dwelling on lady-like accomplishments like sewing, housekeeping and mothering, which we get enough of by day.

There are about twenty or so ladies who came at first to my meetings, but being the West End it turns out they are game for much more than you might expect, not at all 'pan loaf', as you would say, Ishbel, and a good few are my age. There is an intelligent schoolmistress called Miss Ellison, Dr Menzies' wife

Mary, and Mrs Crawshaw, Miss NcNair and Mrs Sweeney who all have good heads on their shoulders.

Rather than sitting knitting and gossiping in the big gloomy parlour, as they did in the days of the redoubtable Mrs Potts, we decided to invite someone to speak to us each week. I started with Kirsty on midwifery and nursing – she has moved over to work in Glasgow now and has a room and kitchen in Partick – and that was easy, and the ladies were fascinated by the details which I shall not repeat in the post. She stood up there on the platform behind the lectern, so upright and beautiful in her best blue suit, and I felt so proud of her. She spoke with a real clarity and vision, for I had always thought nursing to be more about medical advances than the rights of women. Kirsty has a true sense of herself and her purpose, which I feel I lack. And you should have heard the questions she took afterwards. My ears were burning.

Since then, the parlour has been so mobbed we have had to move across the road to the church hall, which is freezing, but we all put up with the cold since it is fascinating, and the dire alternative is sitting at home watching the nights draw in. Next week we have a speaker from the Scottish Women's Liberal Foundation, following the enormous success – one hundred people, Ishbel – of the visit from one of the only two lady surgeons from the Samaritan Hospital for Women, who came to talk about her work. I wish you could have been there.

In the last few weeks, we have been getting increasingly daring about our speakers. I suddenly feel inspired by something and I have spent all my spare time planning the next meeting. A lady who has been taking theology classes at the university came to talk to us about women in the Bible. She read to us from a wonderful American book by Elizabeth Cady Stanton all about the prominent women around Jesus and the great matriarchs in the Old Testament. She talked about Jael and Judith, and Deborah, a female judge, and Miriam who, as you probably remember, was struck down with leprosy when she challenged Moses' sole right to speak in the name of the Lord. Well, taking a man to task is never easy, particularly a religious man, as I can testify.

Yet despite such fates, just talking about these Biblical women makes them stand out in relief. I had hardly noticed them before, and now I keep wondering at odd moments about their lives. It is peculiar that there we had been reading this great book since childhood, and half of it, the female half, had passed us by.

My favourite guests so far have been the artists Margaret and Frances Macdonald (Margaret has just married Charles Rennie Mackintosh who has designed the new art school on Garnethill), who came to us together. Often there can be forty or fifty ladies coming now, half of whom have nothing to do with the church, so I have to go into the hall early each Tuesday and light the fire. We ask for wee donations for coal and the speakers' expenses and the tea afterwards, and anything left over goes into the collection. Kirsty has me on and says we have gone from a church social to a salon, like the French have. God forbid Duncan comes to one of the meetings, but fortunately he shows little interest. Anyway, I went round to see Margaret Macdonald, with Miss McNair who is a friend of hers, before she came to give the talk, and what a flat the Mackintoshes have on Mains Street! She gave us tea and a nice ginger cake in front of the fire and showed us round the rooms, some of which were half finished. The walls are all whitewashed and the floors covered in cream carpet – how she manages to do her paintings and gesso there without leaving a mark I do not know. Every piece of furniture is as simple and perfect as could be, and there are inlaid stained-glass or metal panels with elongated roses in the fireplaces and cupboards. There was not an antimacassar or a whatnot in sight, just a feeling of enormous peace, all that space to live in and think.

Despite the refined surroundings, and those strange skeletal women with long, flowing hair that she paints (they call it the Spook School here), Mrs Mackintosh was perfectly down to earth and has hands that look like they were made for kneading dough rather than holding a paintbrush. She gave us an entertaining account of the goings-on at the new art-school buildings. There is an animal room directly off Dalhousie Street, where the students are given classes in drawing live animals, not just dogs and sheep, but she says they have borrowed a camel and even a boa constrictor from Hengler's Circus down the road – rather them than me. There are other fancy additions: they have not only electric lighting in the studios, but electric clocks and even 'electric thrones' for the life models to stay warm (quite a different thing from the electric baths at Peebles, I expect). Mrs Mackintosh says she will take Kirsty and me on a tour of the building one day.

Meeting women who are artists, surgeons and suchlike, who are so engaged with the outside world, gave me a vision of all these doors opening before me, full of light, yet I could not leave my present life, my daughter, my husband, to walk through them. I sit back here and catch glimpses from the kitchen. Then it dawned on me that every one of these women who have come is childless, and the Macdonald sisters are the only ones who have married, that perhaps you need to be barren to have the room to think and act, and now I no longer have that choice. Not that I regret having Isabel for one minute, but it gives me pause for thought.

That is quite enough girning, I think, considering that I really am in very good spirits. Give my best to Mr Dalyell, and I have enclosed Mrs Minto's tablet recipe for the children. Write soon,

Your loving sister,
Agnes.

Chapter Nine

20 October 1999

There I was, naked, surrounded by barren career women contemplating the curve of my ass. Just like Agnes's menagerie of lady speakers, the women drawing me all had professions, but they wanted a man and children as well, so I suppose that much has changed. But were these movie PRs, bond dealers, and purveyors of designer ravioli, all struggling to keep the charcoal off their gilt-buttoned suits, happy with their lot? No, or they would not have been attending a beginners painting class at the New School in an unlikely attempt to expand their horizons, code words for trying to meet marriageable men. Little did they realize that the only viable man who would reliably attend the Wednesday class was the lecturer, a septuagenarian misogynist (of whom I am very fond).

After three years as a regular life model for evening classes, I knew that up to half of the twenty students would be gone for ever by the next month. The single women were sure to lose enthusiasm first, since the two male students who had turned up had little potential: one was gay, the other grim. Take my advice, girls, I thought. Go to the 'Semiotics of Coffee: Beverage as Cult' lectures instead. Go to the *film-noir* appreciation series, for art gets done best alone, and you would–be breeders will not find what you are searching for here. Thus I mentally berated the class between three-minute poses as they made panicky sketches of my body.

The deal with Garrett Hughes, the art teacher, was that I did fifteen minutes of poses in the manner of a classical statue, but afterwards I got to read a book in one comfortable position for the rest of the class. The money was steady, unlike the varying amounts I earned painting those faux-classical murals in private apartments. Garrett paid well, in cash, free acrylic paint and canvas (an enormous saving), and occasionally some dope, which did not fully make up for the fact that I had to bare myself on the platform twice weekly on a sticky Indian bedspread over a sofa lacking springs. Who knows who or what had been there? I carefully laid my robe under my body and went back to a pile of Agnes's letters I'd been toting about. Reading them was more a labor than a labor of love, but I now wanted ammunition in case she attacked again. Within pages, however, my toes went purple from the cold.

'Whaddabout an electric throne, Garrett?' I shouted, interrupting him as he patronized another heretofore competent career girl, tossing her painstaking first sketches dramatically on the floor.

'An electric what?' he said, watching the woman crawl about picking up the sketches.

'Throne,' I explained, with a short reading from the letter, that a hundred years ago, life models were treated with proper respect. Garrett snarled that I would stand more chance of getting the electric chair, but then went out to fetch a fan heater.

Basking in the warmth, I put my brain into neutral

and floated. I could see Garrett prickling with disgust as the students asked him dumb questions about where to get the best wooden carrying case for their paints, and which was the finest, longest-lasting paper or canvas for preserving their masterpieces. Those students generally stuck the class about three weeks, until they discovered it interfered with their Spinning bike sessions or aero-boxing. Even the ones who stayed were roundly dissed in the bar afterwards by Garrett who would sneer: 'See yourselves in Tuscany with little sketchbooks doing adorable watercolors of olive groves, don't you?' The students thought he was joking. 'Do you think it's the fucking Toujours Provence school of art here?' But in his retirement, he needed the money as much as me. 'Wouldn't know gesso if they ate it,' he would continue.

But I felt, despite his general air of carnapciousness (an onomatopoeic Scots word meaning crabby, that I'd learned from Agnes), there was something rather vulnerable about Garrett: the way he had gotten so skinny at seventy-two that his trousers were held like a clown's in the air around him by suspenders; the frayed collars of his overwashed flannel shirts; and his persnickety habit of carefully cleaning out soup cans of graded sizes to perfectly fit his various brushes. Garrett was an abstract expressionist, fairly famous in his day but erased by time, and he still thought painting was men's work. He had only accepted me in his tutorial group ten years ago at Parsons School of Art because the secretary put me down as Albert by mistake. I was the only woman there, against his own better judgement, but he was still a great teacher. He'd been round to 666 Broadway recently to make abusive but useful remarks about my Flesh and

Confinement paintings. Garrett maintained, however, that canvas and paint were quite outdated tools, and if he were younger, he would move into installations: rooms carpeted with real grass, writers burning their own work in tableau, artists publicly frying Barbie dolls, pickling dead cats, etc. 'That's where the money is.' (He was right.)

I took a break when the pins and needles started in my legs, and walked round the aspiring artists in my robe. Curiously, and this was something I had noticed before, they drew me with a touch of themselves. Twenty unrecognizable Albertines, each more similar to the painter than the model. The men drew me in sub-Braque or Picasso style, signalling intellectual pretensions above draftsmanship. The women's complexes about wrinkles, fat thighs and large breasts were displayed in their ill-executed art. The round or bulimic painted me fatter than I really was, and the thin painted me thinner. Perhaps they had looked so much in the mirror that every image of woman was mixed up with themselves. I put this to Garrett. 'Bull,' he said, far too loudly. 'They just don't look properly when they draw.'

I was itching to get out of the class, and Garrett had to tick me off for being overtly wriggly during the last fifteen minutes. I was meeting Leonardo Ianucci at eight, not for dinner as promised on the postcard, but for a drink and the screening of the rough cut of his Rikers documentary. Still, who was I to complain? I hadn't seen him for two months, I hadn't had a proper date for seven months, and, for those of you still counting, I hadn't had sex for 224 days. In other words, like the women of Beginners' Life Drawing and Painting, I was desperate.

I shot into my jeans as soon as Garrett cleared his throat to start ending the class, stuck on some lipstick in the foul students' bathroom, and ran over to the bar on Greene Street. Leonardo was in a booth at the back. I felt my stomach lurch in anticipation. I hadn't known I was that interested. He was wearing a black leather jacket, same as me, and, yes, the sunglasses. At night. In November.

We kissed cheeks stiffly and I ordered a beer. Then, just as I was considering an inappropriate remark about sunglasses indoors being the province of hormonal adolescents and *Vague* fashion editors, he took them off. Leonardo's eye was surrounded by an oval of slightly raised purply-red skin. I fought to concentrate on what he was saying about the Sundance film festival. Instead, I stared.

'What's wrong? Oh, my eye. You haven't seen it before? It's a port-wine birthmark. I'll have a Dos Equis,' he said to the waiter. 'So what you been doing these last few weeks? You do any more of that weird belly-parading stuff for your work? And can I see the paintings sometime?'

I wasn't fastening on what he was saying, because I was trying not to stare at his face. 'Sure, whenever you want. Whatever.' I paused. 'I was thinking about that eyepatch you had the first time I saw you, the pirate thing. Why do you wear it if you don't mind people looking?'

'For posing around. For the camera. Using one eye makes me concentrate better. No distractions. And it looks kind of freaky too, so no one hassles me in the street. There was a time, mostly, I have to say, in my overlong adolescence, when I always wore sunglasses or a patch and I even tried cover-up for a while. But then I just decided it didn't matter that much.'

I couldn't decided whether I found his beat-up boxer look very attractive, in an *On The Waterfront*ish way, or repulsive. I pursued the details. 'Another thing. The dog. Did you particularly select him for the patch round the eye? To match?' I half grinned.

'No, it's my neighbor's dog, and he abandoned it when he left New York. You ask pretty direct questions,' he said, turning the beer bottle round and round between his fingers and looking me straight on.

I felt embarrassed. 'It's to do with no longer living among civilized society. If I had an agent, a gallery, a buyer, a life, then I would still, by necessity, have some manners, but when you've no reason to be polite to people any more, you lose the skill.'

He laughed, but in fact I was deadly serious. Not only had I fallen out of civilized society, but at one point for about six months I actually changed time zone, sleeping later and later each day until I was getting up well after lunch and working into the night. My mornings disappeared, and I had retrieved them only partially and recently. I still hadn't got a watch.

We left the bar and walked in the dark across Union Square. Two vans were still being packed up after the greenmarket, full of pumpkins and squashes, and huge bunches of red fall leaves: the country north of here must be covered in bare tree stumps. The remaining smells of hot apple cider with cloves and cinnamon that made me long for upstate New York and the Berkshires, the places where real couples with real incomes went for weekends of real passion. And there I was hanging out with some thirty-five-year-old who spent his weekends behind bars for pleasure. Prospects were not good. Leonardo bought a paper cup of apple cider just before the guy emptied the urn, and I realized that this was as near as I was going to get to a fall foliage tour. We shared it on a bench since we were early for the screening. 'I'm so fucking nervous,' he said. 'What if they hate the whole film?' He slumped forward in mock, or possibly real, despair. Men are such drama queens. Generally, when they express these sort of fears, it is a sign of supreme self-confidence. They just need a little bolstering. But, to my surprise, I found myself crashing through the touch barrier and squeezing his shoulder, feeling that a physical gesture was required to reassure. (Besides, I wanted to touch him.) How was I to know if his film was appalling or not? 'Just be cool about it,' I said. 'From what you've said, no one will have ever seen anything like it.' I felt that covered all possibilities.

We arrived at the film office. The Rikers screening was in a tiny hot room with fat plush seats. There were a couple of people from PBS, who had partly financed the documentary, some fat plush men from cinema distribution, and some artsy types. Leonardo had put his shades back on again and stripped (pleasingly) down to his white T-shirt, in intentional contrast to the men-in-suits that he was schmoozing so assiduously. He introduced me to people but I had nothing to say to them. I felt like a spare part, so I sat down in the second row, took my jacket off and rolled my shirt-sleeves up. I waited alone, and felt a sore need for popcorn.

The grainy words came up: *On Rikers Island: Summer*

1999. The title music was a ska song, 'The Lunatics Have Taken Over The Asylum'. I suppose this made the film's point abundantly clear. Leonardo came to sit beside me in the dark. Suddenly, I was thrown back to pre-prom age, when such a gesture still meant something. My stomach went tight and my pheromones began to frolic. 'I've schmoozed all the necessary people,' he said in my ear. 'Now, enjoy.'

'Well, enjoy is quite the wrong word,' I whispered (unsubtly) ten minutes into the black-and-white film. 'I mean, I didn't expect Rikers to be charming or even photogenic, but neither did I expect my guts to heave like this.' Leonardo smiled cheerfully. On screen one of the inmates of the world's largest penal colony – an articulate, engaging man – was explaining why one of the best home-made weapons was two razorblades stuck parallel in an eraser. 'You get a double cut, see,' he said, demonstrating on an orange, 'and it's almost impossible to stitch up. Leaves a helluva scar.' Cut to a lucky fellow inmate with aforementioned double scar traversing his face. Turn up volume on Neil Young-style doom music.

Just then, I felt the hairs on Leonardo's arm touching mine, which in turn activated the hairs on the back of my neck and caused a bodily chain reaction.

'Then there was this kid who was stabbed to death with a Biro,' added the prisoner. 'Pen right in the fucking heart. Ugly mess.'

His arm was just barely brushing against me across the arm-rest, so lightly I was not sure if he had noticed.

'Methamphetamine's the thing to have. Trade it for gear, a long call on the payphone, new sneakers. You

swallow it in a condom and shit it out day or two later
– if it doesn't burst.'

There was no question that he was really, publicly,
leaning his bare arm against mine. It was incredibly
warm. I thought I might collapse, one way or another,
either from screen violence or lust.

'The white guy down cellblock four. He's been Van
Gogh-ed. You know, they cut his ear off.' More doom
music. Shot of ear stump.

And that was it. I mean, the film went on (and on),
but the extent of what can barely be described as a pass
was this: his arm touched my arm.

The credits came up, the lights went on, and Leonardo was carried off by a bunch of fawning film
executives, squealing words like '*verité*' and 'raw power'.
'I'll call you,' he said, air-kissing me perfunctorily,
desperate to get out. I pushed the bar on the back
emergency-exit door and slipped away, while Leonardo's
entourage went out the front, to a particularly good
sushi restaurant on Sullivan that I could never afford. I
felt dumped. I felt like shit. I wanted him. I needed a
drink.

I knew that after the art class Garrett would still be
in the White Horse, a sixties' haunt he had not quite
kicked. I wandered over there. Garrett, being much
married, much divorced, and much mistressed in his
time, is not the worst advisor on the low motives of his
own sex. His interpretations are, at least, more accurate
than Nosmo's. That night I found him sitting talking to
some regular up at the bar. He took one look at my
downcast face and ordered me a Rolling Rock.

'What is odd about this man Leonardo,' I informed Garrett, 'is that he is not merely a slow mover. He is positively infantile – cute postcards, long lunches, and then he combines his first date, so to speak, with an important screening full of people he wants to impress, shows off and touches arm-hairs.'

'Arm-hairs?' asked Garrett.

I explained and continued, 'What is incongruous about all this is he talks as though we're already coupled. Introduced me to people at that screening like I lived with him or something. But then he goes and fucks off.'

'The mind is willing but the body is not?'

'Or vice versa.'

Garrett made the practical suggestion that I should invite Leonardo to dinner, or for a drink, which was, he had heard, how normal people began relationships.

'And then there's this birthmark. I know it shouldn't matter but it does.'

'Ah, that might explain his fear of rejection,' said Garrett, stealing a drag of my cigarette.

'Naah, he copes fine with it,' I said. 'But there's something bizarre and attractive about a small deformity.'

'You like him because he reminds you of those weird people you paint, all scarred in various ways. Appeals to you women in the Frieda Kahlo school of psycho-art, those pictures that showed her own pain, operations and crowns of thorns on the surface.'

'Crap.' I smiled.

'Or else it's the mark of the devil. Invite him round to number six six six and see if he fits in.'

★

Number 666, I noted the next day, was not the place to bring anyone. Wanda and Meredith, her bossy assistant, were reaching untold levels of panic, for soon they would die, or not, depending on the reaction to the Wanda Wong Spring Show. Wanda was shouting down her mobile phone, while Meredith was stuffing paper into the fax and telephoning last-minute invitations at the same time. 'I have to get false nails by tonight,' screamed Wanda. 'I can't meet the public with bitten stubs. Book me an appointment now.'

Meredith dragged Wanda off to the tents at Bryant Park, and had someone do her nails in the town car on the way. Nosmo and I followed a couple of hours later to provide family support at Wanda's show, attired in what we considered our most appropriate items. In my case, this was a black nylon zippered dress and jacket, with hobnailed boots. Nosmo saw fit to wear a narrow suit with an orange shirt and matching tie, a lime green pullover slung casually over the shoulder. He carried a pearl-handled cane and had also grown a narrow pencil moustache for the occasion. 'Subtle,' I said nastily, causing Nosmo to sulk the whole way in the taxi.

We genuflected to the security men and made it into the tent with its runway down the middle and bleachers for the fashion press to cheer from because, as you know, they are never critical. Nosmo was greeting people all along the front row like he was minor royalty. 'This is my first fashion show ever,' I told him.

'Oh, my dear,' said Nosmo, horrified, 'well, we must introduce you to people. This is Stacey Kitsch from *Harpers*, and Eloïse Motavalli from *Elle*, Tom from

Barneys . . .', but here, he lost me. 'Nadine, darling!' he squealed, and went off in a flurry of air-kisses to roost among the ladies-who-lunch. No wonder he always smelled of women's perfume when he came home. I was left suspended in a seamless conversation between Stacey, Eloïse and Tom.

'. . . Kim goes out to LA all the time because she's got some love-interest there and do you know she never turns on the air-conditioning in her car . . . Oh, hi, sweetie . . . You can just imagine that amazing long red hair streaming in the wind,' began Eloïse.

'She's fabulous, she really is a fab girl but you know about Isiah – I mean, you have to schmooze your clients to some extent but he . . .' continued Tom, from behind his shades.

'. . . he's just so critical,' overlapped Stacey. 'Sooo cutting, especially if they're fat.'

Then I lost track of who was saying what as it melded into a three-way monologue: '. . . into his apart-ment and I asked: "Where are the books? He's so minimal he doesn't read . . . what a sweetheart . . . to a certain extent anyone schmoozes, but this is outright contempt apparently he's had to move loft space . . . that girl should really stick to black, don't you think?'

Half an hour later, the show still had not started, but the conversation looped pointlessly on and on around me, with no one paying any attention to what the others were saying. I had considered myself pretty shallow until I met these people, so now I became not merely cheerful, but smug in contrast. The lights went down and Nosmo slid in beside me singing to the tune of 'A

Partridge In A Pear Tree,' ' "Three A-list actresses, two super-models, one aging rock star, and twelve moneyed ladies-who-lunch." Not bad for a front row.'

Behind the scenes Wanda, who had been surviving all day on a diet of M&Ms, Prozac and espresso, had collapsed shaking in a chair, biting even her false nails, too terrified to start the show. Meredith had taken over, and everything became incredibly well organized. The giant pink neon Wanda Wong sign lit up at either side of the entrance to the catwalk, and the sound-system suddenly boomed with David Bowie's 'Suffragette City'. The sleazy lyrics made me unaccountably nervous.

Down down the runway came the white silk Votes for Women sashes made into a tackily short A-line skirt, topped with a waisted purple jacket and an acid-green driving hat held on by a chiffon scarf. The Bowie song, of course, was more about the merits of short, sharp and brutal sex than the suffragette movement. It left me with a strong feeling of dread.

I wasn't sure if Wanda's show was going to scrape over the taste barrier, and I had an edgy feeling I'd desecrated something by handing over Agnes's clothes. I hadn't known then that Agnes had been so serious about the suffragette stuff. The next model was better, in an ankle-length straight skirt, with Votes for Women running down in violet and green, and a jacket with leg o' mutton sleeves, in the same pink upholstery material I'd worn to that dreadful party. 'I'm back on Suffragette City,' roared the sound system. The black model was also wearing a Votes for Women sash across her chest, in case anyone had failed to get the message.

Eloïse-from-*Harpers* had. In her notebook she was writing, 'Super-Retro, Victorian stuff???' I could have explained the true source, but I scowled at her instead.

Then came some high-necked white shirts, again with leg o' mutton sleeves and long hobble skirts with zips from top to bottom, which I quite liked. They were topped with straw boaters, featuring plastic cherries the size of apples. The models also wore plastic cherry earrings. There was a round of applause.

'It's in the bag,' said Nosmo, pleased.

The music had by now turned to scratchy music-hall records from the turn of the century. There were long, demure aprons, which turned out to be shorts from behind, and then bikinis in suffragette green, violet and white, worn – inexplicably – with fake fox-fur stoles in the same colors, showing little beady eyes.

Stacey was sketching and writing: 'Ironic take on early fems. Why such limited colors? NB apron look.' I felt embarrassed, though perhaps Agnes might find this ironic take on her wardrobe amusing. I was just hoping to hell she wasn't going to make a personal appearance.

The evening wear was pretty stunning: long purple dresses with black lace underneath, lime silk gloves, which fake-buttoned to the elbow, that were ripped off with a rasp of Velcro and applause. Then came the disaster. Even I had not considered Wanda would go that far. But there were striped dresses and narrow pants in Edwardian prison arrow material. The arrows were shrunk and restyled, but they still looked like uniform.

'Wow,' said Stacey to Tom.

'Awesome,' he said.

I found myself sweating with panic and horror. I

suddenly remembered that the silk Votes for Women sash had been wrapped carefully, almost tenderly, in tissue paper. I turned to Nosmo. 'Don't you think this is utterly tasteless, when all those suffragists died after hunger strikes and force-feeding and stuff?'

'Nah,' he said. 'It's an amazing statement.'

I couldn't look. They were wearing handcuff bracelets and ball-and-chain earrings. 'What the fuck does Wanda think she's doing?' I moaned.

'I dunno. You gave her the idea. They're loving it – look.'

The audience was now giving a standing ovation. Wanda came out to take a bow in a swarm of models who seemed twice her height. Everyone stormed on to the catwalk to congratulate her, and I slipped away.

'Coming for dinner?' asked Nosmo. 'We're going to the Room first – they do great fusion food – and then the Taxi Club after.'

'No,' I said, upset. 'I think I'll just go home.'

I was all peopled out, as they say. I sat in the taxi marveling at the levels of superficiality. I was feeling like a sleazeball for my own part in it all, but then I reasoned that Agnes had not, at least visibly, been at the fashion show, so she might not know a thing about it, or indeed care. And there was always the possibility that she didn't exist. I had a couple of glasses of wine in the kitchen, ate a can of cold baked beans with a teaspoon while reading the gossip section of the *Post*, and felt better by the time I headed for bed.

I switched on the little bedside lamp, and suddenly saw the wedding photograph in the pool of light on the shelf. Agnes's gaze now appeared to be directed at me, and it was no longer half ironic. It was livid. Some movement in the periphery of my vision made me look over at the trunk against the wall. It was half open.

I knew she was there long before I felt the warm breath on the back of my neck and shivered with cold. I turned round and she was standing inches away from me in the shadows: the same face, the same hair, the same eyes at the same level. The same beginnings of wrinkles under her eyes. Like a twin.

What had I done to raise her? What had I done to deserve her? I felt sick. I sat down on a pile of canvases.

'Do you mock me, Albertine?' she said, her lips tight, steely. 'Do you know what you're dealing with?'

I couldn't speak.

'Well?' she said, like a schoolmarm.

I began a stuttering explanation, but then I couldn't see the point of continuing. Agnes was clearly dying to let rip.

'You and your under-educated, ignorant friends have no sense of the past. In fact you've no sense at all, no comprehension of integrity, of a cause worth fighting for, have you? Your songs with dirty words—'

'Hey, don't blame me for Bowie,' I interrupted.

'Your stupid clothes . . . I find it wasteful, so wasteful the way you go about leading your insincere, ephemeral wee lives when you could do something worthwhile, something that mattered. I didn't fight for you for this. And this man isn't your solution. Nor the so-called friends you live among here . . .

And thus she continued, until, like us mortals, she apparently felt better for getting it out of her system.

I interrupted Agnes as the flow of pious invective lessened. I apologized, emphasizing that I had no idea how far Wanda would go in her quest for the cover of *Women's Wear Daily*. I also pointed out that Wanda had not been harassed by the ghost of Vita Sackville-West when she did a parody of her gardening clothes. It was then I suspected that Agnes did not do irony.

'Do you mind me asking something?' I said, in a resigned voice, and for the first time she smiled, her face lit up, and she seemed a different person. 'Could you just give me an idea why you're here? And possibly inform me when, in the future, you will be here? Could you tell me what, precisely, the agenda is?'

'Why'd you think I'm here? You know why I'm here. Your conscience should tell you that.' She half smiled again, her lips turned down with suppressed amusement. Perhaps she did have some vague sense of humor. 'I'm just keeping an eye on you. I don't want you making mistakes at this time in your life. Your no' the first, you know.'

'What do you mean?' I asked.

'You should know already.'

I was getting quite irritated by then. I thought maybe if she relaxed a bit, if we sat down together, she might be less cryptic, in both senses.

'Fancy a cup of tea?' I said.

'That would be nice, dear,' said Agnes, and followed me down the corridor to the kitchen. But the bulb had gone in the long corridor through the loft, and the shadows ate her up. By the time I reached the kitchen door, she'd gone again.

I was mightily narked off. I checked the walls, and I considered checking inside the fucking teapot, but she'd completely disappeared. A more professional phantom, unlike this one conjured up by my late-twentieth century diseased mind, would have at least finished the conversation. I chain-smoked three cigarettes while finishing the bottle of red on the table, and wondered if I should see a doctor pronto.

Chapter Ten

Dowanhall Road, Glasgow

10 June 1902

Dearest Ishbel,

I am so sorry to hear that Mr Dalyell has had malaria and no wonder with the dreadful, uncivilized places he has to go for his work. Those strange foreign epidemics I read of in the *Herald* make Glasgow's rickets, its bandy-legged children and its tuberculosis here seem no longer extraordinary, just mundane.

Duncan has not been in the best of health either, and if it is not one thing with him it is the other. Isabel had the chicken-pox for a week, not badly apart from a bit of greeting and scratching, but Duncan caught the shingles from her and has not been able to bear anything touching his waist for two weeks. Of course, he still insists on preaching, and getting a proper suit on, when no one can have the slightest idea of the agony he is going through. And then there is his stomach ... but I could fill a book about that. Anyway, even though he is getting better he has been carnapcious for days, snapping at the slightest thing, and I am afraid that this week the slightest thing was me arranging to go with Kirsty to see Mr Keir Hardie speak at the Metropole on Sunday night.

It is most curious, because I told him some days ago

that I was not going to the Sunday-night service and he
said that was fine. Then when Kirsty arrived to pick me
up, full of excitement about Mr Hardie and chatting
about all his doings, Duncan went rigid with rage, and
asked to see me alone in his study. 'What do you think
you're doing, woman, going to worship at the feet of
some irresponsible rebel filling people's head with
foolishness?' I explained that Mr Hardie was not a rebel
but had been an elected member of Parliament for some
years, and he was also a Christian socialist, as were
many others we knew going to the meeting, so it was
not the most inappropriate way to spend Sunday night.
He pointed out to me that the first Mrs McPhail had
never missed an evening service. 'You don't know where
your duties lie, do you?' he continued.

I wanted to throw one of the first Mrs McPhail's
precious china shepherdesses at him, but instead I told
him not to fache himself, which just made it worse.
Then, as he started shouting, I took the family Bible
from his desk and opened it at the book of St John and
read out: 'The man that says he loves God, whom he
hath not seen, and loveth not his brother, whom he
hath seen, the same is a liar and the truth is not in him.'
That is what Mr Hardie will be talking about tonight, I
said. Then Kirsty gave a loud knock at the door, saying
we would be late if we did not catch the next tram.
Duncan stood at a loss. 'Just get out of my sight,
woman,' he said at last.

(He never seems to complain about Kirsty's
behaviour, which is strange, but perhaps because she was
brought up by her aunt, he keeps a certain distance
from her. Or is he afraid of her, what she might say?

Kirsty has her own independent life, but I am his wife, in his household, and he thinks I am his property.)

We went anyway, me dithering between being ashamed and being angry, Kirsty telling me not to worry. (Mrs Minto told me afterwards, barely hiding a wee smirk, that Duncan had given strong warnings on the evils of heathen socialism from the pulpit that night.) The man who says he married me for being a fighter has found that when it comes to the battle our respective faiths diverge, and that makes me sorrowful.

Anyway, let me tell you about the meeting, which was set up by the Clarion Scouts, of which Kirsty is a member. (I am not sure to what extent she is a fervent socialist, or whether she just enjoys the Clarion Scouts' bicycle rides and rambling in the country with all those eager and principled young men.) You have probably read about Mr Hardie in the newspapers over there, but in the flesh he is just so impressive. He is full of energy and power, and has a voice that rouses souls – in fact, he most inappropriately reminded me of Duncan at his best in the pulpit.

The theatre was filled with three or four hundred folk, from the best-dressed and educated down to a few shipyard workers and rough-handed girls from the weaving factories. Mr Hardie talked about the role of the new Independent Labour Party, and how it was the first to represent working men – and women; about the need for universal adult suffrage, and plans to substitute a state insurance for the terrible Poor Law. (Daily I see with my own eyes how barbaric that is.) What made me warm to him even more was that he seemed to have a real understanding of the burdens borne by ordinary women, not just low wages, too many pregnancies, poor health and bad housing, but the long hard hours of physical work, cleaning and washing and feeding and clothing a family on next to nothing. The idea that women's wages were to supplement a male 'breadwinner's wage' was a farce for widows and abandoned wives who had nothing else to live on. The result is this simple, he said: women feed their children and they starve themselves, year in and year out.

It turned out that Mr Hardie was sharing the platform that night with a feisty wee woman not even five foot tall from the Glasgow Suffrage Society. Miss Annie Belshaw was her name, and Kirsty said she had been one of the first lady accountants in Glasgow but had lost her job after she refused to stop 'behaviour incompatible with the reputation of the business' – selling suffrage and socialist literature on her Saturdays off on a corner of Sauchiehall Street. They lost a fine accountant, but the Suffrage Society gained a fine speaker who also does the books.

Miss Belshaw began by explaining that now that women have the vote in Australia and New Zealand, Parliament no longer has any moral or logical reason for denying the vote to their sisters in Britain, and she went on to talk about individual rights – oh, Ishbel, I wish Duncan had been there to hear her – and how the concept of spiritual equality put forward by the Church, everyone having equal access to God, encourages moral responsibility. 'And we cannot exercise that responsibility properly if we are declared irresponsible by the present law,' shouted Miss Belshaw, only her hat visible over the lectern. She listed those excluded from voting in the Reform Act of 1832: 'criminals, lunatics, women and children'. Grouped with warped characters, and undeveloped ones, women, she said, were a resource unused in political and social life. 'We are like seeds which have never been watered, not dead but merely dormant, awaiting our time.'

She suddenly pointed up to Glasgow's coat-of-arms with the motto 'Let Glasgow flourish' on the poster above her head, with the bird, the bell, the fish and the tree. Then she said (I was taking notes on the back of the programme for you by then): 'We are like the bell that never rang, the bird that never flew, the fish that never swam, the tree that never grew. Women will not flourish until this government frees them from this categorisation alongside those who inhabit the madhouse, the nursery, and the jail.'

In a rousing finish, she said we must take the debate to the factory gates, to the town squares and to Parliament. Against all my expectations, I was moved almost to tears, standing in this room of like-minded people, this atmosphere of hope instead of the fear I often sense in the church. Afterwards, we went over to the Clarion Scouts' rooms near Charing Cross for tea and scones, and Kirsty introduced me to all sorts of people whose names I cannot remember who all pressed various pamphlets into my hands. I felt so ignorant compared to these people, ordinary mill-hands and welders and shop assistants, who had read Marx and Hume and God knows what else in their pitifully short spare time. Kirsty and I walked home arm in arm in the warm June evening afterwards, and I felt as if I was flying; it seemed that all those little thoughts and questions niggling me had been taken by these people and polished into theories and plans for change. It was as though someone had drawn me a map, clear as anything.

I must stop now, because it is past midnight and Isabel, despite being two and a half this month (as she points out often herself), is still getting up at half past six in the morning and causing no end of trouble. I enclose a Paisley shawl, should you be fortunate enough to come upon a chilly evening in your trip to the mountains.

Your loving sister,
Agnes.

Chapter Eleven

22 November 1999

The rain ran down the dusty window like thin grey porridge. Down below, Broadway was in black and white, but for the yellow streaks of taxis. The gloomy climate had inspired my latest painting – I was writing, 'Ripp'd untimely from his mother's womb', in Gothic print in an arch on the canvas. The finished painting was of a fleshy hill. A pair of newborn feet wriggled out of a bloody gash in the skin. I'd originally been thinking about a Caesarean section when I started painting, but I heard just then on the radio about the recent spate of fetus-snatching. In the latest case, a nine-months-pregnant teen had been shot in the head, her belly cut open, and the living baby stolen by her childless friend. As the broadcast finished, I'd felt sickened. Then I slowly painted out the original scalpel and replaced it with a hunting knife with serrated edges. Gothic indeed.

Listening to National Public Radio was no longer soothing, but at least it was company for long hours alone in the studio. I really preferred vaguely literary programs and the meanderings of *All Things Considered* as a working background, because the news was not merely distressing nowadays but positively bizarre. The eleven o'clock morning headlines began: 'The Marriott Hotel at JFK has been comandeered as a quarantine hospital to receive further victims of the airborne plane virus. So far no cure has been found for the deadly virus, found in two Boeing 767 air-conditioning systems . . . In Montana, troops and tanks are still surrounding the steel-walled compound of the Buchananite Sect. A government spokesman said he was unsure how far the underground warren extended, although defectors have reported an enormous network of tunnels, filled with supplies of food and ammunition to last for at least a year after the millennium . . . Deaths from drug-resistant tuberculosis have doubled in New York city compared to last year . . .'

The mystery viruses and tuberculosis reminded me of Agnes's description of an equally rickety, tubercular Glasgow. I must ask her what she thought next time she rolled in, or walked through a wall, or whatever. I was beginning to see as I plodded through the letters how the stroppy suffragette Agnes I knew and didn't particularly love had developed: Miss Red Skirts on Clydeside and all that. In a lot of ways, however, my sympathies lay with Duncan: both he and I agreed that Agnes was not an easy person to live with. For instance, I considered my paintings to be radical, or sort of feminist in their own way, they were about women's lives, after all, but Agnes had a somewhat narrow conception of art and women, I reckoned. She was all noise and fury, when there was nothing much nowadays your average Manhattan career woman needed to get noisy and furious about. We'd drunk the potion of Feminism with a big F, and thrown the bottle away, forgetting the recipe. I was preparing a series of definitive arguments on this subject in my head for her latest appearance, when

Wanda burst through the door waving her hands in the air. 'Disaster!'

'You broke one of your new false nails? The fifty-dollar ones?'

'No, stupid. The social work inspector just changed her appointment from tomorrow. She'll be here poking round the place in an hour. What'll I do?'

I laid down my brushes and switched off the radio. 'OK, we gotta be calm. I'll tidy the living room and hide the worst of Nosmo's pornography under the bed, and you get changed into some adult clothes.' Wanda, perspiring with fear in the November cold, was wearing a fake crocodile boiler suit. She did not look at all like an appropriate mother-figure for a Chinese orphan. She looked like a hostess from an S&M club.

Wanda needed the home-inspection certificate to proceed with the adoption. Already, social workers had asked her all sorts of probing questions in their offices about her attitude to parenting. For the home visit, Wanda had called in industrial cleaners to get rid of the seven years of grime and dustballs that had accumulated since the three of us moved in, so the kitchen and the bathroom could almost be described as hygienic. She had also – I thought this was pretty thorough – bought some real food, fruit, vegetables and stuff and put it in the fridge so it looked as if we cooked rather than going out or ordering in. The fact, I reckoned Wanda's baby would fall asleep most nights in restaurants, lulled by the sounds of expensive plates and pretentious talk, and would get a taste for puréed sushi at about six months.

I started clearing up the living room, those special touches like putting the little packs of Rizla papers away in drawers, and hiding the roaches deep in the trash. We left my room the cesspit that it was. After seven years, I had decided to get out: not really at Agnes's suggestion, but because I thought art and squalling brats didn't really mix, and I would be stuck at home with the kid, the au pair and the Fisher Price and Playskool junk, instead of having the whole apartment to myself. Besides, I felt I had grown out of Nosmo and Wanda, and I wanted to kick the habit of feeding off the remains of their vapid social lives. I think Wanda was secretly relieved: she and Nosmo could play Mom and Dad more easily, and she had gained an enormous playroom for the kid. 'No actual change in purpose for your room, then,' Nosmo had said rudely.

I also had a vague idea that if I moved out of 666, I might minimize the apparition of antsy suffragettes in my existence. I mean Agnes wasn't exactly the devil at the sign of the devil, but it was just over a month to the millennium, and I thought it might be prudent to get out of there in case she came up with something truly spectacular. Somehow, by changing my physical positioning in the city, I thought I might force my stagnant life to alter in some unexpected way too.

I wasn't going far, just over to Broome Street where Garrett Hughes had offered me the top floor of the six-story downtown warehouse he'd bought in the days when such buildings were dirt cheap. The room was enormous and empty, with a black-painted cube at the side containing a bathroom, a sink and a microwave, but as a studio, it was perfect. Garrett had used it to house various mistresses and students (often one and the same for him), but it has been empty for months, and the rent was cheap. The floorboards were covered in dust and paint, but the room had skylights and industrial-sized windows with views – when the pollution haze allowed – over the Hudson river to the big Colgate clock on the New Jersey side and the Statue of Liberty.

Nosmo was staying put, quite keen on acquiring a part-time share in offspring. He was fantasizing about pushing the stroller round Central Park, having a good excuse to visit FAO Schwarz, and already he and Wanda were designing one-year-old Hallowe'en costumes for the parade. But for the purpose of the social worker's visit, Nosmo had agreed to pretend he didn't exist: 'I'm just certain I'd say the wrong thing when they asked me about being a suitable male influence. Better just be discreet about my presence.'

In his room, I censored half the bookcase and stuffed the more erotic literature under the bed. I packed his suits together into one small closet – he was going to be difficult about the crushed Kenzo – and left the larger closet open and empty so the place looked like a guest room. Amadeus was lying purring on the bed, and for good measure I removed his leather collar with silver metal spikes. The cat tried to scratch me in what could not be considered a child-friendly manner. I chucked it roughly on the floor and glanced round for a final check. An enormous black penis in profile caught my eye. Gay cliché or what? I took down the photograph, added it to the sinful cache under the bed, and went out into the hall.

'It's been Bowdlerized,' I announced to Wanda, who looked more like her old headmistress than herself, in a grey suit, tan pantyhose and make-up. 'You look gruesome,' I said.

117

'That's the idea,' said Wanda.

Wanda put her old teddy bear in the crib she had installed between the purple walls where her office used to be. Her aluminum desk was disguised by a red cloth as a diaper-changing table, although with the virulent walls and red floor, it looked more like an altar for human sacrifices. 'That's all I've got. No clothes – I mean, I don't know how old she's going to be. No point in getting an entire layette in the wrong size. Have you got some, you know, lady-like shoes?' I had supplied some horrible pumps just as the doorbell rang.

The social worker turned out to be an enormous black woman trapped in skintight trousers, a lurex top and combat boots. A yellow feminist symbol dangled from one ear, and the other held three studs. She immediately behaved like a realtor rather than a social worker, running around the loft with a clipboard checking that any flaking paint was not lead-based, complaining that the hot water was set at too high a temperature and might burn children. When I crept into the kitchen for a coffee, the social worker had her head in the cupboard under the sink and was saying, 'You can't keep pans in here. What about rust, and leaking dirty water from the pipes?' By the time I left with the mug, she had sat Wanda down at the kitchen table and had begun a curious interrogation. I shut the door and listened outside.

'As a Chinese-American, what incidents of racism do you remember from school?' started the social worker.

'Well, not a lot, really. I mean, I was the only Chinese kid in the class, half Chinese half Jewish to be exact, so no one paid any attention to my race. If anything it was the opposite. I got extra attention, I was special. I mean, we're talking a nice middle-class suburb near Princeton.'

'No, no, but you must have experienced underlying, subconscious racism. How did you confront that?'

'Oh, sure, now and then, maybe. I don't know. You cope,' said Wanda.

'Look, you're about to bring up a Chinese girl in a tough, racist, sexist city. Unless you understand what you've been through as a minority, you can't help her. You've got to keep her in touch with her traditional culture . . .'

'The traditional culture of abandoning girl babies?' asked Wanda.

Fortunately, the telephone rang at this point. 'It's for you,' shouted Wanda, sticking her head out of the kitchen, and to her surprise almost directly into my face. She rolled her eyes in distaste in the direction of the social worker and shut the door.

The caller was Nancy Klinger with a plan for the evening. 'You wanna go reclaim the word "doll" from the men who have appropriated it as a derogatory term?'

'What? Try to make sense.'

'D'you want to come with me to the first meeting of the New York Dolls, a networking group for women in the arts, culture and media in Manhattan? I read to you from the blurb before me on the bright pink paper: our fellow travelers include New York City's most famous revisionist feminist who wants to create an Old Girls' Network, and Vagina Dentata, an African-American *a capella* group, a philosophy professor from Columbia, and that woman who made the three-hour feature film on ironing as metaphor. Apparently, we are going to "rootle around in the *zeitgeist* toybox" and swap business cards.'

'Wow. Pretentious or what?'

'That's the whole idea, Albertine. But it might be worth it. We get to swap contacts, ideas, and probably, for all I know, lists of single men. And there is good news. The meeting is to be held in that cocktail bar on East 9th Street, so we won't have to face the situation sober.'

'OK, you won me over,' I allowed. 'But what do Dolls wear?'

The answer at the Red Light Bar that evening seemed to be that New York Dolls wore black leather jackets (eight), executive business suits with high heels (eleven), rubber dresses (one), tortoiseshell Armani spectacles (five), and a 'Fuck the Shut Up' T-shirt (one). Kate Spade and Prada bags outnumbered Hermès and Vuitton nineteen to four. We sneaked in at the back – it was already eight p.m. – and ordered red wine at the bar. There were forty or so women in their twenties and thirties in the room, all talking at once. It was a bit like seeing yourself cloned. Nasty. Nancy and I huddled, waiting for proceedings to begin.

'Did Wanda get her certificate of cleanliness and goodliness today?' asked Nancy, unbuttoning her Mao suit in the heat.

'Yeah, her sense of racial oppression wasn't quite acute enough for the social worker's liking – she says she's working on that – but the flat was safe enough. Not much they could complain about.'

'Good. Wine's tongue-stripping, isn't it? And this guy you've been seeing? Is that going anywhere?'

'It's slow progress,' I said, fishing some cork from my glass. I explained that although Leonardo had performed successfully telephonically from various locations recently, I hadn't laid eyes, or indeed hands, on him since the film screening a month ago. I explained that we had touched arms, and that this erotically charged couple of minutes had been sustaining me since then. I confessed to being weak-kneed and weak-minded.

'Boy, that's not much to go on,' said Nancy, screwing her face up. 'You've been pursuing this guy for more than three months and you've yet to see him buck naked. Weird.'

'Yeah, you're telling me. My new theory is he's a virgin. At thirty-five.'

'Mmmmn, possible these days.'

We ordered more bad wine and tried to spot television anchors in the crowd. 'Nannncyyy!' came a scream across the room. We were attacked by a blonde Amazon with dark red nails. It was, indeed, New York's most famous revisionist feminist. She enveloped Nancy in Paloma Picasso perfume and what seemed an excessively large number of breasts.

'Darling, I am so glad you could make it, everyone's here, Jane from ABC, you remember Angela from Ms, Ruby Dish from Los Angeles – she's big at ICM now, you know. And who's this?'

Nancy introduced me and explained about my paintings, while I wriggled with embarrassment. The Revisionist Feminist turned a full-beam smile on me and stretched out her hand. I felt like I was being blessed by the Pope or something, such was the intensity of the woman's love-bombing stare. 'That's really insightful. I am just *so* glad you're here,' said the Revisionist Feminist. 'Well, you *must* meet Zindsi Hawkes, she's organizing an exhibition of women artists called Wicked Women, and I'm sure you'll fit right in.'

'What did she mean by that?' I asked Nancy afterwards, but got no answer, since the meeting had finally begun. A *café-au-lait* supermodel with intellectual pretensions had brought her own camera crew – the latest accessory – but was told to send them away since they were men. Then the Revisionist Feminist forced each woman in the bar to stand up and give her name, rank (job) and feminist credentials. The television anchors and university lecturers rose without fear, smiled charmingly at the Dolls, and sold themselves like the finest washing-powder commercial. I was astounded: these people had moved a long way from modesty. When my turn came I just said I painted and sat down. The Revisionist Feminist turned her smile on full again and cajoled: 'But you haven't mentioned the exact nature of your work. It's fascinating,' she advised the room. I was pissed with Nancy for bringing me here: I'd come just to watch, not to be humiliated. I dropped out a few more sentences like an ice machine forcing out cubes.

The aims of the Dolls were then discussed: they would have monthly meetings, provide contacts for each other, help younger women get work experience on the Old Girls' Network, give speeches, put out a list of female dial-a-quotes for the press, 'a Goddess Rolodex to counteract the White Boys' Rolodex', and generally be 'power feminists' rather than powerless ones.

Out of the corner of my eye, I saw a face I recognized beyond the crowd, scowling and black as thunder. It was Agnes, arms folded, leaning against the far wall. It looked from her sour demeanor like she didn't approve of Prada feminism but, let's face it, she only had herself to blame for starting it all. Must be lousy when your political daughter grows up decadent and delinquent. I gave her a wave, and she glared back.

Nancy was looking at me oddly. 'You're waving to a blank wall, you know.'

'Yeah, I've lost it. Go on, get me more wine,' I said. 'Everything is becoming too right-on. I feel uneasy, not to say out of place.' Nancy nodded understandingly and took the glasses.

'One last thing,' continued another Doll, dressed by Rifat Ozbek, 'I know it may not sound important but it is. We must get everyone we know to go out and vote in the local school-board elections next week. So few people turn out to vote now that the Christian Coalition and a bunch of right-wing anti-abortionists are gaining majorities in all the boroughs.'

Everybody seemed bored with this except Agnes, who looked explosive, like someone had stuffed a fire-work up her long skirt. My instinct was to duck. A bit unfortunate that they brought up lack of voting when she was around. I tried to remember when I had last voted. Maybe once at art school? Anyway, the choice in America wasn't that great: capitalism, or capitalism lite, so why bother? We were talking presidents with their pants down, not about the charismatic Mr Keir Hardie. At that thought, I looked over to see what Agnes was doing, just in time to see her storming out of the door. I shrugged – her paranormal huffs were now common-place for me – and took an enormous drink.

Nancy took my arm (she's very touchy-feely) and we milled about the crowd. She seemed to know and be known by everyone. I felt like the dull other half until I spotted an old lover of Nosmo's.

'Nance, look, it's Jerry Argent. There's a man in here. Thought that wasn't allowed under Doll regulations.'

'Oh, you know Jerry, too? Well, he's not a man any more. He changed sex last year. She's legit. Works for the art desk on *Vague* now and wears Chanel. That's all that's required to be a woman nowadays, isn't it?'

I ran over to talk to him/her, cheered by a familiar face. Jerry kissed me lavishly. 'Just raising my feminist consciousness, you know how hard it is to get it up,' s/he said, snide as ever. 'This is Zindsi Hawkes.' S/he introduced me to what was probably a woman with a Mohican haircut, red shorts and matching red fishnet tights, which displayed her gargantuan thighs.

'Ah got installations coming out of mah ears,' Zindsi moaned, in the incongruous accent of a Southern belle. I thought she was referring to the Mohican, but she was talking about her Wicked Women exhibition at the SoHo Gallery. 'Ah got melted Barbies, Ah got ice-cream Tampax, Ah got dykes' dildoes stapled to the ceiling, Ah got photographs of female elephant parts but Ah ain't go no real painting. Sounds like y'all may be mah solution. Give me your card,' she ordered. 'Who's your gallery?'

'I don't have a card, or a gallery,' I said, pathetically. I felt so unprofessional, like I was ten years younger than all these super-confident women around me. I found a gum wrapper in my bag and wrote my number on it. 'That's jus' fine,' said Zindsi, taking it with a raised eyebrow. 'Ah'll be calling y'all,' and she rolled away like a tank to talk to someone more important.

I went off to the bathroom a bit oppressed by the insincerity of it all, and unconvinced that the woman would call, ever. Nancy seemed to have been sucked into the crowd. I peed for a pleasing forty seconds and stood in front of the mirror trying to flatten my hair, which had been electrically stimulated by the Doll's meeting into a large red bush. I applied some Nars lipstick in mud brown, and grimaced at myself. I rifled again through my bag, a sort of outpost of the Staten Island garbage dump, and found a piece of paper at the bottom. I stood before the payphone in the lobby, chewing my electric blue nails, getting up the courage to call. The elusive Leonardo was supposed to be back in town, and I thought, in my alcoholic rush, that it was time to go for it.

'Leonardo? You there?'

The answering-machine cut off and he picked up the phone.

'Hi. How're you doing? Good to hear you.'

'I'm miserable. I'm trapped in a room of fashionable feminists and I haven't had enough to drink.'

'Sounds dreadful. I was going to crash out early after this morning – I was on the red-eye from Los Angeles – but I could do with a quick drink if you need one too. Where are you right now?'

He arranged to meet me at the Temple Bar near both our apartments. I said goodbye to Nancy and slunk off into the wet night. Without her umbrella, I was due for a soaking, and East 9th Street had never been my favorite place at any time of day. I started to run. Within seconds a guy towered over me in the dark demanding, 'Smoke or coke?' kind of threateningly. When I refused to buy and walked off, he shouted over his shoulder, 'There's not long to go till it's all over. Might as well live, girl.'

A few streets away, past a wallful of Jesus Lopes posters, I felt calm enough to think (always a risk in certain parts of the Lower East Side when anything less than full concentration on street life can result in disaster). The Dolls had been fascinating as well as horrifying. I didn't think I'd ever been in a room with so many women unless they were naked and sweating in the gym changing room. But hey, unlike Agnes, I saw nothing wrong with middle-class cocktail feminism. Damn sight better than the dull, hearty feminists I knew at art school that thought you were a gender traitor for wearing a Wonderbra, and who were fond of hyphenating concepts like oppressed-sisters-of-color and sex-as-violation.

Talking of sex, I had now been on the wagon, so to speak, for 236 days and nights, so I was jittery with adrenaline as I came within a couple of blocks of the bar containing Leonardo. Naturally, I would not indicate any trace of said desire. I'd long been of the school of complete nonchalance as far as men were concerned. To show overwhelming interest was a sign of weakness, a jinx. Particularly in the complex and slow-moving psychological case of Leonardo Ianucci. That said, by the time I was stopped short by the sight of the bar doors, I was in such a state I'd started imagining him unzipping the back of my black nylon dress and running one finger down the V of skin as it peeled open.

I took a calming breath and my face slammed into a wall of noise and (illegal) cigarette smoke. Leonardo was at the bar trying to order. In a crowd of backs I instantly recognized his worn leather jacket and the triangle of black hair at the nape of his neck, a place that I had specific plans to investigate further. It was ten thirty and he still had his stupid sunglasses on. I touched his shoulder from behind, and he turned round and kissed me full on the mouth. I nearly passed out with shock. The sensation directly and disturbingly affected my entire lower half. Then it occurred to me that perhaps Leonardo was working by the code we'd used at high school: first base, kiss on the lips; second base, bare top; third base, bare below the belt, etc. At the going rate it would be five weeks before he hit a home run.

'Brooklyn lager?' he asked. 'Your hair's all mussed up.' He pushed some damp lengths back from my face. I held the bar stool in case of total emotional collapse and smiled stupidly. I suppose when you're so unused to being touched by someone of the opposite sex, even the smallest thing takes on enormous proportions, like it did when you were thirteen. We sat down at the last table available in a dark corner and he took off his glasses. His eyes had turned from brown to black. His stare was so intense, or maybe just tense, that I couldn't meet it all the time.

'So. Tell me.'

I informed him of my new incarnation as a Doll, and my possible future as a Wicked Woman.

'Don't play it down. Seems like you did a good evening's work there.' (I had.)

We talked on, and Leonardo asked to see my paintings. Trying to sound totally casual, repressing inner screams of excitement, I invited him round the following Friday. 'I'll have finished off the first series by then. Come for a drink. I'd invite you to dinner but I can't cook.'

'I can. I'll bring something with me, and we can talk properly.'

Awesome. He can talk, walk and cook, I thought. What more could a girl ask for?

Then he dumped on me. 'I haven't told you, but there's this job I've put in for, financed by National Geographic TV. I'll know next week whether I've got it. It's six months' directing films on a series of different tribes in Uganda . . .'

Six months. Shit, I thought. Knew there'd be a hitch.

'. . . nomads and others. We live with them for months at a time and follow them across the bush. There's one tribe where when the men have significant dreams, they waken everyone else immediately, shouting in the middle of the night, and they all sit round the fire till dawn trying to outdo one another in interpretations.'

He continued, wildly enthusiastic, while my momentary happiness at being with him plunged flat. I didn't give a damn about the stupid tribe's dreams.

'But in some ways I don't want to go now.' He took

my hand across the table. (It was the sort of touch that would continue in more complex forms later, I knew it.) 'Not right now, but what can you do? I'll never get an assignment like that again.'

I could barely speak, such were the opposing forces inside me to leave the bar immediately, and to stay, preferably long-term. I squeezed his hand back.

'And there are some things I've got to tell you. Stuff I should have explained ages ago when I met you. I meant to tell you before but I thought . . . I was . . . how do I explain? Well, did you ever see stories about this guy, this serial killer called Mr Manners? He used to—'

'Yo. Found you!' It was Nancy and Jerry, exploding in a rumpus from the bar's swing doors. Nancy was well wined. 'Knew we'd find you here. We're taking you clubbing.'

'Oh, excuse *me*,' said Jerry, lookig meaningfully at Leonardo. 'We're taking you *both* clubbing.'

Chapter Twelve

Dowanhill Road, Glasgow

1 June 1903

Dear Ishbel

I am lying in the West End Park with Kirsty under the greenest of new leaves, while Isabel runs wild with her ball. Like a homing pigeon, she always returns to my rug on the grass because I bribe her with a bottle of sugar-ollie water – do you remember us having that when we were weans?

Well, the news is that I have just joined the Glasgow Women's Suffrage Society. After footering about on the sidelines for a year, I thought I should just get on with it and get properly involved. I was terrified about telling Duncan, but in fact he turned out to be resigned to my shenanigans, so he barely paid any attention when I told him, just sighing, 'Aye, do what you will. You'll do that anyway.' Maybe he is getting mellowed in his middle fifties. Whatever, things are a bit calmer now and there is even talk of another baby, much to my surprise. He has taken to Isabel much more now that she can speak properly (I think myself he was repulsed by the boring physical work of bringing up a child, but he is much more minded nowadays to read to her and teach her hymns, yet in some ways he seems more like a grandfather than a father to her.) For me, everything Isabel does is fresh and fascinating, but he has seen it all before three times with his girls.

By the way, Kirsty – she is off chasing Isabel round a tree now – told me when we were up late talking the other night about how her poor mother died. I mean I told you before it was having the fourth child, but I had not realized her kidneys were under such strain from the third one that the doctors told her it was far too risky to have another. But they both so wanted a boy ... Kirsty is still so bitter about it, even though it was fourteen years ago, and she blames her father for allowing it to happen. I just do not know what to say to her, and it is not a healthy grudge to hold. I wonder if that is why she became a midwife, but I am too scared to ask her.

Anyway, on to more hopeful matters – well, someone has to be hopeful about getting women the vote. I have hardly had a minute to spare writing up the reports of the suffrage meetings which are every Thursday up at George's Cross. The more I learn the more ignorant I feel. There is not much talk of the Bible here. Most mock the sham world of the Church and instead they all know their Marx, their Carlyle, their Engels, and talk of Ibsen's *The Doll's House* and how it has changed the perception of marriage.

We draft pamphlets, people from the art school design cards and posters, we arrange lectures and meetings, and some of the ladies travel miles to the hustings at by-elections, even as far as England. I am convinced myself that nothing will come right in this country until women are treated equally with men. The slow progress is so frustrating, though, after all, why should there be anything extraordinary about women having a voice in the laws that govern them? I know you agree with me here, Ishbel, so I will not go on about it, but suffice to say I am fairly brewing with enthusiasm for our struggle.

Annie Belshaw – do you remember I wrote to you about her a year or so ago when she spoke with Keir Hardie at the Metropole? – anyway, she has become my mentor, really, although I am still a wee bit feart of her brusque manner. She cornered me when I was in the women's tea-room putting up posters for our debate on legal rights ('Wife or Slave' was the title, good and provocative and my suggestion) and said I was picking up things so quickly that I should go to the Clarion Scouts to learn to be a proper speaker. I blushed and said I did not have the time, but she said the society had better use for me than putting tin-tacks in notice-boards, and so a week later, I was in the speech-making class.

We go every Tuesday evening to the Clarion Scout rooms, but out of the ten of us, there are only three women: myself, another suffragist, and a lassie from the weaving mills. The rest are men, mostly trade unionists, and one young man who does the books at Slater's and fancies himself an intellectual. The first time, the teacher, a Mr Ellis who is a retired councillor but not a retired drinker from his looks, handed us each a slip of paper with a quote on it. Mine was from Samuel Johnson's dictionary: 'Oats. A grain, which in England is generally given to horses but in Scotland supports the people.' He gave us five minutes to make up a two-minute speech, without notes.

'Right you first,' said Mr Ellis, pointing to the man from Slater's. 'Up at the lectern with you.' The man's quote was 'England is the mother of parliaments' and he went on and on about the separation of powers, quite elegantly, I thought. 'Dull. Flat intonation,' said Mr Ellis dismissively, and waved him down. The poor boy looked quite deflated, and I could feel my stomach knotting away to itself. Next up was one of the trade unionists from Yarrow's, talking about Britain which, according to the quotation from William Booth of the Salvation Army is 'a population sodden with drink, steeped in vice, eaten up by every physical and social malady'. He gave a rousing speech, well over the two minutes, and I felt like clapping. But his criticism was: 'Good, but you can't sustain that level for half an hour. You have to have peaks and troughs.' Then Mr Ellis's fat finger pointed along the row to me. 'Me?' I asked him. 'Yes, you. Are you just here to watch?'

My heart was thumping, but I got up on the box so I could reach the lectern properly. I held on to it to stop shaking, and began, 'Ladies and gentlemen,' read out the quote, started to say something about Mr Johnson's travels in Scotland, and then froze entirely. I just stood there, glaekit and gulping. 'Mrs McPhail,' said Mr Ellis, 'if you agree with Mr Johnson about the Scots, then you shouldn't say another word. Perhaps you do not find his tone patronising?' That got me going. Well, Father was always such a Scots nationalist, and I felt his blood coursing within me, so I just laid into Mr Johnson and his limited understanding of anything north of the Border. Mr Ellis only stopped me when I drew breath. 'Better, Mrs McPhail, better. You've got some fire in you, I see,' he said, with an irritatingly amused look on his face.

Anyway, once we had all made fools of ourselves – the first time is always the worst, as they say – we loosened up and learned about grabbing the crowd, timing, phrasing, repeating certain slogans, and peroration. (It seems to me you're supposed to repeat yourself constantly, but in different words.) Mr Ellis showed us how to stand, not in an aggressive position but relaxed, feet slightly apart, and how to breathe. The other suffragist had a tendency to wave her hands in the air. 'Do nothing unless your gesture means something.' He said we women must try not to wear gloves because that distanced us from the crowd, and if the gloves are light-coloured they look like hand puppets, and he warned me against my polka-dot blouse: 'Makes folk's eyes skelly at a distance.' Hats that shaded the face were useless, he said, and it was better to go bareheaded where possible. Well, I had no idea that dress mattered so much.

I thought the class was hard going at first, but now three weeks later, we are heckling one another to practice dealing with difficult crowds. I get quite carried away, letting everything come out, shouting, thinking on my feet. After the class, I feel like we used to feel when we were little after a trip to the seaside, that airy head and pleasant exhaustion which makes me fall into a deep sleep. Next week we are going early in the evening to stand on a box on Glasgow Green to make speeches in turn to whatever crowd turns up there, and I will report back to you on my public humiliation.

The whole speech-making business made me think about Father, and I thought that although he might have found my cause a wee bit ridiculous, he would be proud of what his daughters have done. There you are, adventuring from Delhi to Calcutta, seeing the wonderful, the mysterious and the horrible, meeting Brahmins, Parias and monks whose nails are so long they grow into the flesh of their hands. And here I am, standing up, literally, for what I believe. I thank God Father never gave us any doubts or fears, never told us that something was impossible. If he had had sons, perhaps it would have been different for us, but I feel he has laid an iron frame of strength within us, and I thank him for that. I miss them both so much.

Anyway, we have important business, Isabel and I. We have to feed the ducks. I will write next week.

With all my love to you all,
    Agnes

Chapter Thirteen

27 November 1999

'Alb, just look at this. Wow. This is the most extraordinary thing I've ever seen,' shouted Nosmo, as I came
into the apartment. He was sitting mesmerized in front
of the television. I kicked the door shut and dumped my
box of wine bottles in the hall. The HSC Home
Shopping Channel logo glared from the screen in the
living room.

'What is it? The largest zirconite friendship ring ever?
Tiaras for dogs? Pubic-hair extensions? Share it with
me.'

'Nah, nah, come and sit down. A bunch of terrorists
have taken over the Home Shopping Channel and
they're forcing it to broadcast their demands live. I've
been watching it for an hour. They're making all those
people selling zirconite rings kneel at the back in a row
and . . .' Here Nosmo cracked up laughing. '. . . ooh . . .
oooh . . . recant all the garbage they've told the unsus-
pecting Midwestern public.'

Indeed, as we watched, a man with an AK47 and a
black balaclava was smashing a display of limited-edition
porcelain baby dolls on the floor. 'Shit,' he shouted,
hitting one camera square on with a 'Tiny Smiles'
Victorian doll, which shattered down the screen. 'This is
the crap you fill your minds and souls with. Capitalist,

136

manipulative trash in a "limited ediiton" of *two million*. Two fucking million. And you, yes, *you*, viewer, you have just paid three instalments of fifty-nine ninety-nine, to own this shit.'

He poked his gun in the back of a terrified telesaleswoman's back. 'Tell 'em how much you pay for these wholesale from . . .' Here he turned the doll over to look. '. . . from fucking Korea. Tell 'em about the child labor you exploit.' The saleswoman gibbered in genuine ignorance and began to cry. 'Oh go back and kneel down,' said the terrorist irritably, handing her over to one of his masked and gloved henchmen. He moved his face into the camera for a close shot. You could see white skin round the eye-holes of his mask. 'Fellow Americans, there are forty days – *forty days* – until the end of the world, and all you can do is buy shit like this, sitting there on your fake-leather sofas with your walletfuls of credit cards.' He suddenly disappeared out of camera range. There was machine-gun fire. He reappeared. 'And if the company even thinks of taking us off air, we will shoot one Home Shopping salesperson for every five minutes of lost broadcast time.' The camera panned over to a giant teddy bear ($89.99) riddled with bullets.

Nosmo was clutching his stomach and hooting. 'Oooh, this is superb. What irony. What timing. Oooh.' As a Home Shopping addict, he knew the quality of such programing very well. 'Superb' was probably a fair assessment of the broadcast.

'But what if they really kill someone?' I asked, wondering if everyone else was losing their grip on reality too.

'Well, if we flick over to CNN Live,' said Nosmo, zapping the channel, 'we can see that FBI agents have surrounded the place and there are helicopters hovering above.'

'Yeah, and what difference did that make to the people in Waco?' I pointed out.

'Good question,' said Nosmo, zapping back to HSC, where the terrorist was forcing a man in a shiny double-breasted suit onto a rowing machine. 'You keep at that till you lose weight,' he said. 'That's what you advertised it for.' He stuck his gun in the salesman's sweaty face. 'Faster, faster.'

I giggled and went to put the white wine in to chill, for Leonardo was coming round to cook dinner that night.

Wanda came bustling in the front door. 'Is the siege still on? I took a cab instead of walking in case I missed any of it. You know we were planning to do a Wong II Wong junior range on HSC?'

Without waiting for answers, Wanda joined Nosmo on the chaise-longue. They looked like a comfortable old couple enjoying a horror movie, except that Nosmo was wearing a long brocade shift. I handed them each a glass of the red wine and took mine into my room. I had my own problems right then, the worst being 'What will I wear?' and the second worst being 'Will this guy sleep with me?' I pulled on some orange velvet jeans, which I suited, but they were cut so narrowly I thought they might burst during what had been billed as a relaxed dinner at home. So I put my regular jeans back on, and added an old green velvet jacket that clung softly. Then I started worrying about my makeup – I'm sure men don't notice any of these things at all – but I aimed eyeliner just above my upper lashes, and immediately smudged it. 'Why bother?' I asked myself in the mirror. 'Why bother for someone who's leaving the godforsaken country next week?' and continued to apply my lipstick with extreme care.

Back in the living room, Wanda and Nosmo were still huddled before the television. 'Do you think it's OK to invite someone round that you hardly know and then make them cook dinner for yourself and your friends? Isn't that a bit much? Shall we offer to go out?' I worried.

'Seems like dinner is all you're going to get off this guy, so we might as well benefit too,' sniggered Nosmo, flicking back to CNN. 'Look, the cops've got gas masks.'

The intercom buzzed.

Leonardo entered, bearing two large Balducci's bags, wearing a baggy black suit with a collarless shirt. He'd obviously been out sliming some film types. 'Hi,' he said, kissing me (lips again). His dog trotted in behind him. 'Seen the Home Shopping siege? I think the terrorist guy wrote a script beforehand. His timing's amazing. But any minute now the whole thing is going to go dreadfully wrong.'

'Yeh,' said Nosmo, shaking hands with Leonardo, who pretended not to notice the curious shift. 'It's so carefully choreographed, and he's playing to both the cameras like a professional.'

Wanda stood up to shake hands too. Her gaze locked on the birthmark, but then slowly toured the long length of Leonardo's body, and officially registered it as well made. I grimaced at her, she's so obvious, and she gave me a vulgar girl-to-girl thumbs-up sign behind his back as he went ahead into the kitchen, saying, 'Well, keep me posted. Gotta cook.'

I poured myself more wine and a tumbler for Leonardo and settled down at the kitchen table. I poured a bowl of water for Spot: the way to a man's heart is through his dog. I was so fucking nervous. He folded himself into the chair opposite. 'Sorry I was too shattered to go clubbing the other night. Was it good?'

'Disaster,' I said, screwing up my nose. 'Don't ask. You did the right thing. I'm sorry we're forcing you to cook. You wanna watch TV and I can start preparing the simple stuff?'

'Hey, I didn't come here to watch TV.' He smiled, and passed me a giant string bag of mussels. 'Give 'em a wash? And, anyway, you can see that sort of stuff any day these past few months. If it's not Home Shopping in Pennsylvania, it's some nuts in Montana. I mean, it's funny and surreal right now but it's only a matter of time before the FBI agents fuck up big time and raid the place and—'

'Yeah, and we'll see the crazy stuff beforehand, but none of the carnage and death afterwards because they'll cut the broadcast, so it will remain no more than a weird movie to most people at home. And then they'll buy the rights and make a movie about it anyway.'

'Precisely,' said Leonardo, his jaw tight, like he was taking it personally. He shook his head from side to side as though he was clearing it out. 'Anyway, forget that. Cookery lesson: Zuppa di Cozze Piccante. Mussel soup. Well, it's more a stew, with chillies, anchovies and tomatoes. Run them under the tap and throw them in that pan with some white wine and olive oil until they open,' he said, waving at the mussels.

'This Mama's recipe?'

'No, Papa's. Learned at his knee in the deli.'

'Oh, you're *that* Ianucci.' Wished I'd found that out before. I was on to a good thing here. Ianucci's Delicatessen in Brooklyn was a vast salami-hung cave of a place with, I remembered, olive oil in what looked like garbage cans. Shame Leonardo didn't go into Papa's business close by instead of filming distant tribesmen who would not know good pancetta if it bit them.

Anyway, I chopped while Leonardo did artsy things like mashing the garlic and anchovies into hot oil 'until dissolved'. Previously, I had not been aware that anchovies were soluble. At the same time, he was grilling slices of polenta, halving figs to go with prosciutto, and unwrapping cheese.

'This is fab,' I said, referring officially to the food but fantasizing for a moment that we were a long-married couple fixing dinner together. We cooked on in what people refer to as companionable silence, but I felt as sexual tension.

'I'm leaving the end of next week, you know,' said Leonardo, delivering the body blow when I least expected it. 'They barely give you a week to get organized, these guys. Bad timing, huh?' He looked up from his chopping to see my face stuck in an ironic downturned smile. He changed the subject. 'Can we go see your paintings and leave this to rest for a while?'

We left the perfect multicolored stew, and the dog followed us. We passed Wanda and Nosmo still glued to the screen. The terrorist was making a long and witty speech to camera about the millennium, without notes. I opened the door to my studio with some reluctance, worried that Leonardo would think me frivolous, or plain pretentious. My work was not exactly guys' stuff. What is it anyway with modern relationships that you have to reveal your work to each other before you reveal your anatomy?

The bed seemed mortifyingly central to the room, I thought, looking through a stranger's eyes. Indeed, it was the only clean patch in the studio, with a canvas canopy strung over it like a tent from the ceiling to keep out the light from the high windows. Except for the large rug near it, there were paint trails everywhere on the floor, and jars of nasty grey and pink flesh colors on wobbly tables – stuff I usually didn't notice. Leonardo wandered along the far wall where five pregnant women were propped, each canvas six feet high. He came to the 'Ripp'd untimely' painting, moved closer and then started back in disgust. He lingered before the truncated woman imprinted red by her too-tight underwear, and then mooched among the pile of smaller canvases without saying a word. The smells of oil and turpentine and acrylic mingled heavily in the radiator heat, and made me feel oddly light-headed. The silence was unbearably tense, so I noisily cleaned out some jars at the sink.

'I see now,' he said.

What's that supposed to mean? I thought. I felt sick with embarrassment.

'Well, I could never quite work out what you were talking about, especially with that fake belly, but I get it now. This is smart. It will also freak people out. But that's what you want, isn't it?'

I had, in fact, no idea how I wanted people to react. It had just happened. 'I suppose so,' I said vaguely, twisting my hair, which was out and about, into a long roll.

He stared at my hair and then right at me, and I became aware of the space between us in the room, in the *bed*room. I held my breath. He had stretched out and he looked poised to cross the gap of two or three feet. Then Agnes walked in from nowhere right between us, her boots echoing across the floor. Naturally, I looked like I'd seen a ghost, which I had, but Leonardo presumed the horror on my face was directed at him. The dog went bananas, barking and jumping. Leonardo backed away and tried to keep on talking, appreciating my brushwork and colors and stuff. Meanwhile, I could only raise furious eyebrows at the smirking Agnes, but I was ready to kill her, if that was technically possible. I got my chance to speak when Leonardo said he'd take the dog outside for a quick run.

'What the hell do you think you're doing? That's the second time you've gotten in the way when he's been around. Just get right out of my face.'

'Now, now, now,' said Agnes, actually shaking her finger at me. I rolled my eyes. 'Just you calm down, dear. That boy's no use to you, or anyone. He's got a past you don't want to get involved with. He's no' a bad lad, but he's got baggage, if you get my drift, and I can tell you from experience that you don't want that. He's no' reliable.'

'What do you mean?' I said, exasperated but interested, too. 'How do you know all this?'

'Ah, that would be telling,' Agnes said, ever-helpful.

'You know, I'm not marrying this guy or having his kids, he's about to leave the country, so I don't know what you're getting so freaked out about.'

'As I said, he's no' reliable. Look at his behaviour so far – always disappearing. Take my word for it, you're making a mistake here.'

'I just don't have time for this,' I growled at her. 'Now fuck off.'

She looked aghast at my language, and disappeared, leaving an annoying little shimmer. I wanted to cry. Why did these things only happen to me? Or perhaps they were not happening to me, which was even worse. I walked shakily into the corridor.

Meanwhile, back in reality, the live siege broadcast had been blacked-out and Wanda and Nosmo were snuffling round the kitchen looking hopefully into pans when I returned. When I informed them that Leonardo was in fact the son of *the* Ianucci, their excitement mounted.

We ate greedily. By the time we reached the cheese course, a squishy Pont L'Evèque, with some Taleggio and aged Pecorino on ciabatta, the inhabitants of 666 Broadway were all in love with Leonardo. For Wanda and Nosmo, the feeling was purely gastronomic.

The kitchen glowed with warm light and alcohol. It was the only room I felt Wanda had got right in her redecoration with ochre walls, mismatched plates and secondhand furniture. Wanda had been talking about her planned adoption of Li An, a four-month-old orphan from Wuhan, a giant industrial town none of us had heard of in China. She left the table and came back with a blurred photocopy of a passport photograph. Half the baby's face was in darkness due to the bad reproduction.

'Isn't she beautiful?' said Wanda. 'I mean, you can't actually see her properly at all but I can tell.'

They each admired the blur. I was sort of pleased that Wanda felt comfortable enough with Leonardo to show off her prized treasure, and hoped she was a better judge of character than Agnes. Wanda was flying out at Christmas to pick the baby up. Leonardo seemed fascinated by the details. He kept asking questions. Either he's broody, I thought, or else he feels a new film proposal coming on.

Nosmo was saying it was best to shop for the baby in the Barneys January sale. 'No point in buying the wrong size at twice the price now, although I have my eye on some perfectly adorable little hats like strawberries.'

Leonardo laughed, but Nosmo took it well. 'The layette. I'm in charge of the layette because I have better taste than her,' he said, gesturing towards Wanda. Wanda gave him a very direct look, which meant shut-up-and-go-to-bed. On cue, they both thanked Leonardo profusely, said he could come back any time soon, and slipped off. I could hear them snickering like teens in the corridor.

Instead of an increase in tension when we were left alone, I felt a release. The dog was asleep under the table, Leonardo flopped into the low armchair by the stove, and I sat on a cushion on the floor. 'Come over here,' he said, barely audible. I slid over and leaned back against his chair. He stroked my hair away from my forehead right down to the small of my spine. I rippled with his touch. It was odd not seeing his face, concentrating instead on disembodied feeling. I let my head fall back, stretched out my neck, and allowed my brain to dislocate.

His sentences fell out one by one. 'I have been thinking about touching you, touching your hair, since I saw you in the street in the summer. Wondering how it would feel.' He had his lips on the crown of my head. 'Thinking about how red it is. How old-fashioned it looks, like hair in a painting. Do you find there's one thing about each person that obsesses you?'

I turned round and reached up to touch the purple birthmark round his eye. It was slightly raised, like a Braille message. I read it carefully. My fingers slipped down to his mouth and were drawn in, one at a time.

Then the night became circular without a beginning, end or middle, filled with dark surfacings and drownings and even acrobatics that could not be individually remembered because they required, at the time, no thought.

Eventually we ended up under the tent of the bed, at perhaps four in the morning. I had a strange, clear sensation, that slightly wave-battered, exhausted high got from a long day at the seaside. The feeling seemed weirdly familiar. I slid off Leonardo's belly and lay in the crook of his brown shoulder, looking at my white freckled skin against his darkness, listening to his breath and idly parting the hairs on his chest illuminated by the street-lamps. I basked in my own happiness.

'I do not have the best of news,' said Leonardo, looking down below. 'I'm afraid this one's burst.'

'Oh dear,' I said. I leaned over and looked closely at the condom packet I'd found earlier in the bedside drawer. Sell by Nov. 1998, it said. (That's what comes of having sex after 241 days without it. You're never prepared.) I passed the packet to Leonardo for evidence and shrugged. 'Well, I'm four days off my period so it should be fine and . . .' My voice trailed off, thinking of worse possibilities than pregnancy.

He saw my face. 'Oh, it's OK. Don't worry about that. I haven't slept with anyone since my wife.'

'*Your wife?*' I sat up straight in bed.

'She's dead. She was killed nearly two years ago. You're the first person I've slept with since then.'

He looked edgy now, waiting for my reaction. I just wanted to put my head under the pillow and avoid dealing with the situation altogether. Instead I lay back slowly beside him.

'I'm sorry I shouted. How awful. What happened to her?'

'I tried to tell you the other night in the bar, but your friends came . . .'

He pulled me back over towards him and wrapped his arms round me. I lay stiffly at first, feeling utterly separate in the physical closeness, feeling the presence of his wife lying between us, watching his face as he talked for almost an hour.

His wife's name had been Anna, and they had lived in Brooklyn for three years in an apartment on Cobble Hill. They had had no children, but both mothers, being Italian, had been set upon rectifying that. He'd met Anna at the wedding of one of his friends from high school, and three months later they'd gotten married themselves.

He drew in a ragged breath. 'Anna worked selling advertising for *TV Guide* in the Rockefeller Center. One lunch-time she had just come out of the Au Bon Pain onto Sixth Avenue, with a *cafe latte* and a tuna sandwich in her hand. A man came crashing into her, she dropped the coffee and was saying, 'You should look where you're—' when he stabbed her in the throat, and then the chest, and by the time the ambulance got through the Friday afternoon traffic jams to the hospital she was dead.'

Leonardo kept his gaze steadfastly on the street-light outside. 'Then the man disappeared into the crowd, and wasn't caught until he stabbed a tourist six weeks later outside Saks Fifth Avenue. He was a serial killer. You maybe heard of him?'

'I remember,' I said. 'The papers nicknamed him Mr Manners. All those tacky headlines. He was the guy who shouted out going into the courthouse, 'People have got to learn some manners,' or something. He kept jostling people on the street and then killing them for no reason at all. Oh, God, there were—'

'Four others,' he cut in. 'It's one of those things you read in astounded disbelief, serial killers, sieges, thinking, New York, it's a dreadful place. And then you discover it's about you. It's about your wife dying at twenty-seven years old on the Avenue of the Americas. You realize there are no certainties anymore, that at any moment everything could end. Stop. Right now.'

I stroked his arm. My throat swelled up, and I blinked, feeling I shouldn't cry. I said nothing because there was absolutely nothing for me to say.

Leonardo, on the other hand, had a great deal to say. His words flooded out. He seemed to want to go through it all again.

'That Friday afternoon, after the police called, I went back to my parents'. My mom was hysterical. My dad and I drank ourselves into unconsciousness. I stayed away from Cobble Hill for a week, except to get my suit for the funeral, an event which was entirely about exercising self-control and not screaming out in public. People kept saying, ' "It'll be cathartic," but when your pain is so raw that's fucking ridiculous.'

Eventually, he had gone home. Of course, Anna was still there. He said the bed had smelled of her and she had left him a last note on the fridge. 'We need milk, OJ and 2 fennel bulbs. Back after 8, XXX.' He had read it and thrown up in the bathroom.

He had kept hearing her in the passageway, or feeling she had just left a room when he entered. 'I would save up things during the day to tell her at night, and only then realize she wasn't there.' Her bank statements and subscriptions to *Glamour* and *Vague* had kept appearing in the mailbox, and some days Leonardo had woken up unsure whether she was dead or alive. When they caught the serial killer, Anna's death became public property again and he had been forced to believe it. He had someone to hate, but it made little difference. He hadn't bought any newspapers during the trial. 'Her sister came and took her clothes away, but for weeks Anna's stray socks appeared, pale blue or white among my laundry.' I felt my eyes watering again, but held myself back, feeling no right to any pain.

Leonardo had moved into a studio in the West Village, hoping to leave it all behind. Six months afterwards, when he was working again, he had gone unthinking into the coffee-shop where he and Anna

149

often had breakfast on Sunday. He'd started crying uncontrollably in the booth and only stopped at home an hour later.

'What was she like?' I asked, sitting up again and pulling the quilt round me, wanting to envisage the other woman in the bed.

'Well, sort of dark and adorable, a little plump and, well, Italian. Catholic. She wasn't that much interested in her career. She really wanted to settle down, have a family, hang out with the extended family. Have picnics on the Jersey shore. We had a lot of fights about that. Lot of fights about me working too much and going away. I mean, maybe it wasn't the most perfect marriage. Maybe it wouldn't have lasted, and maybe it would have got better, but we never got the chance to find out for ourselves. For a while, death made her perfect, us perfect, but I can't live on and believe that.'

Although Leonardo had been unable to read about the trial, a year later he'd found himself increasingly interested in the killers on death row, where Mr Manners presently remained, endlessly appealing his sentence. Leonardo had started making a film in Huntsville, Texas, about the prison clothing factory run by condemned men, all of whom, presumably, had killed an Anna somewhere. He'd been popular with the prisoners. They liked the film. One had even invited him to watch his death by lethal injection, and Leonardo consequently found himself even more against the death penalty than he had been before his wife's death.

'Peculiar, really, the opposite reaction from what I expected. Then I filmed all summer in Rikers, once a temporary resting place for Mr Manners, and now I am as you see me, obsessive about crime and punishment.'

'God,' I said, raising my face from my hands and exhaling.

'I'm sorry to land all that on you. It's not something I've really done before to anyone. It's made me feel better and you feel a great deal worse. But I couldn't not have told you.'

I was exhausted, upset, already hung over and astounded by the strange intimacy I now had with Leonardo – and his wife. Suddenly Agnes's first words repeated in my head: 'When he comes to my bed at night I want to be a true wife to him . . . but sometimes I feel the cold body of the first Mrs McPhail lies between us.' A shadow of the thought must have passed across my face, because Leonardo suddenly said, 'She went out of my head. I forgot her completely for hours. I lived without her last night, properly, for the first time.'

He kissed me into a melted pile-up of emotions, and stroked the tension from my body until it curled softly. He held me from behind and said, 'Need to sleep,' before passing into unconsciousness. I watched him breathing peacefully, his eyes shut, his strange purple mark turned black in the semi-dark, and I felt a twist of dread for no reason at all.

We awoke late in the morning still locked together in the same position, and ravenously made love again in the steel-gray light. After all, I thought practically, there's no point in worrying about a condom now.

At noon, there was a knock at the door and Nosmo appeared with Spot, two coffees, blueberry muffins, and a prurient look on his face. He brought the mugs to the bedside. 'Messy night at the Home Shopping Channel,' he said cheerfully. 'Five dead, including two salesmen, but the siege is over. Can you believe it, though? They're already back on air this morning – tuna casserole special, eighteen ninety-nine including the recipe.'

Chapter Fourteen

Dowanhill Road, Glasgow

17 December 1905

Dear Ishbel,

We are catching up with you Dalyells at last. I am
going to have another baby, after all this time. The
good news has brought a new lease of life to Duncan,
and all his stomach troubles seem to have been
forgotten. More like he has transferred them all to me,
because I have been a bit peely-wally and off my food,
but that is the price you pay, and I know you know
that yourself, Ishbel, from long experience. We were
sitting at dinner the other night and I had cooked
brisket and onions in a white sauce, Duncan's favourite,
and I put great platefuls in front of us and realized I
could not touch a thing. I could only take a wee bit of
the mashed potatoes. Meanwhile Duncan was sitting
there chewing away making plans for 'the wee lad'. He
thinks it is a boy again, and talking about whether we
could afford the school fees for Glasgow Academy, or
if he might get a scholarship somewhere. And I said to
him, 'Well, the baby is probably small enough right
now to sit in your teacup, so shall we worry about the
school later?' He laughed, which makes a change.

Duncan told me it was fifteen years, yesterday, since
his wife died. I could hardly believe it was that long,

because I am still aware of her presence in the Manse every day. She was a quiet, rather dull woman, according to Kirsty, but there is a little charcoal sketch of her still on the mantelpiece in the front room, and Duncan, I know, keeps a lock of her hair in a silver snuff box in his desk drawer. Poor Duncan. They ought to be growing old together instead of him having a young troublemaker about the house like myself.

Anyway, new life is on its way, and although it can never replace that which is lost for ever, it does provide a terrible, caterwauling distraction and a new source of love when it arrives. Last time I remember I prayed every night until Isabel arrived, but now I no longer feel the duty or the urge. What will be, will be, and there are so many other questions on my mind that even God cannot answer.

Every time I walk out into the street I am assailed by the unfairness of things. I saw a tramp being taken away by the police, dead with the cold, early yesterday morning on Byres Road when I was out getting the messages, and last week when I was in the town I gave tuppence to a woman without any legs who was sitting on a sort of trolley, begging. (Maybe we should recognize that we have a caste system here, too.) Then I go back to Hyndland and see some of the women in the church who have spent the average man's monthly wage on a hat to wear in God's house, and I wonder, I wonder more and more.

I try to talk to Duncan about it, but he always brings the conversation round to charity, and I do not think there is enough goodness in those people's hearts for charity to change the world. Nor am I so narrow-

minded as to accept unquestioningly the voice of the
growing stack of Independent Labour Party pamphlets
supplied by Kirsty and hidden in my bedroom drawer,
but I have been quietly reading Marx's critique of
capitalism and there is some good sense there, I know it
in my bones. Those answers go beyond an hour of piety
and charity in the collection plate once a week. If
women had a say in the world, I am sure far less of this
would happen.

I do not suppose you will have seen anything much
yet about the suffrage demonstration at the Free Trade
Hall in Manchester, for the story may not yet have
reached India in detail. But the reports that have come
up to Glasgow have been fascinating. You know I
mentioned a few months ago about a wee group down
in Manchester, the Women's Social and Political
Union? I told you about Mrs Pankhurst's Suffrage Bill,
the one backed by Keir Hardie, being filibustered to
pieces by that eejit of a Member of Parliament in an
endless discussion of whether motor-cars should have a
rear light as well as a front light. Well, the whole
business obviously irked the Pankhursts and the WSPU
more than anyone thought, because they caused a fair
bit of trouble thereafter.

It all started in October when the Liberal Sir
Edward Grey came to speak at the Free Trade Hall in
Manchester, and refused to meet the suffragists'
delegation. Christabel Pankhurst and Annie Kenney, the
one that used to be a mill-hand, then settled themselves
among the audience in the hall, and at a crucial
moment, a little white Votes for Women banner
popped up above their heads. Miss Kenney stood up

and asked, 'Will the Liberal government give women the vote?' but her question went completely ignored while others were answered. She kept shouting it out, and then the men beside her roughly pulled her down and one of the stewards stuffed his hat over her face. Then, during the vote of thanks, Miss Kenney got on her chair and shouted again. There was complete uproar. The two women were dragged screaming out of the hall by stewards and policemen. Miss Pankhurst tried to spit at a policeman, and hit one too, just before they were flung down the steps of the building. Meanwhile, a carnapcious Sir Edward was saying that suffrage was 'not a party question' and 'not a fitting subject' for the meeting.

They were arrested, and chose Strangeways Gaol over fines (in the Third Division, in prison dress and eating prison rations, brave women), and what started as a polite question became a national scandal. Of course, everyone says the Cause has been put back dozens of years by their unruly behaviour as 'wicked and brawling women', but I have never seen so much written in the newspapers or talked about, and I think it has done us no harm.

So when the Prime Minister came to speak in Glasgow recently, why, we were inspired to similar action. An extraordinary wee pudding-faced woman, Mrs Flora Drummond, arrived from Manchester (although she is a Scot from Arran) to organize the protest against Mr Campbell-Bannerman. Kirsty and I made cotton Votes for Women banners, dozens of them in case they were taken away from us, and prepared to heckle. The hall was full, and we caused a proper stramash, although no one was arrested. (Imagine what Duncan would have said! I did not dare tell him we had been there.) The *Herald* just noted the day after that there had been 'a number of unfortunate interruptions' during the Prime Minister's speech. Mrs Drummond holds a grudge against the state, since she took the examinations to be a postmistress but was banned from the job for being under the five foot two regulation height. Despite her size, she was, however, a fine match for the Prime Minister. I think the WSPU are right: there is nothing like causing a bit of trouble to get some attention, and perhaps the more polite Glasgow Suffrage Society should consider such action. Certainly Annie Belshaw thinks so, and is increasingly rebellious about 'genteel politicking' as she calls it. We shall see.

Down Sauchiehall Street, the shops are all filled with toys and decorations, and I am off to search for some coloured wooden bricks for Isabel (she will not touch her dolls) and something in the tobacco and pipe line for Duncan. I hope you have already received the parcel I sent a couple of months ago. Yours is here already, and many thanks. As the brown fog comes down and the nights draw in I often dream of what it must be like to spend Christmas at your house, with the plantain trees at each side of the door – I do not even know what a plantain looks like – and the pillars of your porch wreathed by flowers in our bleak mid-winter.

Wish Jennie, Allan and Ian and Mr Dalyell the best in the New Year,

Your affectionate sister,

Agnes.

Chapter Fifteen

5 December 1999

A plump man was dripping repulsively onto the screen of the Stairmaster next to mine. Blinking red lights indicated how macho he thought he was: all at full power. I'm strongly against sweating in the gym myself, so I picked a gentle twenty-minute hill-climb, which would about last through the pages of *Vague*. On my other side, the Addict had been on her Stairmaster for at least an hour, with eyes only for herself in the mirror, ignoring the growing queue behind her. Each time I came to the Pump (rare event), the Addict was there, her hip-bones preceding the rest of her body, her shoulder-blades hanging out behind, all this perched on muscled stick legs.

Indeed, the Addict had been in both my 'abs and buns' classes at the gym this week, although she had no buns to speak of whatsoever. I had been forced into this undignified race for taut buttocks after Garrett Hughes set up a massive mirror behind my ass in the life-drawing class, and I watched the students doubly replicate my sags and cellulite in broad charcoal strokes. There no doubt about it: I had developed a thirtysomething backside without noticing. Now, after two bun-shaping classes, I could barely sit down, let alone pose. Also, my body was on view to a wider audience now that I had a

158

lover (however temporarily) who was giving me sleepless nights one way or the other.

The plump guy in the Apple Bank T-shirt stopped spraying me with sweat and went from his Stairmaster over to the treadmills. I gave him a baleful glare in the mirror and mopped my arm exaggeratedly with a paper towel. The banker set the treadmill at top speed too, and grunted off, already purple in the face. Five minutes later, just as I was deep in another article about John Galliano's summer-house, there was a strangled grunt from behind, and the banker plopped full on his belly. The treadmill delivered his body to the end of the belt like a suitcase on an airport carousel. One or two people, including me, stopped working out and went over to him.

'Outta the way,' said one of the Pump attendants, shoving me aside. 'Don't touch him. Heart-attack.' With difficulty, he rolled over the banker's body and noticed his T-shirt. 'Probably insured. Check his locker and get an ambulance,' he said, to another employee. The attendant then made a pathetic attempt at resuscitation, but it was clear that the banker was a goner, and soon he was gone. The Addict was back on the Stairmaster as the paramedics went out of the door. Within five minutes, the ex-banker's treadmill was occupied by someone else.

I couldn't believe how cool and callous everyone was. I mean, I don't like sweat-spraying bankers, but I thought it would be only decent to stop working out. Besides, I felt nauseous. I went to have some water and a tea in the gym's café downstairs. I'd gone off coffee. Poor guy, I thought. If only he had stuck to exercises like drinking beer and playing golf this would never have happened. Only in New York can being a few pounds overweight matter enough to lose you a business deal or a job – or your life. In the office behind a glass wall just opposite the café, I could hear the gym manager bawling down the phone, 'I don't care if it's seven thirty. Just get me the lawyer. I want to know what to do with his records right now ... Of course his family will fucking sue. They always do.'

In the changing rooms, I stood under the beating shower for ten minutes, until the hot water jellied my brain. I don't know what was with me, but I was tearful and edgy, probably since this might be the last time – for good? for a while? – that I would see Leonardo. I'd only spent three nights with him, but they were what parents call quality time. I had a severe case of love or lust – the different strains can't be distinguished so early in a relationship – and now he was about to disappear. He had a couple of hours before he caught the overnight plane to London and then on to Uganda. 'Fuckfuckfuck-fuck,' I bawled under the sound of the water. I felt vulnerable, peeled and ready to bruise. 'Should never have given him the time of day in the first place. Stupidstupidstupidstupid.' I thought it best to make a hysterical scene alone in the shower rather than embarrass myself publicly later. By the time I got dressed (with care, in my new brown suede jeans), I felt drained but calm.

We were meeting in the Furniture Shop, a basement bar filled with comfortable old armchairs on Houston. I got there early and chilled out in a corner with a Brooklyn lager. I started a cigarette and couldn't finish it. Leonardo strutted in, a parody of the explorer in desert boots, his leather jacket, a bandana round his neck, and jeans that were cut tightly across the crotch. I wanted traditional lust in the dust there and then. I was poleaxed by physical craving. He hugged me first, which was worse than being kissed, closer somehow.

'Travelling light,' I said, embarrassed into cliché. He had one nylon bag.

'Don't need much by way of clothing, but I do have antibiotics, snake-bite antidote and forty packs of chewing gum to trade. Another beer?'

He seemed kind of ridiculous with his snake serum and his desert gear, like a Boy Scout dressed up for camp. I felt a tenderness in the pit of my stomach for him. I told him about the fate of the plump at the Pump, and he told me how picky National Geographic TV was about getting the right sunset. 'That's why we need six months for three tribes. Color co-ordination is all important. It's sort of glossy-magazine TV.' We completely avoided mentioning what was on our minds.

Eventually, the conversation withered into silence. Leonardo took my hand. 'You all right?' he said, looking down at my stomach. 'You're not . . .?'

'Yeah, it's all fine. It's spotting, just started today.'

He looked pretty relieved that I wasn't pregnant. For some reason that really irritated me. I changed the subject, tried to fill the empty space.

'Hey, what happened to your dog?'

'I've given up the sublet and taken Spot to my sister's kids. Don't suppose I'll get him back.'

'Least you didn't have him put down.' I was babbling now, trying not to get upset. 'Nosmo knows this actor

161

who married that woman novelist, Campbell Johnson. Do you remember, their apartment was all over the lifestyle pages, and there were lots of pictures of her accessorized by their fluffy Scottish terrier called Kiltie? She said, "He's like a child to us," and then they got divorced and because neither of them could be bothered to keep him, they had Kiltie put down.'

'Another victim of a modern media romance.' Leonardo drank up his beer and shrugged. 'Suppose I should be making tracks. I can't phone really regularly from where we'll be, but I'll try to write. If you want you can write back *post restante* to the National Geographic box at Kampala Central Station Post Office.' He rushed his words. 'Or not. See how you feel.' He pushed my hair back and held my face in his hands and looked right at me.

He seemed tense. His face darkened. He started to speak and then stopped abruptly.

'Sure, I'll write you,' I said, trying to sound as casual and unbothered as possible. (Why? Why wasn't I more straightforward and honest?)

We walked outside and he hailed a cab.

'I'm sorry I have to go right now. It's a bad time, when we . . .'

He held me close for a long while and I felt my eyes fill threateningly. You can't cry if you've only been with a guy for four days.

'I'll miss you,' I said quickly, before my voice did any cracking.

'Me too.'

'Then the taxi door slammed and he disappeared over the Williamsburg bridge into the night.

I went back into the bar to wail in the washroom.

My running mascara made tribal designs down my face. What had I expected? He wasn't my husband. He wasn't even my boyfriend. He was an emotionally repressed guy who was still getting over his dead wife. It had been a lousy three-night stand, so why should there have been any profound declarations? If he had used the words 'I love you' I wouldn't have believed him anyway.

I stomped home grumpily, past annoying Christmas decorations in the shop windows along Broadway and a sandwich-board man wearing a sign saying 'The Beast is Coming' done in dripping red paint. Back at number 666, Nosmo was at the door on typical irritating form.

'Why, honey, you look like a girl who has just lost her sweetheart to the Foreign Legion, and fears that he will become hardened and bitter in the desert.'

'Shut up and die,' I said, marching towards my room, suddenly incredibly relieved I was moving apartment in a few weeks.

'Your mom rang,' continued Nosmo. 'She wants to know what days you'll be down in Palm Beach for Christmas. She invited me too, but unfortunately I was forced, by a previous engagement I just invented, to refuse. She says you have to ring her back tonight so she can get the rooms ready.'

'That's all I need right now.'

I put on my tartan pajamas because I needed comforting, and lay on top of my bed without moving. My breasts felt sore and in my nipples there was a tingling like pins and needles. I stared at the tented roof for half an hour, feeling drained and weird. I wanted to talk to someone. Not Nancy, not Wanda and definitely not Nosmo. Then I considered Agnes. I was still pretty annoyed with her, but she was, after all, what you might call a co-member of the Dead Wives Club. I suppose that was partly what all her dramatic warnings were about, and perhaps she really did have some line on Leonardo, something that would make it easier for me to forget about him. 'Agnes?' I said quietly, feeling stupid. 'Agnes?' There was no response. I checked the trunk, but it wasn't occupied. Perhaps she was bugged about me swearing at her last time. Perhaps even my personal ghost had abandoned me. 'Where are you? I want to talk.'

Nosmo came in without knocking. 'You've started talking to yourself. I heard you. You're hallucinating.' He gave the too-kind smile of a psychiatric nurse. I considered slugging him. 'Your mom's on the phone again. It's only nine thirty, you know, so I couldn't pretend you were asleep.'

In the living room, Nosmo, with Amadeus pacing his shoulders, was watching a documentary about the New Crusades against Islam. Thousands of nutty American Christians with scarves covering half their faces had declared a new holy war against Mecca and were telling the reporter about their plans for a terrorist bombing campaign to bring in the millennium.

'No Mom,' I said, staring, amazed, at the TV. 'I can only stay four nights.' She brought up the fact that my delightful brother loves his parents enough to stay for seven whole days. 'I know Brent's coming for a week but I just don't have that kind of time. I've got to get back on the twenty-seventh, I've got an exhibition to organize,' I lied. In fact, there was no exhibition forthcoming. The noxious Zindsi Hawkes from the SoHo Gallery had been round last month to inspect my stuff and had kept a contemptuous snarl on her face throughout. I hadn't even bothered to be polite to her. I'd just left her alone with a pile of the paintings, which she'd looked at for about a quarter of a second. Naturally there had been no word from the Wicked Women exhibition.

As I hung up, the recruits for the New Crusades were filmed training at some secret location in the Catskills, in full Desert-Storm-style garb. They were shooting at cardboard targets with added Arab headdresses. 'The Ragheads have bombed American passenger planes. They've bombed our World Trade Center. They've bombed American air-bases. It's time to avenge all that. If the government won't, we will,' said the leader, his head blacked out by the camera.

'Seriously weird,' said Nosmo, as I plopped down beside him on the sofa. 'And this is nothing to what's going on out there, in the streets. Crusade-wise, I mean. Do you know I was attacked by two EvangelAngels yesterday? They got me, either side against a wall outside Grand Central Station, and said, 'We want to talk to you about God.' They were both six foot two and they leaned over me, potential violence in their staring eyes.' (Nosmo always talks like he's already written each anecdote for a magazine. Which he usually has.) 'And they both had halitosis. I kept saying I was Jewish, but they had me there for ten minutes. I was just so pissed. I had to buy one of their leaflets to escape.'

Three days later, the EvangelAngels got me, too. Like some plague, they'd multiplied by the Biblical hundredfold. I was getting off the D train at West 4th Street, right at the end of the platform, and about fifteen ugly guys in 'God Squad' T-shirts surrounded me and two other women. They started shouting, 'You have only a month to repent. Repent now. Atone now for your sins.' The other women made a run for the exit, but I was lugging a huge box, a Robochef with attachments, Rose's Christmas present. I was hot already and all these blue berets bore down on me, shoving tracts in my face, chanting. Then I did something I'd never done in my life before. I fainted.

The EvangelAngels at least managed the Christian act of finding me a seat before they disappeared. I had only lost consciousness for a few seconds, but I was horribly light-headed. As soon as I felt steady enough to walk, I went straight up the subway stairs and across to McKay Drugs to discover my destiny. Big girls don't faint unless there's something weird going on. In my case, my period had barely started before it disappeared, leaving not a trace. I went to the counter and bought a ClearBlue pregnancy test. I was shoving the change in my purse when Wanda came up, dragging two over-flowing baskets. I blushed guiltily, even though the test kit was in a paper bag. Wanda didn't notice.

'Have you seen all this baby stuff the adoption agency told me to buy for Li An?' she moaned. 'I've got eighty diapers, four cans of Enfamil, Baby Tylenol, creams, wipes, dozens of different bottle teats, baby bath, jars of mushed carrot, antibiotics, and I'm a hundred and fifty dollars lighter. We've got to live in some gross hotel for two weeks, and I don't suppose they'll have anything.'

We took a taxi the few blocks home because we

were so laden with bags. The horrifying sight of the Pampers and Huggies had nearly brought on another faint, as the reality of what had (probably) happened percolated my brain. I rushed to the bathroom as soon as we arrived. 'Result in one minute! One hundred percent reliable even the day you miss your period!' it said cheerfully. I peed on the stupid stick, and then turned away to stare at the bloodless face in the mirror. Behind me, two inexorable blue lines appeared in the test windows.

I went into the kitchen, a pall of dread trailing me. Wanda was making coffee, and chattering away about leaving in early January for Wuhan to pick up her baby, going on about the weeks of adoption bureaucracy she expected in China. It was perhaps the last conversation I wanted to have. But Wanda had her own worries and needed reassurance: 'Problem is, she's five months old, but I've no idea what size she'll be because sometimes they get the age wrong and sometimes they're really small and underfed. I am, in fact, in total panic about the whole thing.'

Not as panicked as me, I wanted to say. At least Wanda made a conscious choice to acquire her baby, whereas mine was thrust upon me, so to speak.

Wanda had been worrying as much as any pregnant mother. 'How can I be responsible for someone else when I can't cook and I still forget my own mobile phone number?'

I roused myself from my foul mood to provide the support she was seeking. I imitated the social worker: 'These are questions of repressed immaturity which you should have considered some months ago, Ms Wong.' I hugged her. 'Of course you'll be fine. It's that terrible sense of duty and responsibility that takes over, so they tell me, forcing you to cope. If thirteen-year-old mothers in the Bronx can do it, so can you.' We? I pushed my coffee away. It tasted burned and disgusting, but perhaps that was the hormones.

Wanda continued, 'I keep having this dream where I get given the baby, but it's only about four inches long and it lies in my palm and stares at me, and I cup it in my hand and it leans against my shoulder. It's not curled up and fat like most babies, but more adult-proportioned. I keep forgetting it and leaving it places because it's so small. Then I wake up and panic.'

'Believe me, she won't be that small. You've seen the photograph – she's definitely two feet long. It's not as bad as that. They make so much noise you can't forget them, and I guess somehow they enter your subconscious, so you're always thinking about them.'

I plaited a strand of my hair. What on earth was I saying? What did I know? Worse still, Wanda's talk of four-inch babies made me nauseous again.

'And what if she's ugly when they hand her to me? What if I don't feel any maternal bonds whatsoever?'

'I dunno. Babies are usually squashed-looking and ugly, but Chinese ones are cuter than most. I don't think everyone instantly makes a bond. I know lots of women who keep planning to throw their babies out the window for the first three months and then make friends with them afterwards. You just have to believe you're destined for each other, and then it will work.'

'Yeah. You're right. Wish you were coming with me.'

I hugged her again. 'It'll be just fine.'

Wanda went off to put away her stores. I went resignedly off to the phone book to look up Planned Parenthood to put a stop to my unplanned parenthood. Despite my professional and artistic interests in pregnancy as a concept, when it came to conception itself, I was less enthusiastic. Sure, I wanted kids one day, but not today. Sure, I thought, if I had a home, a job, a husband, a grip on sanity, I might have considered keeping it, but now? Certainly, I knew *who* the father was, but I didn't know *where* he was, or really *what* he was, so he was not going to figure much in this decision. Besides, I felt pretty matter-of-fact about abortion then: I didn't like it, but I'd dealt with it before. I felt it was barely worth running through the arguments for and against again.

In my four years at Parsons, my girlfriends and I had been through this a lot, and I don't think one of us regretted it. Abortions were an inevitable part of our twenties, our student life, particularly for the ones who were just starting out in their careers. I'd taken my friends home in taxis from the Sixth Avenue clinic and supplied Advil and comfort, just as they'd come round when I'd had an abortion seven years before, and brought me, I remember, a great carrot cake from the deli and some dope for the (negligible) pain. I lay in bed all afternoon like a queen, munching and puffing happily, feeling the hormones-from-hell already draining away and my body resurfacing into normality. I cried only once, when I was drunk a few weeks later, but I didn't doubt my decision for an instant. I still don't. Of course, no one says that publicly. Too shocking. Who was it who said, 'If men had abortions, they would be a sacrament?' It's different if you're poor and try to get one somehow, but for even half-affluent women, abortion is a convenience they never talk about. It's five hundred dollars or something now, not cheap for a starving artist, but at the clinic they take American Express, Mastercard, or Visa – on which, in the most unbefitting way, I get air miles.

Just after I'd finished sorting out my initial consultation, the phone rang again.

'Yeah,' I said.

'Hi, it's me. I'm calling from the hotel in Kampala just before we leave really early.'

'Ohmigod.' I sat down on a stool. I had, I realized, never expected to hear from Leonardo again. 'Hi, how are you?'

'Well, Kampala's a shithole, the cameraman's a woman, which I didn't expect, and we're taking in dozens of Walkman radios to bribe the tribesmen to co-operate. Sounds pretty old-fashioned, in a way. Anyway, I wasn't ringing to tell you that. I was ringing to say how happy I've been the past couple of days and nights . . .'

A beep came indicating call waiting.

'I couldn't think what to say to you the other night in the bar,' he continued, as the beep came again. 'You want to get that?'

'Yeah, hang on and I'll get rid of them.'

I changed lines.

'Hi, Albertine? It's Zindsi Hawkes. Ah'm on mah mobile. Hey, listen, we're going to be using y'all in Wicked Women now, but Ah need you to fax me a list of—'

'Can you just hold on? I got another call.'

'Jesus, Leonardo,' I said. 'It's that woman from the SoHo Gallery. She wants to exhibit my stuff.'

'Cool. When?'

'In January. Anyway, I had a wonderful time too. I wanted to tell you also, I mean I—'

'Look, gotta go. My money's running out. Yes, they still use coins in phones here. Operator won't take my AT&T card number. I'll be thinking about you a lot and—'

Then he was beeped into oblivion by the Ugandan telephone system.

Zindsi Hawkes was still there: 'Look, Ah don't have much time. Ah'm leaving town tomorrow, so fax me a list of six paintings, perhaps three of those Confinement ones, and three of those gross trailerpark women. They'll all have to be framed, but Ah need the titles and dimensions by fax so we can allocate space in the gallery and do the catalog before everyone goes on holiday and Ah must also have a hundred-word CV from y'all, OK?'

'Uh, OK,' I said, and meekly took down the fax number before being dismissed.

I was shaking when I put down the phone. First thing I did was get a beer and a cigarette (which, of course, I then didn't want), and the next thing I did was to start crying. We can blame the hormones, but I was in serious shit. I cursed the entire call-waiting system. I cursed Leonardo for being affectionate. I cursed Zindsi Hawkes for timing herself so badly. I cursed myself for not saying anything to Leonardo. Then I just cursed.

My life had forked, like a tongue.

171

Chapter Sixteen

Victoria Infirmary, Glasgow

14 March 1906

Dear Ishbel,

I have terrible news. I have lost the baby. The poor wee thing had only been there for five months and it was a boy, too. I saw him, he was like a tiny doll he was so real even though the nurses tried to make me look away and they wrapped him in a cloth and took him away forever. I wanted to hold him so much and I still want to hold him, a little thing with no name. How can they call this a miscarriage, a mistake, when it is a birth and a death? I cannot calm myself. I don't know what to do, Ishbel, I am lost and screaming inside and I have to tell you, I have to pass on some of the pain. You and Kirsty are the only people who will understand. I have been on this ward for 12 days now and there are women here much worse off than myself, there are women here who are dying after childbirth, so I cannot let them see me cry. I wait until it is dark and the ward is full of coughs and snores and then I can surrender to my hurt.

Little Isabel is in a complete state because these starched old matrons will not let children visit on the ward. Kirsty smuggled her in once to the visitors' room, but she is only four, after all, and she cannot understand why I have disappeared. She will be an only child now, for the doctors have told me that my womb is too weak to hold another baby, and the same would happen again.

The physical pain was almost a relief, taking my mind off the real agony. My fever has gone and I am not so weak now and they are sending me home at the weekend and Kirsty is coming to stay to keep an eye on me. But Ishbel, Ishbel, I have milk here for this wean, I am full of it and there is nothing to suckle. I feel so bereft, as though someone has cut off one of my limbs leaving a numb stump, and I still keep trying to move it even though there is nothing there. I feel so abandoned, by everyone, by my son, *my son*, by God, by Duncan. He has come faithfully to see me very day, but he cannot be doing with hysterics, he says every time I cry every time. When the doctor told him about the miscarriage Kirsty said it was as though a shutter came down on his face and it went stiff and blank. 'We must accept what is God's will and we must pray,' he said to me. I could only turn my face away and look at the green chipped paint on the wall. I no longer believe in anything.

More than anything in the world I wish you were here. I miss you so much, Ishbel.

Agnes

Chapter Seventeen

24 December 1999

So that was the letter that really did for me. It was visceral. I lay on my bed and wept. I wept for Agnes, for her baby son, fully formed but small enough to fit in a teacup, as she once said. I looked at her wavering copperplate, the sloppy sentences so different from her usual disciplined prose. I was sickened by her literally godawful husband. I was no longer an observer of her life, just as she was of mine, but a participant. I wanted to hold her, if only she had been there, but perhaps her grief and loss was a century old and barely felt now.

Of course, empathy wasn't exactly a problem for me, being seven weeks pregnant. I was crying for myself, as much as for Agnes, and my emotional state was so hair-trigger that I had blubbed at a *Lassie* rerun on television the night before. Why, you ask, would I have been watching such a thing? I had been trapped in my parents' condo in Florida for four long days, to mark the family feud known as Christmas. There wasn't just a baby roosting in my belly, there was resentment, too. Resentment that I had to spend time in relative hell. I got up to have another pee, an hourly occurrence, in what my mom refers to as 'the ensuite' and lay back crabbily on one of two single beds. Within hours of coming home, if the Seagrape gated community could be described as home, I always slumped back into the role of difficult teen. I still believed that returning to the parental fold actually caused my hormones to revert back to dangerous adolescent levels anyway, but being pregnant made the chemical cocktail extra volatile.

Every time my mom or dad asked me a sprightly question, even an innocent one about my work, I became sullen and uncommunicative. The more I was questioned, the more I was chivvied to play tennis or have a drink by the communal jacuzzi, the more I shriveled away from the banality and into silence. Pleading tiredness, which was the truth for once, I'd holed up with the household's back copies of *People* magazine and a selection of Agnes's letters, while my parents and my brother Brent went to the beach. Even then, I had barely time to think, thanks to my family's desire for togetherness.

It was bad enough being in sunny Palm Beach for Christmas, but it was worse sharing a room for four days with Brent, the prodigal son. His main faults are that he is (a) twenty-five years old (b) a merchant banker (c) a snorer and (d) an asshole. He also talks too loud, laughs at his own jokes, windsurfs, plays competitive sports like they matter, and carries a six-pack everywhere like a handbag. My parents think he's God's gift. Literally. Brent's testosterone and my record childbearing levels of human chorionic gonadotropin were in direct confrontation in the small guest bedroom that holiday.

'We're back!' said Brent, striding in wearing his psychedelic bermudas.

'Uh-huh.' I didn't even look up.

'Time you got some color on your face, Albie. Get

175

your bikini on and we'll go out to the pool for a quick one before dinner.' How come he gets to call me 'Albie' but I don't call him 'Brentie', I suddenly thought.

'Don't want skin cancer. Didn't bring a bikini,' I said, still not raising my head from an article on Hollywood's premier pet salons.

'Oh, you can borrow one of mine, pumpkin,' said my mom, coming in. This was physically possible. Through dint of obsessive aerobics and progressive surgery, my fifty-three-year-old mother is a trim size eight. Her motto is: 'You're never too old for Spandex.' She held out something small and fuchsia-colored with large cups. I peered into them.

'I'll never fill them up.'

'Oh, almost, honey. You know I only had teensy-weensy implants.' She pointed her pointy little rocket chest into the air to emphasize this. She leaned forward to confide: 'I had to go back to Dr Murkoff for a replacement in September. One went hard and the other stayed soft. I felt all lopsided – least that was what your dad said.' She tittered. I mean, no one titters nowadays, but my mom still manages.

'C'mon,' growled Brent. 'Hurry up.'

I changed and followed him down to the pool – better than being trapped in a small space with him. I looked down at my white stomach, which was suspiciously bloated, not through actual baby but because the hormomes had shuddered my digestive system to a complete and queasy halt. I was, however, pleased to note that my breasts, though painful, actually filled the bikini for once. (Why my mother thinks fuchsia pink goes with red hair I'll never know.)

I managed a few desultory lengths. Brent went off to the Seagrape bar (a community amenity just like the identity checks when you drive up to the gate) and got some piña coladas, large plastic cups with a swirl of shaving foam on top and a glacé cherry. I nearly heaved directly into the pool, but instead held the cup and pretended to sip.

'Seeing anyone, then?' said Brent.

'Nope.'

'Seen anyone, even?'

'Nope.'

'I've met this woman at the gym, Marlene. She has got one amazing body.'

'Just the one?'

Brent didn't notice. 'She just moved to Chicago and she has this great apartment in a high-rise overlooking the bay. Some view, man, and she wants me to teach her windsurfing this summer. You know, that gym is chick central, I'm telling you. Her shorts are so tight you can see the little mound where . . .'

I let him drone on about Marlene and her various mounds. Then he went on about the White Sox or Red Sox or whatever. I shut my eyes and lay on my back in the sun, risking ten minutes of freckling. I thought about the fact I was not only in a family way, but also up the junction, up the duff, knocked up, and to cap it all I had a bun in the oven. But the main problem was that I was with child, but not with partner. I didn't really have any feelings for the baby. After all, there was no sign it was there, other than that I felt crap. This baby was not wanted, not by me and definitely not by its father, who had made himself as scarce as possible and was about as

177

committed as a passing ram in a field of sheep. Not like Agnes, who so wanted that child, and lost it when it was on its way to being real, not the kidney-bean-sized, nauseating blob that was causing me all this trouble. It was funny, because last time I had an abortion, I don't remember being sick, or my breasts growing, or my stomach bloating, or getting so emotional. I kept working and smoked valiantly for the six weeks, and then it was gone. No mess, no anguish. Should have been the same again, really, one night in bed counteracted by one morning in the clinic. Still, I had a day fixed for the abortion in New York, 28 December, time to recover before New Year, indeed the new century. I stood up courageously, and dived into the pool.

It was Christmas Eve. All round the world, people were celebrating the birth of a child fathered by a guy who mysteriously disappeared. Typical. I empathized with the Virgin. We watched the holiday specials on television. The evening news was showing carol singers at a snow-covered Rockefeller Plaza in Manhattan. 'Religion just seems so inappropriate in Florida,' I said. 'It's just too fuckin' hot.'

'Don't be ridiculous,' said my mom, clearly irritated by my swearing. 'Palm Beach is becoming a great center of Christian revival. Your dad and I are going to the ChurchMall midnight carol service tonight, aren't we, Dad?' My parents still refer to one another as 'Mom' and 'Dad', rather than Carol and Albert, even when their children are not there.

My dad made a responsive noise through the bag of tortilla chips and salsa he consumed in their entirety every night. What with golf being his only exercise, in retirement he was doubling in size, while my mom, but for the permanent silicone parts, was shrinking. She not only went to the ChurchMall for services, but throughout the sweaty summer she was a member of the MallWalkers club, Spandexed Palm Beach ladies who met and marched three air-conditioned miles round the mall each morning wearing lip-liner. I'd been to my first ChurchMall service the year before. When we'd arrived, there were men in fluorescent jackets directing us to parking spaces, because the congregation was expected to be ten thousand. I wasn't sure whether the crowd, outfitted almost entirely in Gap shorts, would pray or do the Mexican wave.

'Last Christmas of the twentieth century,' said my dad, who specializes in the obvious. 'You sure you don't want to come?' He went out with the progidal son Brent to the balcony to grill a dead animal on a skewer and another wave of nausea hit me as the smell wafted through the screen door. Why the hell was I there? Why did I come every year for this farce, the claws of duty sunk deep into my back? Look, I thought, if I met my parents at a party, I wouldn't ask for their phone number. It isn't a generational thing – I've plenty of older friends like Garrett – it's just the way my parents strive for mediocrity and respectability. What was there to say to them that Christmas? There was nothing to say and everything was left unsaid, just as it had always been.

'Do you like the new sofa?' asked my mom, laying the table. 'Yeah,' I lied. 'It's sort of wild Western, isn't it?'

'It's after a Navaho Indian design. We had it shipped after our holiday in Santa Fe, and then I got the cushions here, and the Native American blankets from a catalogue.'

Appropriate for this prison compound on a dead swamp, I thought, while actually saying, 'I suppose the new orange and turquoise color scheme is kinda Western, too?'

'Salmon and pistachio, actually. You should know that, being an artist.'

'Yeah, right.'

If we couldn't agree on interior design, we certainly weren't up to a conversation on the ethics of childbirth and abortion. Perhaps other people discuss such things with their parents, but I thought if I even opened my mouth the pastor might be called in to counsel me, and I would probably be forced to join the ChurchMall teenage mothers' support group.

We sat down to eat at the table, covered in, yes, a Navaho cloth. I told them what I thought might be cheerful news: that Wanda was adopting a Chinese baby from an orphanage, perhaps at this very moment. But again I'd underestimated the clutch of the Christian right on the ChurchMall.

'Well, that's wonderful, Albie, but she'll be a single mother. It's not good for a child not to have a male role model,' said my mom.

'Well, there's Nosmo. He'll be around, taking a share of the work.'

Dad spluttered in his beer and some landed on his Ralph Lauren polo shirt. 'A gay father is no father at all. What does the girl think she's doing? A deviant, not a man.' He saw my livid face. 'I mean, I like Nosmo personally, but—'

'Right, forget it. These are my friends and it's none of our business,' I spat.

Dad could see I was raging. He took a big bite of steak and simultaneously tried to change the subject. 'You know, I play golf with this executive from Gillette when he's down on holiday . . .' I could see the steak fibers writhing on his tongue as he talked with his mouth full. '. . . and there's a great design job coming up redoing those disposable-razor five-packs. Design something millions of people would see every day. That would be some opportunity for you, eh, Albie? Make some real dough for once, and it would be full time, with medical insurance, pension, everything. Shall I put in a word for you?'

'Thanks, Dad, but I already work full time.'

He went silent and took an extra helping of mashed potatoes from the serving plate.

Despite Brent's sports monolog for the rest of the meal, the atmosphere remained tense, and my parents went off to the ChurchMall early. 'Mince pies beforehand,' said my mom, too cheerfully.

'Let's watch TV,' said Brent, as they left. We sat at either end of the Navaho sofa, with a sort of no man's land between us. He surfed the two hundred channels, a long process, until he hit a sixties' version of Mia Farrow. 'Oh, wow, it's *Rosemary's Baby*, just starting. I love this retro stuff.'

I slid out of the room as the hairy devil bore down to impregnate Mia and threw up in the bathroom.

Afterwards, I sat on the carpet and leaned against the bath, surveying with horror the faux art-deco fittings and wallpaper with pink and silver swans. God, I was dying for a cigarette, but they made me feel sick too. I walked out onto the deck for some fresh air and quiet. This was a mistake. Down below at the Seagrape communal jacuzzi, middle-aged couples appeared to be wife-swapping and drinking beers, judging by the hysterical laughter and screams of, 'Ooh, don't, Darren. Don't you dare.' There was barking from the two giant Rottweilers that patrolled the perimeter fence. They had probably just eaten some poor Cuban illegal immigrant. A posse of mosquitoes descended on my bare legs, and a bug the size of a golfball flew by. I went indoors to bed.

In the middle of the night I was roused by Brent's guttural snores. When we had shared a room on vacation as kids, I'd forced him to wear one of my bras backwards with two tennis balls in the cups when he went to bed. This contraption prevented him rolling over on his back and snoring. It was most successful, but unfortunately Brent only bore the humiliation for a week. Then I reverted to throwing sneakers at him. I stuck my head under the pillow, and slipped grouchily between waking and dreaming.

The dreams of pregnancy are psychedelic, like nothing you normally experience, and you remember them all, because your sleep is so disrupted by the need to turn over or pee. That night my bed became a dark mahogany four-poster, carved on the back panel with a coat-of-arms. The design was in a shield shape with a bird, a bell, a fish and a tree cut into the wood and the words 'Let Glasgow flourish by the preaching of Thy Word' underneath. I was holding onto the end of the great carved bed, staring at the shield across the sheets, standing on the floor. No, not standing, sort of squatting, pulling down on the Gothic frame. Behind me, there were shady people in the room. I could hear them whispering, but I was concentrating too hard to look round. I felt an urge to push, push hard, and I could only look at the shield in front of me, faintly hearing someone – Agnes, yes, it was her voice – saying, '. . . the bell that never rang, the bird that never flew, the fish that never swam, the tree that never grew, the baby that never . . .'

There was no pain. I bore down and there was a pop. I felt something the size of a Florida grapefruit burst out from between my legs, followed by a fish feeling, a feeling of something flowing easily, the size of a small salmon. I didn't look down or behind. One of the shady women in the room was dealing with that.

Later, I woke up alone in fresh white sheets in the big Gothic bed, and felt an enormous lifting of my spirits, a flow of relief through my body. The shield was the only sight I could remember from the previous night. I turned round to have a better look. Yes, there it was, carvings of a bird, a bell, a tree, a fish and a grapefruit. Wonder what they mean, I thought, luxuriating in the crisp bed-linen of the dream.

Brent snored at full decibels again, and I really woke up in nasty polyester-mix sheets and found myself scrabbling to hold the outline of this dream in my head. It seemed important to grasp. I successfully silenced Brent with a well-aimed Nike and dozed off again.

'Fuck,' was the first word I said, when I woke up on Christmas morning. My pillow was wet from crying in my sleep, and I wanted to complain about the heavy-handedness of whoever had supplied my dreams. I felt like I'd been raided by Pro-Life (Glasgow branch) in the night. I was very ratty.

'Mnnm?' said Brent. 'Oh, yeah, right. Happy Christmas, Albie.

'Happy Christmas,' I said, smiling hideously as I slid into the bathroom to retch once again.

The smell of buckwheat blueberry pancakes came from the kitchen, their wholesomeness clashing with my mom's nuclear-strength perfume.

'Happy Christmas, darlings,' she said, kissing me and Brent, who was already pouring maple syrup on his four-stack with bacon. (Like father, like son. Brent would be a porker, too, if he didn't work out.) I fortified myself with dry pancakes and felt my stomach settle. I wished I was with my grandmother Rose instead: she has a wild septuagenarian all-day party in New Jersey every year. I called her, but there was already a call waiting.

My mom gave her special all-inclusive smile. 'Now, you will come to the eleven o'clock service? It's always very accessible on Christmas Day, and the children's choir singing carols is just adorable.'

Brent and I found ourselves in the back of the half-timbered Bronco, experiencing the same irritable and unwilling feelings we had had as kids being forced to travel with our parents. At the church, my dad parked in the C-area of the mall's multi-story, and we walked over to the huge building, which looked like a sports astrodome but for the cross stuck on top. We went up to door D on the second level, where one of the ushers in a royal blue suit was directing people. 'Carol, Albert, welcome, and Merry Christmas!' he boomed, shaking hands. 'And these are the kids down from the big city? Welcome to the ChurchMall!' I picked up some ChurchMall leaflets to read while we waited, including *The Christian Garden* and *Advice and Help for Young Moms*. The usher directed us to good seats in the front row of the mezzanine, while the digital sound system played a carol medley. On every seat there was an envelope for the collection. I idly opened mine and discovered a credit card slip, where worshippers just filled in the number and God debited their accounts. It said He also took cash.

The sound system made trumpeting noises, reminiscent of the music heralding the compère of a TV game show, and the handsome host, or rather the pastor, appeared on the stage. 'My friends,' he began. He was wearing the same Ralph Lauren tie my mom had bought my dad for Christmas, and a sleek-cut suit. His tan was Florida perfect, and I knew, even from two hundred feet away in a crowd of 9,894, that he buffed his nails.

The pastor churned out some Christmas platitudes, gave a reading from the Good News Bible, which sounded like it had been written by an advertising executive, and we stood up and sang 'Good Christian Men Rejoice' and 'Silent Night'. Then the children's choir performed 'Away in a Manger' out of tune, and the congregation said, 'Awww', in one voice after they finished. I looked round for the emergency exit.

Before I could make a bid for freedom, the pastor rolled into his sermon: 'Today, of all days, is a time to think about the family, not just the Holy Family, but our own lives at home. Because the family is the building block of our society and our church here. But there are growing forces out there, beyond our community, which threaten the traditional family: the media, liberal politicians, gay rights campaigners. They all have an anti-family agenda which is often an anti-life agenda, too.'

He paused to slick back his hair. 'My friends, we know in this ChurchMall that we respect our women, that we respect them as workers and homemakers. We know there has been more change for women in the past few decades than there has been since the birth of our Saviour, and we all appreciate the positive aspects of those changes. But the women in this congregation also know the difference between being feminine and feminist. They know that God made men and women different to fulfill His purpose. Out there in the media, there's an anti-Christian agenda, an anti-family agenda.' He thumped the lectern and there were nods and murmurs of assent from the congregation and my parents. I reckoned I'd have to push past ten people to reach the end of the row.

'Feminism has encouraged women to renounce marriage, murder children for the sake of convenience, and seek spiritual insight from witchcraft. As we pass into the next millennium, this is the time to cleanse ourselves of such poisons, and end this increasingly Godless modern age, in which women claim a "moral right" to murder their young.' He pounded the lectern again. 'There must never again be a time when witches and infanticides . . .'

I charged out of the front row, repeating 'excuse me' ten times, and ran up the stairs past the usher to the door. People, particularly my own family, turned and stared.

I sat, fuming, on the steps outside door D. If there

was anything to make you keen on infanticide, I thought, it was the policy of Florida ChurchMalls Inc. These people had clearly been brought to medieval extremes of belief by the southern heat curdling their poor northern souls. And what made me more irritated was that I knew, and I'd known inside all morning (all month?), that I was going to keep the goddamned baby.

I was not sure whether to credit this decision to Pregnancy Dreamworks Inc., or to Agnes's miscarriage, or to my parents for being so suitably horrified by single motherhood, or to the fact that I was just so much older than last time, and that I knew the right man might not be worth searching for. He was probably extinct as a species. I didn't hold out any, never mind great, hopes for Leonardo, but genetically, things could be worse. At least he wasn't ugly, he wasn't dumb, and he hadn't run to fat. In my mind, I had long ago separated fathers from children: there was no reason that a child should not come first, and a suitable father-figure be found for it later, if possible.

Then there was that great improbable, the wave of plain need to have a child, to love something that loved me back, simply. Something I hadn't felt seven years before, because it wasn't there. I wondered if I had known, subconsciously, that the condoms were past their sell-by date all along. I wondered why I'd never thought to get the morning-after pill. All this pointed suspiciously to a decision already made. So, emotionally, a baby seemed a brilliant solution. Intellectually and economically, I knew it was an extremely bad idea. I couldn't think how on earth I was going to pay for it. I wouldn't be able to work with a screaming baby or a destructive,

187

paint-eating toddler in the room – my patience is dangerously low even with adults – but neither could I afford a childminder. Maybe I'd have to get a real job. I mused on, as the Christmas choir continued, sickly sweet, inside. At least I knew about pregnancy and childbirth. I was well read on the subject, thanks to my work and my obsession (I was beginning to admit that a little to myself). Actually going ahead with the business would be pretty cathartic.

I found myself humming as I headed into the multi-story parking lot to wait by the Bronco. I could hear the pastor booming out his final address, more witchcraft, infanticide and lesbotic evil, no doubt. I made a mental note, although I would not be using their services, to give a small donation in the pastor's name to Planned Parenthood. Just by the door was his parking place, marked out with fresh white lines and a sign on the wall saying 'Pastor Searle'. Well, looky here, I thought. Our charitable pastor has a great big shiny Mercedes 700. The acreage of pristine white metal attracted me. I found my hand reaching into my bag for my pink lipstick and writing across the hood of the pastor's car: 'What if the Virgin Mary had believed in the right to choose?'

Chapter Eighteen

Dowanhill Road, Glasgow

30 October 1907

Dearest Ishbel,

I am sorry I have not written for a month or two, but it seems as if there has not been a moment to spare. I have been running around like a scalded cat on suffrage business. I cannot tell you how delighted we are here about the latest addition to the Dalyells. I think Rose is a wonderful name, but your hands must be full with four bairns on the loose, however wonderful this ayah woman is. I am just after putting a wee dress and bloomers in this packet for my new niece. I do not envy you all that mothering, though. Now that Isabel is at primary school down the road, I have had time to devote myself to work for the Cause. Duncan is tired and tolerant about it all, and I still help him as much as I can round the parish, but increasingly I am drawn to the political life.

Much as I regret that Isabel will never have any brothers and sisters around her own age — well, Kirsty is a half-sister — it does mean I have hours of freedom to do what I will most of the day, and Mrs Minto is always there, installed in the kitchen and as immovable as the range. So for the first time in my life, I have been down to London! It was so simple, just stepping on the brown train at Queen Street. We slept in bunks, got morning tea from the porter, and by then we were there. I went with Kirsty, and we negotiated buses and trams no bother – well, it was no more frightening than Glasgow, armed with a map – and we visited the headquarters of the Women's Social and Political Union in Clements Inn.

It was a Monday, and they were having what they call an 'At Home' meeting. Christabel Pankhurst stood on a chair and talked to the women about all the events of the past week. She knows her politics, and she has a sharp tongue. They call her 'Queen of the Mob' because she is such a crowd-puller and handsome with it. Then someone else spoke from Manchester. We spent two days in meetings with suffrage organizers, and shouldered home a mountain of pamphlets on the train. But Kirsty and I did take ourselves off for an hour early one morning, while everyone else was having breakfast at the house where they were putting us up, and went to see the Houses of Parliament and Big Ben, when the morning mist was coming off the river and the boats were sounding their foghorns. For some reason, we started running across the bridge over the Thames, and I felt oddly wild and free when policemen in curious English helmets looked at us strangely.

Since then, I have been working with Helen Fraser of the WSPU to set up a branch here in Hillhead. As you know, there are enough genteel ladies here with time on their hands who would like to do more than keep house. We are also advertising the meetings down in Dumbarton Road, so we are not outwith the reach of ordinary folk. Already, there is great interest in the cause and we are attracting new followers now we have split from the Labour Party. Myself, I think that the causes of socialism and suffrage are absolutely compatible, but the men at Westminster seem unable to hold two ideas in their heads at once.

I have never thought much of artists, but Helen Fraser is so clever and elegant, dressed in clothes she has embroidered and designed herself. She is obviously talented but has given up much of her work to be the Scottish organizer for the cause. Although she designs banners and suchlike for the movement, she has put her artistic pleasures aside for the sake of politics, and she works, I have to tell you, like a navvy. She believes in direct action – 'deeds not words' is the motto of the WSPU – and she does not waste a moment. We are going to Aberdeen together in December to hear Mrs Pankhurst speak. I went through to Edinburgh with her for the huge suffrage demonstration down Princes Street three weeks ago, and last month we went to meetings at Kilmarnock and Springburn, where I made my first speeches to ordinary folk in the streets: quite a different business from preaching to the converted at meetings.

How I wished Kirsty had been there, but she works all hours on her rounds and could not come. In Springburn, I stood on a cart draped with our banners before a crowd that was less than friendly. There were young lads jeering at the front, shouting, 'It's a man ye want,' and old wifies with no interest in the Cause just out for the spectacle. I thought my knees would give way, and the speech I had prepared on a few bits of card seemed far too bookish and complicated. So I fell back on religion; having thought I had put the Church behind me, all those days in the pews and at Sunday school suddenly came to my aid.

You know the passage from Amos that says, 'They shall build houses and inhabit them, and they shall plant vineyards and eat the fruit of them. They shall not build and another inhabit; they shall not plant and another eat.' Well, I used that in a speech to these farm women, factory workers and housemaids to point out the unfairness of their situation: they are producers, workers with no control over the means of production, no right to decide how their country and their industries should be run. They do all the work, but are not rewarded by benefits like the right to vote.

Those Biblical images, those well-learned, well-worn passages that have been with us since childhood, are a rich and powerful source of understanding and emotion, a fine tool in this new work. Probably listening to Duncan at Sunday service has given me some wonderful material – I feel slightly shamefaced that he does not fully comprehend the use to which it is now being put. Helen, who has been speaking in public for years, says you always do better with what you know best, keeping it simple. There was a piece in the *Herald* the other day, quoting some elders of the Church of Scotland who were moaning about the supporters of Votes for Women being 'unChristian agitators who sport their petticoats on platforms and bring shame to their sex'. Well, they cannot have heard my sermon on suffrage from the back of the cart in Springburn. Besides, most of the women I meet in this movement are as religious privately as they come; they just do not have time for the established church.

Anyway, I am enclosing the new *Votes for Women* magazine, which was launched this month from London, just to give you a taste, and I am sending you a WSPU button so you can shock all your finest acquaintance out there. The royal purple colour stands for freedom and dignity, white for purity in private and public life and green is the colour of hope and emblem of spring.

The word spring has reminded me to put in this photograph a man took of Kirsty and me when we were taking a dauner in the Botanic Gardens – note Kirsty's aigrette feather hat from Copeland and Lye, and my reversible coat. Quite the thing, we are, and not a petticoat in sight.

With best love to all the weans,
  Your affectionate sister,
    Agnes

Chapter Nineteen

31 December 1999

I was in the Spring Street bookshop, lurking in the pregnancy and childcare section. I noticed it had been moved to accommodate the encroaching New Age Religions section, which was pullulating with nutcases. Last summer I'd spent a great deal of time here among the pregnancy shelves with a cushion stuffed up my dress. Now, with an invisible two-inch, ten-toed fetus up there, I was inexplicably worried someone I knew would catch me with an embarrassing book, and I would have to explain that research had become reality. I grabbed *What to Expect When You're Expecting* from the shelf and hid it under a copy of *Granta* until I reached the till.

It was 31 December and the next day, apparently, the Dark Ages were to begin again. At least, that was what it said on the front page of the *Daily News*, and who was I to doubt it? I took my reading matter over to the Dean and Deluca cafe on Prince to indulge the complex cravings that had replaced morning, afternoon and evening sickness. At the counter I ordered a cappuccino ('Caffeine *does* enter the fetal circulation,' lectured the pregnancy book) a carrot muffin, and an enormous lemon tart ('No calorie is as empty, and therefore as wasted, as a calorie of sugar,' it added.) I only gained this information after I'd started eating and drinking. I felt kind of guilty, but not, I reasoned, as guilty and psychotic as the rest of the world. In the last week, the *News* told me, 1,562 Americans had committed suicide singly, and 124 in groups, mostly in silly costumes. 'People who tend to be pessimistic get ever darker. It's an enormous event tunneling through the *zeitgeist*,' explained the article. Indeed, the cream of the cult world appeared to be planning to dress up in long white robes and shoot themselves at midnight in isolated but well-armed farmhouses throughout the world. The mass suicides would peak as the first twenty centuries ended, as would international champagne consumption. To my enormous disappointment, page five revealed that Jesus Lopes had emigrated to Cuba, taking his silver lamé suits, the entire funds of his Second Coming tour and a seventeen-year-old male aide with him. Sensibly, he had bailed out just before the Day of Judgement.

You could tell the Dark Ages were upon us again, said a columnist in the newspaper, 'because of the growth in corruption, deprivation, violence, medieval-style ignorance, religious bigotry, fornication and extra-marital pregnancy.' That's me, I thought, pleased to be included. I felt upbeat about having fornicated and brought a child into the new Dark Ages. It sounded pretty cool.

A woman sat down next to me. I went on reading. 'They do a lovely carrot muffin here,' said a Scots voice. 'I've never had a muffin like this before.'

I raised my eyes slowly, resigned. (And secretly slightly puzzled that the undead ate stuff. Could people see the muffin (*my* muffin) disappearing into thin air, bite by bite?)

'Hello,' I whispered, looking round for eavesdroppers. 'You've not been around for, ooh, I guess forty days and forty nights.' I looked questioningly at her.

Agnes smiled at me. She was wearing that reversible coat, from the photograph, over a long black suit. On her lapel was a purple, green and white suffragette button. She looked thinner, more weary. 'Well, you've been busy, eh?' She stared meaningfully at my stomach.

'What do you know, exactly? Do you know stuff even when you're not around?'

Agnes brushed some crumbs from her skirt and didn't answer. Then she grinned conspiratorially. 'Liked what you did to that minister's car,' she said.

That really threw me. Was she some kind of modern, pro-choice feminist? Did suffragettes know words like pro-choice? And had she been in Florida? Was she omnipresent? Then a worse thought occurred: had she watched us together in bed? I felt ill. I wasn't just being haunted, which was bad enough: it was as though she was peeling my skin off and performing a sort of living autopsy on me.

I got angry (again). 'Would you mind explaining what your purpose is? I mean, are you just trying to be helpful in an ancestorish sort of way, or are you the ghost of feminism past or something? I mean, what's your angle here?' Agnes was clearly tickled by the ghost-of-feminism-past idea, and laughed. I couldn't believe that no one else could hear her or me, but all around, New Yorkers were focusing on their sole interest: themselves.

'Well, dear, I'm just here to help as much as you want. You don't seem to have anyone else, least of all that happy-clappy mother of yours,' she began. 'You've made your decision, and you just have to stick by it. Now, you have to get a proper job or something to support that wean that's coming, because that Italian man that's away will be no use, I'm telling you. That Leonardo will always be attached to that wife of his he lost. I know from experience. Now, let's think what you could do.' I told her to hold on a minute, but she continued, 'You've done the right thing getting out of that flat you were in with those two fashionable types. Bad influence on a child, there. You've got to get your feet on the ground if you're looking after someone else's life too. I always say . . .'

God, she was seamless. And opinionated. I wanted to talk to her about all sorts of things, about the baby she lost, and not just the one I'd gained, thanks in part to her, about Duncan her husband, about why she ran from one religion to another feminist one. After all, I had this window on her changing life too. But she was only interested in ploughing into the future, not the past.

'The baby,' I said, as she paused in her lecture. 'Your miscarriage . . .'

'No use worrying about that now,' she said, 'though I was a wee bit down for a while at the time. It happens. Anyway, we were talking about you.'

'No, *you* were talking at *me*,' I said, glowering.

'Well, if you feel like that, dear . . .' She paused. 'You couldn't go and get us another one of those carrot cakes, could you?'

I went off to the counter. Maybe she didn't carry modern currency. Typically, by the time I got back, she'd dematerialized, leaving me with a dozen unanswered questions, a constant feeling of being watched, and a carrot muffin. I sat down and stared at it, and time slipped sideways. Had Agnes been there at all? Had I bought a second carrot muffin, or was this the first, uneaten? Had the entire conversation been imagined, riding high on the hormones of pregnancy?

Anyway, there seemed to be a pattern of conversations broken off, and whenever I rejected Agnes's advice, her ability to stay in the here-and-now diminished. It was as though I was conjuring her, as though she came from something in me. I sipped the dregs of my coffee and thought that the most curious thing was that the ghost business had not freaked me out more. By the time Agnes snuck into my world, things were already so weird she didn't really stick out. I wasn't scared of her now either: she looked too much like me; she had become strangely safe and familiar. Her presence wasn't the problem; the reason for her presence was. Why me? Why now? And why did she never finish a conversation?

I surveyed the cafe just in case Agnes was hovering in the crowd, but there was just a bunch of SoHo types who seemed to have become as unhinged as the newspapers they were reading. There was an odd, hysterical atmosphere about the place, not due to phantasmic apparitions, but because people were worried about being invited to the right party, particularly when the end of the world was nigh. I was going myself to the Revelation party in my former apartment at 666 Broadway. 'Shame to waste the address,' Nosmo had said, 'particularly in the short but pleasant period that this will remain a Pampers-free zone.' While Wanda was worrying herself sick, Nosmo was going through a sort of second adolescence before his light parenting duties set in. He had insisted that everyone come to the party dressed as Biblical characters. I was going as Jezebel in purple and scarlet, with snakes in my hair for good measure. Nosmo and his new boyfriend Ned would appear streaked with fake tan as Adam and Adam, clad only in vine leaves from the deli. They had invented two blasphemous cocktails called Gog and Magog. 'We will be cast into the bottomless pit before you can say Happy New Year,' I had warned them, last time we talked on the phone. 'There is no doubt that we will be on the A-list for retribution. In fact, I already am.'

Before the party I walked back to my new apartment at Garrett's on Broome Street in light snow, past the green globes glowing over the subway entrances in the dusk. I felt strangely whole, inexplicably happy. At last there was a point to my existence, a good reason to avoid jumping in front of a subway train because there was nothing better to do of an evening. I didn't have a Great Cause, but I did have a tadpole inside me which would turn into a beautiful prince, or a frog. Whatever.

I reached in my pocket for a much-handled, crummy postcard of an elephant, which Leonardo had sent me back at 666. Not that the card said much, but its very presence was reassuring. Leonardo wouldn't yet have received the letter I'd sent him last week. Not that it had said much either, certainly nothing about what was lurking ever larger in my mind. Just thinking all the time about fornication and extra-marital pregnancy was making me a bit loopy, but then someone told me that you really lose 10 percent of your brain cells when you're pregnant. It's true. The baby eats them, or they die off, or something, so that by the time you give birth, you're pretty much retarded. But then the cells grow back again within three months. I reckon it's like being pruned.

Because I had lost my mind I had also lost the keys to my apartment, so Garrett had to let me in. Mysteriously, he was wearing fishing waders and smelled of whiskey. I didn't ask. He silently and reproachfully handed me my key-ring, which I'd left in the door. Upstairs, the apartment was cool, in both senses. The corridors of his rickety warehouse were freezing, but the rooms, separate workshops on six floors, were gigantic and could be warmed with serious effort. Being on the top floor with the view over the Hudson was wonderful on the occasions the lift worked. This was not one of those occasions. Still, compared to my previous quarters, I observed panting up the stairs, the place was sumptuous. I had a sort of skylit workshop-bedroom at the back of the fifty-foot room so paint contamination was limited in what Garrett referred to as 'the utility cube' – the kitchen and bathroom. Then the living-room part stretched into the night through huge windows at the side and the front. Furnishings were a ripped leather armchair from a dumpster, the increasingly burdensome trunk, a table with three different chairs, and two of Garrett's old paintings I'd selected, choosing the colors like wallpaper from a roomful downstairs. I sat in the armchair, my chair in my apartment, and grinned.

The child I was bearing had an unreliable mother,

an absentee father and an inconsistent income, but at least it had somewhere cheap to live, I thought, plaiting black rubber snakes from Toys 'R' Us into my hair. Better still, I'd at last have a guy (I was convinced it was a boy) to hang out with who was easygoing and uncritical. But financially I foresaw problems. Garrett had said I could pose in his evening class right until the end of the pregnancy. Indeed, he seemed amused by the idea, unlike me. I thought I might get a few more tacky mural commissions for dining-room walls on the Upper East Side. I might even do the unthinkable and sell a painting at the Wicked Women exhibition. I'd only sold a painting twice before. In seven years, my art, my real job, had netted me a total of $1,400. Yes, that's an income of $200 a year. So I was not going to be in the business of having a full-time executive career and a nanny. 'Never mind,' I said, out loud in Agnes's Scottish accent. 'Cross that bridge when we come to it.' There was no response, so I put on purple lipstick to match my skintight dress and took pleasure in this last chance to look really slutty.

At midnight, that millennial moment we'd all been waiting for, I found myself splayed on the chaise-longue in the arms of Nancy Klinger. There were worse arms to be in, I reckoned. Nancy's costume consisted of black jeans and a too-small T-shirt, which said VIRGIN. We kissed in the New Year passionately (very passionately in Nancy's case, I was just enjoying some human company), and I wondered precisely what changes Nancy had planned, sexually, for the twenty-first century. Then I told everyone what I had planned for the future, and their mouths hung open like drawers. I was pretty pleased: I felt I'd temporarily upstaged the century with my news. After I convinced them I wasn't joking, we drank to me, and the first fetus of the next millennium. I then embraced a shocked Wanda and both the Adams, and toasted them in Magog, which was largely based on cheap sparkling wine. I kissed Delilah (a supermodel by day), four Satans (one a banker with an enormous fake red penis – what can I say?), and John the Baptist with a tray round his neck to carry his severed head (only quite funny).

It was the first New Year's I could remember when I woke up before noon, and without a hangover. Indeed, I felt perky. I thought I might even paint something. I lay in bed considering what, and turned on the television at the end with my toe, since the remote had been lost in the move. The lunacy began: '. . . in what appears to be a collective suicide and killing in two Canadian villages by the religious sect Temple of the . . .' I changed channels. '. . . parties booked the Statue of Liberty, the Empire State Building and chartered the QE2, but hardcore millennial scholars say the new century does not begin until the first of January 2001.' I zapped again. '. . . spoke of an impending global disaster, the magic of fire, and of catastrophe and ruin . . .' And again. '. . . of computers in every state have gone down with the date change, leaving businesses, banks and . . .' Zap. '. . . not since nine hundred followers of the Reverend Jim Jones were killed with poisoned Kool-Aid has . . .'

'Shut up. Give me Home Shopping. Give me fashion. Give me cute wildlife programs,' I shouted, irritably toe-surfing. I hit the off button with my heel, and calmed down looking at the pattern of winter sunlight on the wall opposite. I made a New Year resolution to give up caffeine and television, both of which made me jumpy. Then I went into the kitchen and brewed myself a big mug of Italian mocha. On the fridge, like any normal person, I had magneted pictures of my friends and family. These included that artsily sepia photo of Agnes walking arm in arm in the park with Kirsty, both in weird hats. It was at that point it dawned on me, my neck still tattooed with Nancy's lipstick, that Kirsty was of much more importance than the letters revealed. Agnes was, more than likely, a dyke. Whether she knew it was another question.

I wondered, not for the first time, why she'd picked me to haunt. Or why I'd picked her to haunt me. Perhaps it was the time, the cracks at the turn of this century and the last, or just my emotional state that made me open to such things. (I preferred, and prefer, the theory that I was more receptive and sensitive than most people to the other theory: that I was nuts.) I wondered also if Agnes was up to speed on stuff like the Internet, television, and the latest restaurants in New York, or whether she was still stuck in the early 1900s. I pondered, over a second coffee, on the nature of the haunting: the irregularity of it, the unfinishedness. I was three-quarters of the way through the black-ribboned pile of letters, and it occurred to me then that Agnes's visits might end when I finished them. It seemed logical, in an illogical, and possibly entirely imaginary, situation.

Still, in many ways Agnes was an inspiration. A thought occurred to me, and I went downstairs to Garrett's kitchen, a scary unhygienic place I normally avoided, and borrowed all his odd teacups, mixed, chipped and mostly from the Sixth Avenue fleamarket. I ranged them tidily on a shelf, and began a rough outline of each on the canvas and filled in the pattern on each neatly. Sitting in one cup, the one with violets on the side, I painted a five-month-old fetus, fully formed with a big head and that translucent pink-red seashell skin they have. The early-afternoon sun came low through the back window, and I worked all afternoon, delightfully alone in a almost silent city where everyone else was still in bed.

The cup business got me thinking about Ida and the coffee grounds. What better way to start New Year than a psychic consulation with Ida? I mean, I had more reason than most to believe wholeheartedly in such things. Ida Petrowski's my spiritualist. She does readings of the future by telephone, and my girlfriends and I consult her for a laugh every month or two. I risked ringing the Bronx number. Ida has a half-Bronx half-Russian nasal accent, which is nearly incomprehensible. She came straight on the line. 'Nyahh,' she said, which meant yes. 'I've been up for hours, honey. It's Him.' Him was the unnamed husband. 'He's still lying there. When He gets up, I'll kill Him. Now what can I do for you? A reading? Ring me back in five minutes. I gotta find my slippers and get the cawffee going. I've just been sitting here watching the nooze on television. Tragic, ain't it?' Ida read futures in coffee grounds, and she was, in my and my friends' experience, 99 percent correct. It had begun as a joke, but many now considered Ida a reliable service, and happily sent the twenty dollars in cash in an envelope after each reading.

I called back. She had a cup ready. 'Nyahh,' Ida said, which meant well, well. She sounded speedy and caffeinated. 'I gotta lot to tell you. Gonna start at the top here with the near future, next few weeks, say? I gotta pattern here I've never seen before with you, Albertine, looks like money, plenty of money coming to you. Has someone died and left you something? No? Nyahh, it looks pretty fortunate anyway, it's an upward curve to the rim. Now I'm moving further down. I gotta question: you started putting on weight? Thought you said you was skinny, and I see one big girl here. Be careful what you eat. OK, OK, never mind the fat, maybe what I'm seeing here is you doubled, a kinda shadow. You gotta twin sister? No? Nyahh, well, moving along, we're talking later this year, maybe the summer, and again I've got good fortune. I got fame and fortune here, maybe you'll win something, but whatever it is makes a big difference to your life, then there's a big zigzag, followed by another. Don't know what that means, except a big change, I mean, like, we're talking major change. Then, last of all, there's this funny mark, kind of star-shaped, sort we used to say was the mark of the devil in the old country, but nyahh, could be benign. On the whole it looks good for you. Happy NooYeah. Nyahh. And did I say it's twenty-five dollars now? Noo century, noo rates.' I thanked her, hung up, and put the cash in an envelope.

Five days later, I was still pondering over rich and distant relatives who might pass away and leave me a small trust fund. None came to mind so, as a precaution, I bought a lottery ticket at the corner shop as I walked over to the SoHo Gallery. I was supposed to supervise the hanging of my paintings in the Wicked Women Show, which was opening next week. A few other artists were there, making temperamental scenes and demanding more and better space on the floor and in the Wicked Women catalog to display their genius. A sweet, bespectacled guy installing the stuff left them all cat-fighting, and took me over to a blank wall in the far corner of the back room. 'This is yours,' he said, looking edgily at his new client in case I burst into hysterics at the unpromising, half-hidden site by the washrooms. 'Fine,' I said. I had never advised on hanging before. I felt pretty professional. 'Well, all five in a row, close together at nose level. My nose level. That's it.' The installation guy looked astounded. 'You are the first sane person I've met all day,' he said, through gritted teeth. There was no sign of Zindsi Hawkes, I noted with relief. 'She's more a creative than practical force,' he said, smiling conspiratorially.

From a distance, my paintings propped against the wall looked like five enormous pink flowers. It was only close up that you saw the gritty trailerpark detail, the scars and sags and scribblings on the flesh. I felt distanced from them, like they'd been painted by someone else, but I also felt a twinge of pride. I went to check out the competition. Pegged on a washing line across the room was a twenty-two-legged set of pantyhose, the very last pair molded perfectly for balls and a penis, all in California tan. Below that, in a small refrigerated glass cabinet, there were, as promised by Zindsi, ice-cream Tampax, used and unused, made from vanilla and Cherry Garciaflavored Ben and Jerry's. This sight immediately brought on a last bout of morning sickness. I plopped down queasily on a chair covered in some sort of black poodle fabric. Then I realized it was an exhibit. I looked at the label. 'Pubes', it said. This is very silly, I thought, passing life-size photographs of what I assumed were the private parts of lady elephants.

I found a real chair in the reading area and sat until the nausea subsided, leafing through *At Your Fingertips – The Care and Maintenance of a Vagina*, a humorous collection from *Hysteria* magazine, at $5.95. I observed my fellow exhibitors – I would not necessarily describe them as artists – arguing for space. 'How dare you refer to this exhibit as "that bunch of dolls",' one screamed at the poor installation guy. 'I heard you, don't think I didn't. You have no idea about the significance of Barbie in this culture.' She then moved 'Hot Flush Barbie' and another Barbie with an added penis and a monocle on to a pedestal right at the front of the room. I got the feeling that the installation guy, who had taken off his glasses and started eating them, was about to throw everybody out and just get on with it, but he merely said, 'OK, next?'

The only paintings apart from my own were pastiches of Norman Rockwell with the happy family in the diner, the mom showing a little chest hair. I thought they were pretty funny, and I was also impressed by a woman who had carefully made up different Sara Lee cakes from the mixes, installed them in potholes in Manhattan streets, and photographed them as a set of still lives titled 'A Woman's Work is Never Done'. There were also some posters from the Guerrilla Girls, campaigners for women artists: 'Do women have to be naked to get into the Metropolitan Museum?' asked one. 'Less than 5% of the artists in the modern art section are women, but 85% of the nudes are female.' In the coffee bar at the back, an electronic announcement board showed the following statements in an endless loop: 'MEN ARE 48 PER CENT OF THE POPULATION AND THEY NEED YOUR HELP / PARTS OF THEIR SEX ORGANS ARE AMPUTATED AT BIRTH / THEY DIE 8 YEARS SOONER / THEY HAVE TO EXPOSE THEIR BREASTS IN PUBLIC.' The installation guy suddenly appeared by my shoulder and looked at the moving letters with resignation. 'This has not been easy for me.' He sighed. 'Normally I hang nice black and white photographs.'

I smiled. 'Yeah. I can imagine.'

I didn't realize how much one sympathetic conversation from a non-hysterical artist would mean to the installation guy, because I missed the launch party, lying at home with a stomach upset. I sent Garrett as a scout instead, and he came back hopping with delight.

'I thought your paintings looked great, especially well set off by all the bullshit around them. They had them on the first wall as you came in. They were the first thing that hit the eye after some stupid dolls. I didn't know what you meant about being in some back room. Incidentally, what price did you put on them?'

'Three thousand dollars each. For fun.'

'Well, they've all got red stickers on them,' said Garrett. 'They're all sold.'

Chapter Twenty

Dowanhill Road, Glasgow

14 December 1909

Dear Ishbel,

The blinds are all pulled down and the house is thick with gloom. Duncan will not have any daylight in his bedroom, for he says it gives him a headache, and his condition has not improved. Dr Menzies, in whom I have less and less faith, says he has palpitations of the heart and must rest absolutely still until they return to normal, but there has been no change in the last three weeks and his pulse remains irregular. Of course, there is nothing to make Duncan more desperate to rush around then being told to stay still, and Kirsty and I are behaving more like gaolers than nurses. The other daughters, Margaret and Lily, have been round, looking as though they had come to stand at the side of a deathbed. They are a dreary, pious pair and sat around in the front room drinking tea with long faces and making doleful conversation — 'It is God's will', etc. They were no help whatsoever and really I wanted to tell them to go and boil their heads. Fortunately Duncan made a fine show of seeming healthy for a few hours, and was quite brusque with them, I am delighted to say. A young minister has come as a temporary replacement at Colquhoun Church for the month and is doing a perfectly fine job. Indeed, I suspect the congregation is increasing, but then it always does around Christmas.

I find it so hard, Ishbel, that I can do nothing for Duncan, and whatever I do is always wrong: his tea is too hot, his bedclothes are bumphled, the stew is not right. He is so frustrated, poor man, that he cannot help being irritable. Still, he is trying everything: you would think he was a spendthrift the way he gets through patented medicines he sees advertised in the newspapers. This week I had to go up the town to get him three bottles of Nerve Tonic at 1s. 9d. each, which he drinks like a fish. I forbore from pointing out the ingredients on the back, the main one of which is alcohol, since he is, after all, a pillar of the Temperance movement. His sickroom looks like a closed-down library or pharmacy, with dozens of bottles and books gathering dust on the mantelpiece. He wants nothing moved and everything within his reach, like some old women set in her household ways. Ishbel, I am at a loss. I do not know how to cheer him up or whether such an act is possible. Isabel at least is good for him. When she comes in from school, they read books together in the quiet dusk.

Kirsty has moved into the spare room to help with Duncan's care, although she often comes back exhausted from a night delivering some baby, and then gets up a few hours later. In fact, with Mrs Minto around, his needs are all seen to, but in some indefinable way I think she feels guilty; she wants to talk to her father, to break through his reserve, but she does not know quite how to do it. He is sixty now, and only for the first time, lying in his bed, do the years show. It is very lowering.

I feel so ashamed, now that Duncan is ill, that I have been running round the country working for the suffrage movement. Maybe if I had kept more of an eye on him, he would not have worn himself down to a frazzle like this. But, you know, things could have been a great deal worse: I might have ended up in gaol after the last suffrage demonstration, and it was only by chance I did not. I am so relieved I did not cause Duncan all that worry.

I have only now come to my senses and realized how irresponsible I was in Newcastle a few weeks ago when we went down to protest during the visit of Lloyd George. I was with the militants, along with Christabel Pankhurst, Lady Constance Lytton and Mrs Brailsford. The police had put barricades in the streets, expecting us, but they had underestimated Mrs Brailsford, who had hidden an axe in a bunch of yellow chrysanthemums, and started hitting the barricade in front of her. Immediately, some policemen fell on her and dragged her roughly off. Then Lady Lytton threw a stone at a car owned by the man who was putting up Lloyd George during his visit, and she was arrested straight away. I was right behind her with a handbag filled with stones, but our target had gone.

Meanwhile, the others had gone off to smash windows. The ones who were arrested refused as usual to be bound over and were imprisoned for six weeks, although Lady Lytton, who is quite weak and unhealthy-looking, was discharged as medically unfit.

The others, and I might have been one of them, went on hunger strike as agreed and the poor things were forcibly fed. Oh, how I felt for them, and I also felt terrible that I was not one of them, but now I realize the strain such an ordeal would have put on Duncan, never mind poor Isabel. (Isabel likes to wander round the house in my Votes for Women sash and her nightgown, and says she is a suffragette like her mother. Fortunately, Duncan is upstairs and cannot see this sight.) Mind you, a couple of those women in prison are married with young children, too, but they believe the sacrifice is worth it.

Kirsty herself shows no sign of getting married and having any weans, although plenty of young doctors have at various times taken an interest in her. She is a quite extraordinary figure, and dresses most peculiarly nowadays, in large jackets and tweeds because she goes everywhere by bicycle. She says the bicycle makes her twice as efficient. But she is thirty now, getting on, the doctors have all found suitable wives, and she is so dedicated to her job. She seems to like being up half the nights of the week in some room and kitchen in a tenement with half a dozen children, the father down the pub and the mother giving birth to another. From her stories, it does not surprise me that Glasgow has one of the highest numbers of infant deaths in the country, what with neglect and dirt and overcrowding and just plain poverty.

Yes, yes, I know you are thinking this is nothing like as bad as India and that family of thirteen you saw the other day, trailing behind their mother like a descending row of stick insects, but we are supposed to be a civilized, sophisticated country here, though you would not think it from what you see. The wee things are weaned on to nothing but potatoes and bread and dripping, so their legs are bent with rickets. There are two- and three-year-olds, Kirsty says, who cannot speak a word because no has had time to talk to them, and they seem to find their playthings in the midden. She said the other night she was dressing a sore and mistakenly left the bottle of rubbing alcohol behind at a clarty tenement down on Dumbarton Road. The next day, she went back and claimed that half the bottle was down the mother, and the other half was probably in the four-month-old since it had slept soundly for ten hours during the day. Probably it was the first relief the mother had had. I told Kirsty she should take her some of that Nerve Tonic next time, and she told me not to be ridiculous.

Anyway, it is wonderful to have Kirsty in the house all the time. In between attending to Duncan, we sit up late putting the world to rights, which you know I am able to do for hours on end, and when she has time she sometimes comes with me to a suffrage meeting. I feel, in some way, that I am having a second childhood with her, going to the theatre and parks, and on outings with her and Isabel, all the things I never did when I first got married. Strangely, as we get younger inside, Duncan seems to get older, and that weighs heavily on my heart. He says he will wait another week in bed, and even if nothing has changed, he will still do the Christmas Day services. Dr Menzies will be able to do nothing against his iron will, if he really decides. I know that through long experience. It is one in the morning now, and I am too tired to write another thing. I can still hear Duncan tossing and turning next door, and I only wish he could sleep too.

Your affectionate sister,
Agnes

Chapter Twenty-One

4 March 2000

For a while there, I hardly slept. The euphoria that I'd felt around New Year drained away, leaving me emotionally empty but physically increasingly full. The novelty of it all had been replaced by trepidation, as I sensed the first nips and twitches of reality inside. There was nothing much to show outside at four and a bit months – just looked like I'd got a little sloppy about the gym, stuck on a Wonderbra, and binged out on Pepperidge Farm cookies. But mentally, it was all happening: I'd wake at five a.m. in the dark, and lie there waiting for the dawn, rigid with unnamed worries. I'd wake up from dreams, screaming: the baby would be made of grayish plaster-of-paris, and I'd drop it on purpose to watch it smash. That night in March, I dreamed of a stone baby, like the effigy on a dead child's tomb, which melted back into flesh as it sucked my nipple – for some reason through my white T-shirt, which became stained with a yellow juice.

After that I sat up panicking, a lump in my throat, and put on the bedside light to check the time: 3.17 a.m. I found myself looking at my T-shirt for the yellow milk stains, but all was pristine above the statement EXISTMYFUTURE398MODERN. Inside I felt black despair. I felt so alone, so lonely with his horrible, unknown burden waiting for me. I lay there restless for about half an hour, and then got up to look out of the windows down at the Hudson and the city lights in the snow and tears started running down my face, although I was making no noise. I whispered his name over and over, as though that might bring him back, or cause the telephone to ring from a bed under a mosquito net in some raddled Ugandan hotel, but nothing happened. My problem was made worse in that I could not even admit to myself I loved Leonardo, and his behavior so far had never indicated he loved me, so I felt no right to grief for the loss of him; just an indefinable ache that he did not know yet, perhaps would never know, that I was carrying his child.

I went to get some Evian out of the fridge, and as I passed the leather armchair, I saw a body slumped in it. I started, and felt the adrenaline of fear rush through me even as I realized it was Agnes. I thought she was dead (well, technically, she was) but then I saw her breathing. She was asleep. Was she in the habit of watching (over?) me at night?

I cleared my throat loudly. She stirred, and her eyes opened. 'Oh. Must've . . . hmmm,' she said, primly straightening herself up.

'Hello. You been here all night? Regular thing, is it?' I wiped the wet off my cheeks I hoped before she noticed.

'Just keeping an eye,' she said, standing up and fixing me with a penetrating stare. 'Up at this time, eh?'

'Yeah.' I sniffed.

'You're having a bad time of it, aren't you, you poor

wee thing?' She seemed about to slip her arm reassuringly round my shoulder, but something held her back.

'Will I come over and sit by you on the bed? You and that baby'll catch your death if you stand around half naked,' she said. I got back under the quilt – it was minus ten outside – and Agnes perched on the side of the bed, gray-faced in a shadowy dress. We talked. It was probably as near as she ever got to a slumber party.

'D'you miss him?'

'Yes. But I'm not sure if there's anything to miss. I'm not sure he'd be around even if he was on the same continent.'

'Well, I did say he wasn't the most reliable—'

'That's not much help now, is it?' I broke in, my voice breaking too.

'No, it's not . . .' she said, shaking her head.

We were silent for a while.

'Well, what's done's done,' she said. 'It's no' the worst thing that ever happened to anyone, having a baby by themselves.'

'I know. I know. I'm just scared.' I heard my tone wobble pathetically with self-pity.

Agnes sighed and looked up at the skylight. 'You'll be fine. You've got friends. You've even got Rose, and she's no' a bad lass. You'll no' be on your own.'

'I know,' I said. 'I don't mind being alone. I mind being lonely.'

'Oh, come on,' she said. 'It's the best thing in the world that's happening to you. The greatest joy. It's the gift all your barren friends want and can't have for themselves. Besides, it's brought you back down to earth. "You were lost but now you are found," as the good Lord says.

'Thought you weren't religious any more.'

'Nothing wrong with the occasional quote.'

I was beginning to feel warm and sleepy. Agnes continued, 'Sometimes, an enormous event, a change of life which seems the worst, brings its own good too. Like when Duncan died and I was still young and—'

'He died early?' I interrupted, jolted partially awake.

'Mm-hmm. But then the second half of my life, my real life, began, and where doors had closed, others opened. And you'll gain far more than you lose in this. Instead of one life, you'll have two, you'll be a mother, and you'll be you, too. And at first you don't think there's room to hold the two existences and you think your head will explode and your bones will crack under the strain, but then, after a while . . .' Her voice mesmerized me, and I fell asleep to the sound, calm as a baby.

By ten a.m. when I woke up alone, I wasn't sure if all this had been a dream, or reality, but since my reality was increasingly dream-like, I supposed such distinctions no longer mattered. But there was a reassuring dent in the quilt where someone had been sitting. Above the bed, the skylight was whited out with snow. I slid further under the covers to contemplate my next move. It was, I decided, time to go public on the pregnancy, and by public, I meant wider public, such as the father-in-question and my parents, since my friends already knew. It was clear to me that too much inner contemplation was resulting in peculiar dreams and probably permanent psychological damage. Outward confrontation would take my mind off it. I leaned over to pick up the phone by the bed to dial my parents. At the first ring, I hung up, and decided to go for a test run on my grandmother, Rose, who is a good deal more relaxed about such things than my mother.

I dialed the New Jersey number, but there were ten rings before Rose answered. 'Hello, dear,' she said, out of breath. 'I just ran in. I was sweeping the path. There's four foot out there, but I think I'll still come into town on the train the day for the Macy's whites sale. Are you—'

I interrupted, 'Pregnant. I'm pregnant.'

'Oh, my God, I'd better see you as well, then.' Rose grew more Glaswegian with the excitement. 'Are you, I mean d'you intend . . .?'

'To keep it? Yes. I'm about four months now.'

'And is there . . . I mean, who is the lucky father?'

'Um, well, there's the question. Can I meet you later when you're here?'

We arranged to meet at noon in the coffee-shop in Macy's basement, where Rose had a coupon for tea and two free cakes that she wanted to use. She selected a big cream meringue, and I had the lemon tart. The situation reminded me of my recent tea-time encounter with Agnes in Dean and Deluca, except that Rose was wearing a tight purple ski-suit and furry moon boots to combat the cold, and carrying three sale bags. She looked like mutton dressed up as *après-ski* babe.

We sat down in a corner.

'So,' Rose said with a broad grin, preparing to relish the details, and the meringue.

'Well, I got pregnant by mistake, and I thought,

I'm thirty-one now, I might as well, I'm not doing anything else.'

'Well, that's brilliant,' said Rose, as though it were the simplest, most sensible decision in the world. 'And your boyfriend? I didn't know you had a boyfriend.'

'I don't. But I'm quite happy about doing it on my own. I have reason to suspect he won't reappear.'

'I see. It's like that, is it? Immaculate conception?' She paused to consider. 'Have you told Carol and Albert?'

'No. I was going to ask you about that.'

Rose sucked her gleaming white false teeth, and pondered again. I knew she would be sympathetic, because there was only five months' difference between my grandparents' marriage certificate and my mother's birth certificate. Such was the case for many war brides who came to America.

'I don't envy you telling them, 'specially now they go to this church shopping center thing they've come over all moral majority. Mind you, you could write a wee note to them, and then put on that answering-machine of yours for a few days, give it time to sink in.'

I agreed this was a good plan. We got down to economics after that. Rose, for all her radical youthfulness, was slightly shocked by my relaxed attitude.

'They need prams and nappies and milk and all that, you know, and you can't get a stroke of work done while they're around. I can give you a bit of a loan to help, if you want.' This was an extraordinary offer from the normally thrifty, coupon-cutting Rose, and it made me feel tearful again. I told her I needed her support more than her cash, and explained about the shock sale of my paintings – fifteen thousand dollars. On the back of my good reviews in the papers, the SoHo Gallery had, unbelievably, offered to represent me. They were also giving me a two-week one-woman show in a slot that had come empty in July, just before I was due to give birth.

'What with the holidays, is July a good month to open?' inquired Rose, always on the ball.

'You're terrible. It's the only show I'm going to get, so I'm happy with it, even if the whole city's in the Hamptons.'

We had another pot of Earl Grey – I paid, since it was not included on the cake coupon – and we talked on about the health of Rose's elderly Labradors (dodgy), the health of Rose herself (fine), and my health (increasingly curious).

'I've been reading those letters from your grandmother Agnes.'

Rose looked up, alert like a sniffer dog. Then she covered herself. 'Oh, now, I haven't looked at them in years. I remember that one written on a scrap of envelope from the prison, must've been smuggled out, oh, and that dreadful one about the force-feeding. You wouldn't have known she was that sort of woman to look at her. Always well turned out, respectable. Kept her money down the back of the settee.'

'I haven't got to that stage yet. I'm at 1910 or so. I never knew all that. Did she bother you in . . .' I hesitated.

'Did she what?' said Rose.

But then I thought (wrongly) that Rose was the most practical, down-to-earth person I knew, and that she would probably laugh if I mentioned the apparition of Agnes. I changed the subject back and Rose started showing me her whites sale bargains. 'If I'd thought, I could've got you some sheets for the baby.' I gagged at the thought, the horribly practical thought, and then we headed our separate ways into the subway.

At home, I took Rose's advice, and wrote a short note to my parents on the back of a tasteful Masaccio postcard showing a mother holding a half-naked baby. Why not get them in the mood? I thought. Then I began the big one: a letter to Leonardo on foolscap, because I knew I would need half a dozen attempts. By three thirty, I found my work acceptable and copied it onto an airmail letter. I thought a trouble shared like that was probably a trouble doubled rather than halved, but what the hell? It would give Leonardo something to occupy his mind in the jungle or desert or wherever he was with this cameraman who had turned out to be a woman. I hedged the letter in terms that would not cause fear and loathing, pointing out that had I looked at the sell-by date on the condom, this would never have happened, and assuring him I would not pursue him through the courts as a Deadbeat Dad. If he wanted to be part of the kid's life, all he needed to do was turn up; I expected nothing more. If he didn't want to be involved, that was fine too. Of course, such statements bore no relation to the truth. In reality, and I had to take into account my addled brain, I desperately craved his return in three months and his affection. I indulged in happy domestic fantasy: I saw us walking hand in hand in Central Park, the baby sleeping blissfully in a sling. I knew I wanted to share the baby with someone. Unfortunately, Leonardo was someone I knew very little about, including his permanent address. And probably he had sent postcards to everyone he knew, not just me.

I pulled on my hairy orange coat and ran downstairs to mail the letters before I could change my mind. I was also going round to Wanda's that afternoon, because she'd arrived the day before, fraught, late, and epically jet-lagged, with the adopted baby from China. I was dying to see them. My run shuddered to a shuffle in the deep snow, which was still falling. There were no cars on the streets, a few psychotic taxis, and some garbage trucks with snowploughs chained on the front. I went into the post office on Varick Street and made sure the airmail letter was stamped correctly for Uganda: the National Geographic, *poste restante* at Kampala Central Post Office. Then I buttoned up every button I possessed, put up my umbrella, and waded over to 666 Broadway.

Nosmo answered the door in his navy silk pajamas, with a big gloop of dried spew on his left shoulder. Over his right was a purple tie-dyed Babygro topped with thick, spiky black hair.

'Shhh. Wanda's asleep. She's been up half the night with the monster here and she's still in another time zone, so I took charge at noon and sent her to bed. Unfortunately, a certain percentage of the milk I put in seems to come back out. Is this normal?'

I kissed him. 'Let me see.' Nosmo put the baby, not a newborn baby, but a sort of medium-to-large one, I thought, into my arms. She was awake, but heavy and floppy. She smelled edible. I felt a first blast of mothering hormones. 'Hello, Lianne,' I said, formally. Li An, now Americanized to Lianne, was worryingly perfect, unlike

223

white babies which were, in my limited experience, ugly and blotchy. Instead Lianne had creamy tan skin, pink cheeks and shining brown eyes. She was also fat, reckoning from the rolls at the wrist. 'The hairstyle is most impressive.'

'Gimme,' said Nosmo, snatching the bundle back. 'You're dripping on her. Take that hairy coat thing off.'

We sat down on the chaise-longue – I noticed the orange fake-pregnancy cushion was still there – and we took turns at holding the baby, passing her like a tray of delicate crockery. Lianne neither cried nor smiled, but kept holding on to a yellow bandana. Nosmo said Wanda reckoned that Lianne was more like six months old, even though her birth certificate said four and a half. 'They date 'em when they turn up at the orphanage. This one came wrapped on the doorstep in a beautiful rug with her name taped inside. That was all. Wanda's got the note and the rug. She had it dry-cleaned, sort of like an heirloom for the kid.'

'Weird,' I said, slightly spooked by seeing a real, live baby, and wondering if the nasty twitches in my stomach were at all the same thing. 'I'll go make us a coffee. Looks like you need it.' I left Nosmo trying to change the baby's diaper. He was putting the Pamper on backwards, but I didn't know that then. The kid screamed.

'How come,' I said, bringing back the mugs and pointing to the bandana, 'she holds on to that yellow thing all the time?'

'Dunno,' said Nosmo, looking like he'd lost the instructions. 'That's weird too.'

'She holds it because it's kind of the first thing she's ever had of her own,' said Wanda, entering dramatically in her bathrobe. 'She grabbed it from me in her cot in the hotel after two days, and she's sucked or held it ever since.' Wanda hugged me. I'd missed her. I felt reassured that someone was in the same shit as me. She looked about twenty pounds thinner than before leaving, due to motherhood and native Chinese food. She checked Lianne to see if she had survived Nosmo's care. 'I changed the diaper with some difficulty, but I did get seven ounces into her,' he said, proudly waving the bottle.

Lianne gave her mother a large smile, making it clear she discriminated against gay men and people with bristly orange coats that matched their hair.

Wanda looked ecstatic at this preferment. 'She didn't smile at all for the first week when we had to wait and go through all this paperwork. She didn't cry at first either, and then she was hysterical on and off for twenty-four hours. I was desperate.' Wanda still seemed shaken. 'I thought it was the change to American formula from this milk and rice-flour sludge they get, but the same thing kept happening to the other parents adopting in the hotel. The hotel was a nightmare, hot water kept cutting off. Anyway, apparently it's sort of shock. The babies suddenly realize it's for real – they're outta there and they just start screaming, probably with relief. They know that when they cry someone's going to do something about it at last.'

Wanda was off on a monolog about the orphanage, one of many in Wuhan. She got out photographs of a gray concrete building with a weedy yard, a shelf of hundreds of tiny shoes – the saddest sight – and a room full of cots with a bad copy of a capitalist Mickey Mouse on the bare wall. 'I went with a bunch of other parents to visit the orphanage and take pictures in the rooms they let us into, so Lianne would at least have some history when she grows up, and these little girls kept coming and grabbing our legs, holding on like we were a passage out of the place. It was awful. And, let's face it, no one's going to take a three-year-old who's been deprived of affection – not that they're nasty, there's just not enough staff to go round – when they can take a baby without the same damage.'

I wondered what she meant by damage. I'd been reading my dictatorial childcare manual *What to Expect in the First Year*, so I knew that a five- or six-month-old baby should be rolling, grabbing things and maybe even trying to sit up. I wondered why Lianne remained a soft blob on her mother's knees, but I didn't say anything. Wanda continued, 'Lianne had this cot with nothing in it, no toys, no mobiles, just a quilt, among twenty other cots, a mesh forest in this room. They just prop up the bottles on a pillow beside their heads, and if they learn to suck, they survive. Otherwise they die. It's fucking awful. I had nightmares afterwards. I'm going back to adopt another one, once I can remember my own name and remain fully awake for more than thirty seconds.' Her courage made me ashamed.

Wanda had gone on a tour of China, starting in Shanghai, before she completed the adoption in Wuhan. She'd thought she would pass unnoticed as a native, but she realized she was too tall and all her clothes, even her jeans, were too well cut. She stuck out like any other tourist. At the hotel, she met other hysterical and nervous middle-class parents, half of whom seemed to live on the Upper West side and behaved like it too. She immediately felt comfortable and realized she was Manhattan by instinct, rather than Chinese. 'I did get a feeling they picked out the strongest, best-looking baby for me because I was half-Chinese, but that could just be parental bias. Still, took me two days to get her to hold anything, and she's only now growing muscles in her back and learning to push on her arms and legs because I put her on the rug every day in the hotel. When she smiled, at last, I cried for about half an hour, which stopped her smiling for another two days.' Wanda sounded as if she was about to burst into tears again.

I changed the subject, aghast at the debilitating effect of new motherhood, and gave Wanda a box, which contained an extremely small pair of red cowboy boots.

'Fashion victim already,' said Wanda, pleased. 'These are completely useless right now. Thank you. Shoulda seen what she came in. Kept them too.' She fetched a bag contained three smelly handknitted jumpers – 'they like to boil their children' – a little cotton padded jacket, and pink padded trousers with an enormous split crotch. 'Makes changing the diaper easy, and in the streets, you see little kids squealing and their mothers just set them down and they pee.'

'I want to know,' I said, joggling Lianne, who remained stony-faced on my lap. 'What did you think when you first saw her?'

'Well, all the parents waited in the hotel corridor, and we went into this room to get the babies one by one. A nice, nurse-type woman came over holding this enormous bundle of clothing and said something I didn't understand. Then she tried to speak English. "You doctah," she said, which I thought meant we had to see a doctor. But then she handed me the laundry bundle and there was a little face in the middle of it, which looked exactly like my own baby pictures, and my throat closed up and I couldn't breathe and I could hear someone crying, and it turned out to be me.'

I felt my eyes watering, too. Nosmo said he better get some proper clothes on and slunk off. Lianne burped.

'So,' said Wanda more steadily, looking at my barely rounded stomach in my ski-pants, 'you got all this to come. Don't know what's more traumatic – an eighteen-hour flight with a screaming baby, or an eighteen-hour labor. How do you feel anyway?'

'Fine. Kind of normal now, not at all sick, but like someone has stuck a baseball in my stomach. I feel it when I roll over on my front at night. And I keep having these weird dreams where I drop the baby or it turns to stone or something.'

'Oh, I had tons of them beforehand too. Normal anxieties for irresponsible people like us. When's your due date?'

'July sixteenth. Another four months of worrying.'

'Well, don't worry about practical things. You can inherit all the clothes Lianne will have grown out of. Lots of the stuff I bought was too small already when I got there. And, you know, when I get a proper child-minder in three months, maybe we can share some days.'

I thanked her and looked heavenwards. It was just like the ChurchMall teen mothers' flyer said, 'Go ahead and have the baby and God will provide.' I smiled.

I took Lianne while Wanda went off for what turned out to be an extremely long bath. Lianne was showing no signs of sleepiness, so I tried to persuade her to crawl or at least do a push-up on the rug, leaving enticing rattles just beyond her reach, but the baby remained stubbornly immobile, and began to wail. What the hell do you do with babies anyway? They don't *do* anything. They just lie there. I lifted her to the window and explained about snow, and pointed out a yellow cab jammed and revving on Broadway. 'Ga, cha,' babbled Lianne. 'Yes, that's right, car,' I said, giving her the benefit of the doubt. 'But practice "taxi". It's more useful for living here.'

The phone rang. 'It's for you,' said Nosmo. 'It's Nancy. She lost your new number at Garrett's – apparently you're unlisted – but I said you're here.' He handed me the portable and stomped off. I put Lianne in a football hold, and managed to get the receiver up to my ear. 'I'm holding Wanda's new baby. Hang on till I get to the sofa and establish proper co-ordination.'

Nancy got full baby details, and then asked me to come with her that night to Henrietta Hudson's. She'd selected me as her companion because she did not want to go alone, and I only had a few blocks to walk in the snow.

'That's that lipstick lesbian bar, isn't it?' I said, warily. 'Never been there.'

'I'm not sure we use the term lipstick for it, but I'll let you off if you come.'

'Who's "we" exactly?' I asked, but Nancy rang off.

By ten o'clock that night I was more keen on getting under the quilt again than schlepping out to be Nancy's stooge but, on the other hand, you never knew when a new experience might result in some material. I put on my Timberlands, and thought I would probably blend in very well as I walked up Varick. I liked this weather since muggers disappeared, EvangelAngels went to ground, and the streets held a moment of silent white perfection before they turned to dirty slush.

I realized as I crossed Hudson that the sign above Henrietta's said 'Bar and Girl', which I'd instinctively read as 'Bar and Grill' before. Of course, Nancy was late, so I had to stand nervously at the bar sipping my beer for five minutes. It was pretty empty, and no one was paying me any particular attention. Everyone else seemed to be couples. I looked round hopefully for such paintable clichés as tweeds, monocles and leather, a sort of living Otto Dix portrait, but the women were all dressed like me in big sweaters for the cold. Nancy appeared shaking herself like a dog in the doorway, and her padded Mao jacket, jeans and short hair suddenly entered their natural habitat.

'Hi, Albertine,' she said, hugging me. 'Been at a meeting of the New York Dolls. You should come again.' I grimaced. Then she spotted some other people. 'Joanie, Florence, hi, how are you? We'll be over in a minute.'

'Exactly how long,' I asked in mock horror, 'have you been cruising joints such as this?'

'Oh, a few months. And I'm not cruising. I'm just making friends, you know, sisters.' Nancy face was twisted in an ironic grin.

'Uh-huh,' I said, wondering if, as a sister also on the shelf, I should just think, What the hell? and change sexual preference too. It was, after all, in my blood.

Chapter Twenty-Two

12 February 1910

Dearest Ishbel,

Thank you so much for sending the telegram back – it made me feel less alone in the world, knowing you knew, knowing you were there. The days since have passed in a strange dream, and the pain only cuts through to the quick when I see Isabel's tired, pinched little face as she struggles off to school in the morning, pretending everything is normal. Kirsty has been organizing things, talking and writing to the lawyers, the undertakers, the unhelpful Church of Scotland, while continuing to work, and I do not think she will know what has happened until she stops and stands still. Mrs Minto's reaction has been to withdraw into silence, something which has never occurred before, and she makes enormous pots of stew and cock-a-leekie soup every day, which no one is able to eat in the mute kitchen. She has been with the McPhails for thirty years and knows no other home, and I think she is dreading moving in with her sister, but what else can we do? I cannot keep her on with only a widow's pension from the Church. A Widow's Pension. That makes it seem real and horrifying. Here I am, a widow at thirty years old.

Ishbel, I must tell you this, not so much because you want to know but because I want to tell, because only in the retelling will this vagueness harden into reality. Duncan died in the place, I suppose, he would have wanted to die, in the pulpit of Colquhoun Church. He had refused to stay in bed, and called Dr Menzies a quack to his face, and actually seemed to be managing very well, as though he were back to normal, and his colour returned almost as soon as he stepped out of that gloomy bedroom. He would not let anyone near him to check his heartbeat, and went about his regular business for three weeks from Christmas. Only he must have known was was happening, those irregular beats tapping, but he chose not to hear them. He was on fine form during the sermon, the old Duncan, his eyes filled with fire, his voice full of fire, too, and brimstone, and then suddenly he took a breath, and it was his last, and he slid to the floor. I was in the front row, and I ran up, thinking he had fainted – well, to survive you prevent yourself from thinking the worst – but when I saw his blue face, his half-open eyes, I knew that the Duncan I loved in my own discordant way had gone.

I was shocked to the core, but at the same time glad he had his belief and had gone with it. For days I wondered, How could he suddenly be here at one side of a second, and not be there at the other?

How I wished I still held a shred of that belief at the funeral. Having once been as religious and as convinced as they come – after all, we got through Mother and Father's deaths together, and somehow I had God to talk to, there was something to hold me up. But up there, on the windy Necropolis, beneath these dark tombs looking down on the grey city, I lost all hope. Everything seemed so barren. I kept looking round for some sort of chair of faith to sit on, and not finding it there, and missing it painfully. It was damp and the cold crept into your bones and soul; the grave was a sea of mud, a wreath of hothouse flowers shrivelling by it. Kirsty, Isabel and I all supported each other, and it was all I could do to control myself and not scream into the wind.

It was such a waste, Ishbel, such a stupid, arrogant waste. If he had stayed in bed a bit longer, if he had retired and not rushed on with his work, Isabel might still have a father.

14 February

This morning, two weeks after the funeral, Kirsty and I went up the hill of the Necropolis again, feeling that in all the suddenness and horror of the funeral, we had not properly said goodbye. We took a pot of snowdrops up to plant nearby, and they will flower again next year and the years after. It was crisp and weakly sunny, and we sat arm in arm on a grave by the mound of fresh clods scarring the grass. Below, the factory chimneys were pumping out smoke, and we could see over to the four church towers above the West End Park, and down to the ships at John Brown's and Yarrow's. We cried, but it was an odd sort of grief, it was as though something in us had uncorked and years of tears were flowing out, and sometimes we laughed at remembered times too, in that half-hysterical way you do when you are heartbroken. Afterwards I felt an enormous relief, cleaned out, wrung out, but I also felt a shadow hanging over me had gone, and I looked out at the pale horizon and the rooftops and thought, Well, where next?

In a practical way, that has turned out to be Largs down on the coast, because we have to leave the Manse by the end of the month – the Church is very strict about that. The McPhail family has a two-bedroom flat in a red sandstone tenement on Nelson Street there that Aunt Edith left them when she died last year, and Duncan never got around to clearing it out and selling it. It is in a horrible state of disrepair, but there is plenty of room and Kirsty claims you can see the sea from the bow window. I have never been there myself, but I see no reason why we should not take it – there is nothing else. I want to slough off the old clothes of Glasgow and begin anew.

Kirsty says she will come and live with us when she manages to get a job down there. She says Isabel and I are her family now, and I am happy beyond words to have her with me, and not to have to live on my own. It is like having a sister and a best friend rolled into one. I have just had a little torn-faced man round from the furniture salesrooms, taking notes of everything and offering us something between a fair price and a pittance for it all. I would rather see it all go, but for a few armchairs and books and Isabel's bed, because it was never mine, and I never liked the heavy dark stuff and all those stupid wee china ornaments. There is some plain furniture that the old aunt left, and Kirsty says we might as well start out with that. She is as determined and stubborn as her father when she wants to be, but I am fond of that.

I do not know what I will do, but I must earn some

money somehow, and I am going to talk to Helen Fraser about the possibility of a small wage from the WSPU. They afford two pounds per week for some people and I could edit the suffrage magazine and leaflets from Largs, or even start up a branch there. I just cannot get round to thinking about all that just now, but practical needs, like Isabel changing schools mid-term, keep bursting into my mind and must be dealt with. I have not slept a whole night in the three weeks since it happened, and I think sheer physical exhaustion accounts for part of my inability to get any grip on the world. I was cleaning out Duncan's desk yesterday, and Kirsty found me asleep with my head in the drawer, yet at night I will sleep to come, but it slides away every time I look it straight in the face. In the early hours of the morning, I half sleep and hear Duncan preaching in the darkness: 'For without are dogs and sorcerers, and whoremongers, and murderers, and whosoever loveth and maketh a lie.'

How strange it must be for you too, that a man you never met, and now never will, and only knew through my letters, has disappeared, like a word lost off the page.

With all my love,
Your affectionate sister,
Agnes

Chapter Twenty-Three

16 April 2000

'You're doing what?' I said, choking on the goat's cheese quesadilla.

'Going together to a relationship therapist, you know, like a marriage therapist.'

Nancy looked at me defiantly across the table in a dark corner of the Miracle Grill on First Avenue. I thought she was losing it. I said so. 'Hold on, hold on. Am I right in saying you've only been together with Joanie for six weeks, you've seen three movies together at the Angelika, and you're already getting therapy?'

'Yes, that's true but it's a very intense relationship, and let's face it, they don't come around very often.'

'You're nuts,' I said.

'Hey, it's no worse than employing a personal trainer, or consulting Ida's coffee grains.'

'You're still nuts. Does it work? What does it cost?' I wanted to ask if it was purely a lesbian thing, but I thought that might be rude.

'Thirty-five dollars an hour and it's great,' said Nancy, who had the glowing skin and squeaky-clean hair that comes with new love. 'Joanie and I have sorted out a lot. I was sort of treating her like a woman . . .' I snorted. 'I mean, I know she is a woman but I was behaving like your average guy trying to be cool, not calling, all that. Well, you know, I didn't know how to play it. This is not something I've done much before.'

We ordered two margaritas. The barman stared at my fifth-month stomach, bulging out of a skintight dress.

'Gotta problem?' I asked him.

'Uh, no,' he said, scurrying off. I had trained for this sort of hassle back in the days of the fake pregnancy, and I was only having a couple of glasses of wine, or one cocktail a day, but I suppose the barman wasn't to know that. I was dying, however, to nip outside with one of Nancy's Marlboros, but she wouldn't even let me have a drag, and slapped my hand as it crept, entirely of its own volition, towards her cigarette packet.

I was still a bit down. I needed chemical enhancement — it was, after all, what my body was used to. What was really pissing me was Nancy going on and on about the delights of Joanie: how she was a fabulous photographer, and how attentive she was in the sack, details she went into graphically as I was tucking into my spice-rubbed bluefin tuna. I was just plain jealous, I suppose. All my single friends were getting hitched up, admittedly by unconventional methods, but they still had someone. They shared beds and baths and toasted English muffins and thoughts too ridiculous to tell to anyone else. Wanda had Lianne, and Lianne had Wanda and Nosmo, and Nosmo had Ned 'with increasing regularity', he told me smirking, and now Nancy had this Joanie and, worse, was still wearing Joanie's underwear after staying over last night. And what did I have by way of relationships? (I meant earthly ones, and even Agnes hadn't been around for weeks.) What I had was a message from Leonardo, which of course I missed, left on Wanda and Nosmo's answering-machine; another stupid postcard at my old address from him with an African tribal pattern on it, and absolutely no acknowledgement of the fact he was about to be a father. I reckoned that he hadn't received my letters. His postcards weren't exactly revealing or articulate. Lucky he made films. I scowled. I didn't even have a photograph of him, and his face was turning to a blur in my mind.

'I'm being left behind while you're all getting hitched up,' I moaned into my corn and banana fritters – I'd been eating for at least three recently.

Nancy looked up from her espresso. 'Well, you've got Thing coming out soon. That's a relationship.' We had named my stomach-dweller Thing, in homage to the Addams Family.

'Yeah, but our relationship's going to be somewhat limited, in fact internalized, for the next four months,' I complained.

I did think about Thing almost constantly when I wasn't working, and Wanda had told me that actually hanging out with a baby, having it gurgle and greet you when you came home had the same wonderfully debilitating effect as having your first boyfriend: you were totally in love.

'But Thing's taking over my mind at about the same rate it's taking over my body,' I told Nancy.

'I can see that. You've lost your keys three times to my knowledge, and you've got six unfinished paintings on the go. I'm increasingly thinking that fertility's almost worse than infertility. Half the time you don't even hear what I'm saying.'

'What?' I said, just to annoy her.

But Nancy was right. Something had happened to time. It kept sort of melting away unused, while I had undefined thoughts about motherhood. (I'd even considered buying a wristwatch to recapture the lost hours.) For instance, I'd been mooning for hours around BabyGap, the way I had with the fake pregnancy, but this time the sight of a tiny white all-in-one suit stamped with penguins made me almost delirious with joy and fear. Minuscule baseball caps made me cry. I couldn't bear to buy: I just stood around touching the stuff, like an incompetent shoplifter, and bumped into other bulging women with the same crazy, anxious look in their eyes, first-time mothers, who started intimate conversations in a way New Yorkers never did. I was amazed that Thing's non-presence was so powerful, physically too. There were stretchings and creakings and squidlike squirmings. I was haunted from within and without.

I was relating all this to Nancy when Garrett came into the Miracle Grill. 'Thought I might find you both here,' he said, drawing up a stool at the bar and taking off one of the three jackets he was wearing.

'Hi, Nancy.' He started eating all the free tortilla chips. He ate all the time and never put on an ounce. 'I lost my train of thought at home, started mucking around, so I thought I might as well be wasting time properly in company. You left your wallet on the table in the hall. Thought you might need it.' I blushed and put it in my bag. Garrett got some more drinks, while I sat uncomfortably with an alcohol-free beer.

'Now,' said Garrett grandly, 'we have work to do, Nancy. In this muddled state, Albertine will never

239

get round to it on her own.' He took a small sketch-book from his pocket and opened it. 'INSTALLATIONS', he wrote at the top, and poised his fountain pen expectantly.

I laughed, but Garrett really was intent on filling in all the empty floor and wall space in the SoHo Gallery for my forthcoming exhibition. Its provisional and increasingly appropriate title was Confinement. The SoHo Gallery had written suggesting I needed forty major paintings for the space, but I'd only done eighteen, and was progressing not at all, and possibly regressing. Real pregnancy had caused me to lose all sense of distance and objectivity. Thus Garrett and I had rapidly come to the conclusion, talking at midnight in his kitchen, that we would add pregnancy-inspired sculptures to the package. We concluded that the installations had to be either ridiculous or shocking, preferably using female-appropriate materials, and they had to be saleable – 'Nothing too clever,' said Garrett – in order to support Thing through his future Ivy League education.

He supped his beer and announced that the obvious and simplest thing was to make a cast or two of my pregnant body, although they'd wait until I'd gotten larger. (His less-than-perceptive life-drawing students had not noticed I was pregnant until two weeks before.) No one seemed to be consulting me on this.

'Yeah,' said Nancy, getting into the spirit of the conversation, 'and fill the body cast with milk or piss or blood or something icky like that.'

'Nah, nah, nah,' I said. 'No, I want chocolate. Make the cast out of white chocolate. I just crave it all the time.' Amid laughter, Garrett noted down: '1. Cast body in white chocolate. Title: Cravings. Materials: see Ray Washing.'

Then they decided to cast me in Perspex, and fill my belly with a complete girly baby layette: pink blankets, pink sleepsuits, pink pacifiers, pink rattles, pink rabbits, sponsored by Macy's or someone, and exhibit the list on the wall nearby.

From there, we were inspired. (Do you think this is really how everyone does installations, with their friends, for a laugh, and later they label it art?) Large-size pregnancy breasts should not be neglected, I decided, and decided to make some 40D ones – my own were not really ample enough to copy, having little to build on – and somehow have the breast sculpture squirt milk, yellow colostrum milk, in an endless stream. But how?

'Easy,' said Garrett, and wrote down: '3. Sculpt breasts in clay. Title: Dairy Queen – open twenty-four hours. Materials: clay, wall-suspended plastic fountain bowl and pipes from 6th Ave garden center.'

After another round of beers, we came up with a pregnant armchair, done in flowery chintz with a huge upholstered cushion-belly that prevented anyone sitting down. Nancy felt there had to be something scatological or hairy. I said I'd paint a pregnant woman with her hormone-veined legs open in the style of Gustave Courbet – we'd call it 'The Origin of the World Gets a Varicose Vein'. Nancy, giggling, suggested a white lace pregnancy nightie with human chest hair growing through the weave, titled: 'Mom and Pop'.

By closing time, we had ten installations planned. Nancy and Garrett were wrecked, and I was hysterical. But I was also rather pleased, for if the art world was stupid enough to buy such things, then I was smart enough to create them. 'Final thing we need is a soundtrack. Everyone has a soundtrack for their exhibition now,' said Garrett.

'I have that in hand,' I said, and went off home to sleep without dreaming.

The next morning I was in a clinic on the Upper East Side for my first ultrasound scan. No one tells you how great this is. The room was dark, like a cinema, and a Puerto Rican woman (mother-of-five, she added, to induce confidence) was covering my hump with cold gel and wiggling a sort of electronic Hoover around on it. I gave up all pretence to dignity. At first she turned the screen away and looked herself, and I thought, Oh, my God, the baby's deformed, it's got two heads, they won't let me see, but then she swivelled it round, and there was a gray fuzz, a circle divided in quarters.

'The four ventricles of the heart,' she announced, then she moved the machine lower.

'Large femur . . . aorta . . . kidneys functioning . . . bladder.'

The technical list melted me. It was my baby. For real. We were face to face, or at least stomach to stomach, at last. It was flipping around like a caught fish.

'Won't stay still. I want to get you the profile.'

She dug into the side of my belly. 'There.'

It had a snub nose, eyes, an open mouth and it was sucking its hand. A great wave of repressed emotion welled up in me and I started howling. I couldn't stop. I wanted Leonardo to be there, too.

'There, there,' she said, patting me on the head like a dog. 'Now all that sobbing's getting him – I mean the baby – all agitated. Look, there's a foot.'

Indeed, a foot, with five whole toes, waved white across the black screen in a sort of victory salute. I smiled and hiccuped. The woman went off to print up the scan photographs, and left me alone in the room. With her notes. I'd asked not to know the sex, but I'd seen two grapes with a tiny stick on one screen, and I had my suspicions. I couldn't help myself.

I went straight from the clinic to my latest job, which involved the same position of lying on my back with my legs in the air, on boards across scaffolding, painting a ceiling in an apartment in Trump Tower. I wondered what I'd call him. I was keen on really outlandish names like Zebulon, Jackson and Otis but, knowing America, they'd probably nickname him something sensible like Chuck or Bart at school. I painted one of the Italian-style cherubs on the ceiling with my baby's newly discovered profile, but then I got bored and started speeding up the work since I was having increasing trouble managing the ladders and lying flat out on a couple of boards for hours. If Michelangelo had been a woman, the Sistine Chapel would have been done more swiftly and efficiently, I reckoned, and wondered what he was paid per hour. I got five thousand dollars for that Trump Tower job, but it took me nearly two months on and off. Towards the end, I imagined my belly growing until I was trapped permanently between the platform and the ceiling. I hated doing ceilings, but those in the Trump Tower were low, and I needed the money. The asshole lawyer who owned the place came in to inspect and offered more money if I added a Tuscan landscape on the wall. He had the temerity to suggest I looked through his holiday snaps for a suitable view. 'I'm a bit of a photographer,' he said, kindly putting Vivaldi's 'Four Seasons' on the CD for me. I waited until he left the room and chucked a roller at the machine, neatly hitting the off button.

By six o'clock, my back was killing me. I picked up the phone in the apartment, rang the Village Yoga Academy to check the times of their pregnancy yoga classes, and found one at seven. 'Bring a towel and wear something comfortable,' said the receptionist. I'd leggings on, but no towel, so I swiped a nice white fluffy one from the lawyer's closet. He would never miss one in forty.

The Yoga Academy was trapped between a New Age bookshop and a health-food deli. I bought an organic vegetable pastry for dinner, which lurked like a stone in my stomach. Then I paid my nine dollars and wandered upstairs, past the purple niche with the Buddha, which looked like it was asphyxiating in the incense. I'd been to a couple of classes here the year before, when my shoulders went stiff with hunching over the drawing board, and the cure had been instant.

I was early. The lights were down in the class, but I could make out six hippo-like mounds on the floor, some of which were moaning or perhaps chanting. I lay down on my side, breathed in the freshly laundered smell of the thick towel, and let the darkness slide over me. Just as I was drifting off to sleep, the teacher arrived and flooded the room with light. Revealed beside me, her face inches away, was a vast woman in orange leggings and a vomit-green sweater. Her combat boots stood to attention by the mat. There were equally bloated sights ranged around the room. I was horrified: surely, I would never, ever be *that* big.

The yoga began with us 'sharing' our experiences of pregnancy and plenty of 'Om' chants, which I always thought silly until my brain turned to Jell-o. We did a special chant to the Great Mother, whoever she was. But at least the exercises made me feel long and straight for the first time in weeks. The bones in my spine slotted neatly on top of each other again. Shame this has to come accompanied by all the sharing, I thought. We all did pelvic-floor exercises which, although internal, caused Combat Boots' eyebrows to move amusingly up and down. Then we crawled around on all fours arching our backs like pregnant cats, and I was tempted to run for my sketchbook. We finished with relaxation. As we lay on towels with the lights down, the teacher began drivelling, 'Feel free to speak or cry out, or make another noise. Now, feel how rich and blessed you are. Feel your baby, speak to your baby, feel how blessed it is. Bestow gifts upon her or him: kindness, intelligence, happiness, peacefulness . . .'

'. . . ability to cut through crap,' I whispered.

'. . . sincerity. Feel that your umbilical cord is a silver river running between you and your baby. Fill that river with love. Please sit up slowly when you feel rested.'

She turned the lights up. 'We've five more minutes. Has anyone got anything to say? Any suggestions, feelings?'

By that time, I was truly in sharing and interfacing mode and decided to take advantage of the situation.

'Well,' I said, searching for organic woman-appropriate language, 'I'm an artist creating an installation on child-birth, and I'm interested in recording the sounds, the feelings and experiences of women giving birth naturally. So if anyone would be willing to have their partner or companion record even a part of their labor, I would love to hear it. I feel these sounds are an unrecorded piece of history that should be displayed. I feel the meanings of what we say in childbirth have not been fully explored.'

'Yeah, right on,' said Combat Boots.

'Really interesting concept,' nodded two other women.

Four people came up and gave me their numbers. Of course, I'd no interest whatsoever in shared feelings and experiences. What I wanted for my exhibition soundtrack was bloodcurdling birth screams.

Chapter Twenty-Four

Nelson Street, Largs

5 December 1911

Dear Ishbel,

Well, I am loath to tell you this, for I do not know whether you will be proud or ashamed, but I would rather you learn the news from me than from newspapers or gossip: I have served my first prison sentence for the cause. Do not fache yourself, because I am in perfect health and I was only in Holloway Prison for a week, and the experience was more punishing mentally than physically.

My main worry was that Kirsty and Isabel would not know what had happened to me, because I was due back in Largs on the night of the 22nd, the day after the meeting, but fortunately, the WSPU telegraphed all the prisoners' relatives. I had planned for a while to go down to London for the meeting of the 10th Women's Parliament at Caxton Hall, but by the time I arrived the meeting showed signs of turning into something more militant. You may have read, if *The Times* has reached you by now, of Mr Asquith's appalling behaviour over the Conciliation Bill, which riled the ladies beyond words to action. First he appeared to be helpful, by holding a meeting with Christabel Pankhurst and Mrs Fawcett, but he made no promises, and within days he was telling his gentleman lackeys in Parliament that inclusion of Women's Suffrage in the bill was 'a political mistake of a very disastrous kind'. In some ways, Mr Asquith was absolutely right about his political mistake, because it caused as large a protest in Parliament Square as last year.

We all rushed out from Caxton Hall, led by Mrs Pankhurst and two others who broke the windows of 10 Downing Street. There were plenty of policemen ready for us, with batons and horses. Dozens of women suddenly produced stones from their handbags and started smashing the windows of Parliament and some of the ministries. I was down in the centre of the crowd with a Scots contingent, including a nice woman I'd met on the train down, Ina Murray from Wishaw. A great big dim-witted policemen started beating Mrs Murray with his stick on the chest. I was shocked, I had never really seen a man hitting a woman like that before. I elbowed in and stood right between Mrs Murray and the big Cockney eejit, my face stuffed into the silver buttons on his jacket. He knocked me out of the way, and no sooner was I up than I was arrested, along with Mrs Murray. We were both charged with 'obstruction of the police', though I am not sure how Mrs Murray obstructed anything at all.

We were taken with ten others to Cannon Row Police Courts, searched by a grumpy woman with foul breath and thrown without food into communal cells for the night with all sorts of women, many of them prostitutes, to go by their dress, their extrraordinary use of language and their helpful advice about the court process. By nine the next morning, we were taken before

248

the magistrate, who looked flustered by the number on his books that day – I only discovered afterwards that there were 220 women and three men arrested in the protests. He processed us each in a few minutes, offered me a small fine or a week in prison, and I knew it was my duty and our policy to go to gaol. Duncan's face floated into my head as the magistrate was passing sentence, and I felt a burning guilt for a few moments. This whole thing would never have happened if he had still been on earth.

We travelled to Holloway Prison in the infamous 'Black Maria' and for the first time I felt lonely and terrified away from my companions, although I could hear them as we rattled through the streets, trapped in dark compartments, which barely seated one person and smelled of rank sweat and fear. Oh, Holloway is a grim, grim place, Ishbel. I so pitied those who had been given two-month sentences when I looked up at the endless grey walls and the metal doors rang shut behind, closing out the world. Again, we were searched, even our hair, and our money was taken away by hatchet-faced wardresses with great keys at their belts – in a way, it was much as I had imagined, although I have to admit I never dreamed the food would be quite so disgusting. Under Churchill's rule 234A, the suffragettes have much better conditions than the ordinary prisoners, who are fed a pint of watery grey porridge and lumps of bread for most meals, unless they get potatoes or suet pudding. Some days, on our so-called better diet, we were given potatoes and something approaching meat stew, although many identified the meat as horse. The only egg I got must have been months old, and smelled like it too, and the cocoa, which was our supper, often had little strings of meat in it. Clearly the cooks never bothered to clean the pans.

Fortunately, we were on Dx wing, which had been reserved for suffragettes, and many of my friends were in cells nearby, or else we met in the pavilion under the wire mesh (in case anyone jumped from the iron landings). We were allowed to wear our own clothes, although after seven days without a bath this was less than pleasant, but the poor women in the other divisions who we saw on the way to the exercise yard were got up in ill-fitting green or brown uniforms, with the white 'broad arrow' on them. Their dress seemed so humiliating. Our cells, however, were no better than theirs, being barely seven feet long, and equipped only with a straw mattress on planks and rich with bed bugs, a wooden shelf that pretends to be a table, and a stupid wee stool. The smell and the sanitary arrangements I will leave to your imagination. Anyway, it was at night in these surroundings that I lay, cold and sleepless, worrying about home – I felt so alone without Kirsty by me in the bed – and, I have to admit it, feeling a bit sorry for myself. When they put off the lights, too early in the evening, time suddenly stretched in the dark and I had to pace up and down, up and down to fill it. I was so thankful that my sentence was one of the shortest – I did not even get a chance to send off the fortnightly letter allowed.

How we were fêted when we were released! Mrs Murray and I (prisoner number 439) had been expecting to struggle back to our lodgings for our bags and then to the station, but outside the prison gates was a cheering reception committee with tartan sashes, which took us off for baths and our dinner at someone's fine house (many of the WSPU supporters are by no means poor). We were awarded special enamel brooches with a portcullis on them given to ex-prisoners by the WSPU, and we were very touched. We travelled home singing on the train, and Kirsty was there, having waited for hours at Queen Street station. I have never been so glad to see anyone in my life.

I am writing this from Eliot's, I think Scotland's finest tea-room and ice-cream parlour, which looks out across the water from Largs bay to Millport. I am waiting for Isabel to join me from school for afternoon tea as a special treat for both of us, me because I am celebrating the end of my prison diet, and Isabel because she loves the chocolate iced buns they have here filled with cream. I was worried she would be embarrassed by her 'criminal' mother, but far from it: she was as proud as punch and told all her friends at school and even the teachers. Well, it is easier to find support among Scots: what with the Labour movement, there is widespread endorsement of the cause of Votes for Women and most people consider the ends justify the means.

In fact, Isabel considers the whole thing to be extremely glamorous, and has pinned my portcullis brooch to a huge Votes for Women poster she keeps above the mantelpiece in her room. She is nearly twelve now, and treats Kirsty and me as though we were the wayward children. What with me taking the train up to Glasgow on business quite often, and Kirsty working ridiculous hours, she has started getting the tea ready after school. She comes in with the latchkey she wears round her neck and peels the potatoes and puts on the mince or whatever I have prepared. Of course, sometimes we just have a jammy piece or send her down to get us all a fish supper – such are the advantages of not having a man in the house to worry about. We are all so comfortable and happy together now. I am glad to have a daughter who is looking after me, while there is all this rubbish in the newspapers about suffragettes abandoning their children. 'Get back to your babies,' they cry here. So I am sending you one of the latest in a series of postcards we have been putting out of suffragettes at home, 'Mrs Joseph McCabe bathing her baby,' which you may find of amusement.

Of course, this is only the beginning, and I hope that one day people will come to understand that bathing babies, or rearing children, is as important as building ships or houses. Once women get the vote it will open the door to a thousand other changes, like equal wages and the end of women having no recourse but to sell themselves on Sauchiehall Street. I am filled with an extraordinary optimism now: in going to prison I passed through a gate, through fear and dread, and walked out the other side with my head held high. I know now that we will succeed.

Enough ranting – I suspect you think me quite insane, and there are certainly grounds ... Anyway, the best of love to you and all the family,

Your affectionate sister,
Agnes

Chapter Twenty-Five

12 June 2000

Next door to the Wayne Poncho Auto and Body Shop off Avenue B in the depths of the East Village was the steel-doored warehouse where Ray Washing ran his molding and casting business. This in turn financed his other career as a sculptor, which had failed to take off after twenty years. The place looked like a dissecting room: there were severed limbs and heads scattered around, interspersed with metal and plastic tubing and dumpy, humanoid bags of cement and plaster. The warehouse was dank, and stank of wet clay, paint and dope.

'Wassup, Albertine? How's it going?' said Ray.

'Fine,' I said, which meant godawful. It was June, and by my calculations, one Leonardo Ianucci should have been back in town and straight on the phone to me, the mother of his son. 'Surprise!' I imagined myself saying, heavy with irony and child. But there had been nothing. *Nada.* I'd called his sublet, but someone else's voice had been on the machine.

Ray interrupted my thoughts. 'I've been practicing.' He held out a sculpture of his own meaty forearm cast in gray-brown chocolate and pretended to shake my hand with it. 'I only used cooking chocolate. Saving this for the real thing.' He patted a 150-pound case of white chocolate in catering blocks. I studied the arm. 'It's got a bit of a seam down it, but I like that. Reminds me of chocolate Easter eggs.'

We discussed technique for a while. I'd been terrified I'd have to plunge into a bath of cement, with merely a straw to breathe through my nose, and then be cracked out of the mold with chisels. I felt sick with claustrophobia, and I was sure that in James Bond's *Goldfinger* a woman had been sprayed with gold paint until she overheated and died. Cement could only be worse.

Ray patted me reassuringly. 'Nah, nah, we don't do that. We got quick-drying rubber cement stuff. Just spray on this foam here, and it hardens in five minutes, but still gives you time to take a pose on the floor rather than standing up, if you want.' He waved what looked like a pink fire-extinguisher at me. 'Get your gear off and stand just in front of that wall covered in plastic. You want to stay on the plastic sheet on the floor. I don't want this shit everywhere.' I stripped off and stood embarrassed in my nearly eight-months-pregnant state, my once-neat belly button changed from an innie to an outie. An entire class of drawing students had been impersonal, but somehow being naked alone with Ray I felt ridiculous. This was true suffering for art.

Ray seemed not one bit bothered. He walked round me with interest, like was some specially fecund species of cow. 'My, you're getting big. Big mama. I love it,' said Ray, putting on plastic gloves. I'd pulled my hair back as flat as possible into a plait down my back. 'Have to oil the hair too, honey,' said Ray, roaring with laughter as I shined up all over with baby oil to keep the foam cement from sticking. 'And the plait down the back.' He handed me a pair of earplugs, and I felt a lurch of fear. 'I'll be careful round the nose.' I was already suffocating with panic. The baby was hopping round my belly fueled by the adrenalin of my nerves.

'Ready?' He opened the nozzle and began to spray me. If only my mother, my head teacher, or indeed my great-great-grandmother were here (I checked round) to see me stark naked being sprayed with pink foam by a big black man, I thought. The foam cement smelled like bubblegum, and stuck like it too. Perhaps it was bubble-gum.

'Have you ever used this stuff before, Ray?' I asked suddenly.

'Nope,' he said, smiling cheerfully.

He was being very thorough, spraying from above, below, and swirling round my belly. I was pink and knobbly, like blancmange with lumps. Ray seemed to be taking a Polaroid of me, which I assumed must be for his own amusement. The cement began to tighten on my skin. 'I'm stiffening up, Ray,' I shouted over the spurting sounds.

'Great. Shut your eyes and keep your face still while I do it by hand. Don't speak.' He put down the spray gun and applied the rubber cement to my face with his fingers, leaving only my nostrils open to breathe. I started hyperventilating: the rubber layer was making me feel hot and faint. 'Stay calm,' said Ray, laughing. 'Be done in five minutes. Quick, pose on the floor and I'll spray the soles of your feet.' I felt my way down onto my side, propped up on one elbow, with my belly in fine profile for anyone looking down from above. Of course, I couldn't see a thing, blinded as I was by Jell-o.

Two minutes later, before my elbow even had time to ache, I could hardly move. I was paralyzed. I wanted to make a scene, but I could only manage grunting noises in my throat. Meanwhile Ray, whistling irritatingly, started running what turned out to be a round-edged palette knife down the ridiculous frozen pink blob which was me, starting at the head, going round the arm and down the side to my foot. The rubber cement case peeled away like a dead skin, with great craters for my breasts and belly, and I breathed freely again. Ray laid my cast on the floor, one half face down with my buttocks in the air, the other belly up, hinged at the side like Siamese twins. He took another Polaroid of the halves beside me and smiled fiendishly. 'Don't s'pose I'll ever get to do this again to a woman.'

A few weeks later, I came back to see the final result and to pay the not insubstantial check in cash. I'd also paid a hefty bill to the chocolate wholesaler. Someone better buy this crap, or I am in big trouble, I thought. The money from the sale of my paintings in January was evaporating at speed. But Ray had done a good job. He'd reassembled the head and body halves into a whole, and filled the inside with 140 pounds of white chocolate, roughly my pregnancy weight. The edible woman lay cushioned on bubble wrap.

'Ray, you're brilliant. You're a god. This is perfect,' I said, walking round my white chocolate body, seeing myself in three enormous dimensions for the first time. The smell was mouthwatering and sickening all at once.

'But where'd you put in the tube for the molten chocolate?' I asked. 'I can't see a hole.'

'In your belly-button and up your nostrils, hon. You know, like Tutankhamun. The Pharaohs had their brains taken out their nostrils before they were embalmed. I just pumped the chocolate right back up there and kept the heating on, a sacrifice in this weather I can tell you, until the cast was full. Wanted to ask you something, Albertine. Why the white chocolate? Why not the regular brown stuff? It's cheaper.'

'The brown starts to get this grayish-whitish bloom on it after a few months, whereas the white stays pretty perfect. I didn't want to look scruffy by the time of the exhibition.'

'I was worried you might just melt slowly away before the exhibition, so that's why I'm keeping you in my office, because it's air-conditioned in here, and I have to leave it on at night, but I've included the electricity in the bill.'

'Thanks a bunch, Ray,' I groaned. 'And what've you done with the spare chocolate?'

'Gave it to my wife. She makes wedding cakes at home, any time you're interested.' He raised one eyebrow at my now comedy-size stomach. I scowled back.

We went into the workshop to look at the see-through version of me. I'd gone wild in Toys 'R' Us and Macy's baby department, resulting in an unpleasant array of pink plastic junk including rattles, pacifiers, bottles, a furry pink and white bear, a naked doll, tiny shoes and a tasteless hat. Ray had thrown the pink assemblage into the middle of the body cast and resealed

257

it before pouring in the hot clear plastic resin, leaving the items to float where they liked. Pleasingly, a pacifier had floated to the top where my brain should have been, but most of the rest of the layette was in the belly. 'Genius,' I said, hugging Ray. 'They'll think that's intentional.'

Looking at my Perspex and chocolate selves, it occurred to me that it might not be the best idea to invite my parents to the opening of my first solo exhibition because the display of wanton vulgarity and nakedness might complete the rift in our already appalling relationship. Being newly converted Pro-Lifers, they had had to accept the pregnancy as a gift-from-God, but they were livid that I refused to tell them the name and (especially) the race of the father. 'Look upon it as a virgin birth,' I said to my mother, who put the phone down.

Still, the baby was now eminently and imminently real. Viable is the medical word. At thirty-six weeks, with four to go, Thing would be born alive if it popped out now, and would not even have to live for a few weeks like an amphibian in an incubator tank. This meant, at last, that shopping for Thing was also viable, no longer a jinx. I went over from the East Village to spend the rest of the morning with Wanda and Lianne in SoHo because, frankly, I had no idea what the cutting-edge Manhattan baby should be wearing. We trawled designer baby shops, squeaking over stupid little jester's hats, fake snakeskin trousers and Rasta-striped romper-suits. I rid myself of a great many dollars, but however much I spent, Thing would never be able to compete with Lianne who was now perhaps the city's leader in baby fashion: today she had lime green sandals and an orange and pink bias-cut sundress, which matched the ribbon in her Chinese-style topknot. Naturally Wanda was planning a range of WongBaby clothes for next season.

Lianne was getting together her wardrobe for her first holiday, in California, with Wanda and Nosmo. Wanda announced Lianne needed two bathing suits, sunglasses, and 'something appropriate for San Francisco'. They were flying to Los Angeles that afternoon to open a new Wanda Wong store on Melrose, and then Nosmo was driving them up the coast to San Francisco, where Wanda would see her relatives who still lived in Chinatown, while Nosmo would generally misbehave. Their Californian journey and reactions to Nosmo in the Castro with his small Chinese charge were to be chronicled by him for *GM* magazine in an article provisionally titled 'Baby goes to Big Sur'. I thought this was ridiculous, but I didn't say so as I kissed Wanda and Lianne goodbye.

I stopped in the Cafe Babylon to eat on behalf of myself and Thing: a carrot-hummus wholegrain bagel for the baby, and two pecan brownies for me. As I drank a pot of tea, I flicked through the magazine of forthcoming programs at the Film Forum on Houston. There was a retrospective of Roman Polanski movies: *Repulsion; Honeymoon*; oh, yes, and *Rosemary's Baby* again. Amazing how a film from 1968 keeps popping up like that just when you're pregnant with a child conceived at number 666 with a father who might even bear the mark of the devil on his eye, never mind that you're haunted by distant and difficult relatives with (it now appeared) criminal records. I would never have dared actually to go to the film again, but I read the blurb with horrified fascination.

'In the middle of New York City, Polanski invites the irrational to play with the commonplace – and Satan conducts the drama . . . slowly the fear takes root, passing from sentimental comedy to horror. Is there really a black-magic sect in the apartment building? Has Rosemary (Mia Farrow) really been impregnated by the devil, or is it the imagination of a lonely, tormented pregnant woman?' These were familiar questions I asked myself every day – no, not day but night, when I was alone with whatever inhabited me, and often visited by whatever, whoever, haunted me. I hadn't seen Agnes, now known to me as prisoner 439, for some months, and I was increasingly convinced she existed only in my ever-shrinking brain. I shuddered and got the check, from the same waitress who'd been so entertainingly antsy last summer about my smoking. She looked at me in disgust: I was an irresponsible mother, pregnant again, as far as she was concerned.

I walked heavily home, still relieved I hadn't developed that weird, swaying gait apparent in the other whale-women at my prenatal check-ups at St Vincent's. Stopping for a moment to wait for the lights to change on Sixth Avenue, I peeked into one of my carrier-bags and stroked the French matelot-style romper-suit and matching sunhat I'd bought in trepidation. The problem was, what if, somehow, in some way, it did not work out and all those unvoiced, almost unthought, fears were true? I was terrified that I might come home alone and empty from hospital, to be confronted by a pile of adorable tiny clothes and no one to wear them. Thing obviously found this thought offensive. There was a left hook and a headbutt from inside, and what felt like a bite. A bite?

Something visceral made me look up. Someone was staring at me from the M6 bus waiting at the lights. I knew the face in sunglasses was familiar, so I smiled. Then I realized it was Leonardo Ianucci. He started to wave and gesture cheerfully. Then the bus pulled away and shot up the street.

I went wild with shock and anticipation. I ran – well, half waddled – up Sixth Avenue to see if Leonardo would get off at the next stop, but by the time I reached it, the bus was just pulling away and there was no sign of any disembarking passengers. Faint from the exertion, I crumpled on a bench in the playground on the corner and burst into tears.

The shouts and thuds from the basketball court drowned out my gasps, which were bordering on hysterical. I held my head in my hands and thought what a complete screw-up I'd made of everything. Well, at least now Leonardo knew I was pregnant. He couldn't have failed to miss that, especially in the baby-doll dress I was wearing. I'd only realized two weeks before at the beginning of June, when I received a third postcard dated late April, that Leonardo hadn't received any of my letters, or the fax I'd sent with my new address to National Geographic TV, and thus had no idea of his approaching paternity. On the latest postcard, he had written: 'If you do get time to write, the poste restante address is National Geographic, Kampala Central Station Post Office.' It was then I realized I'd missed out the word 'station' every time. I had cursed myself, but not as hard as I cursed myself sitting on that bench on Sixth Avenue.

But surely he'd get in touch soon. The thought calmed me. Then cold logic intervened, and the bottom plummeted out of my stomach. He'd no idea of my new address or phone number, and Wanda and Nosmo would have left for California. Then a worse thought came: why on earth would he assume I was really pregnant? The first time we'd seen each other last year, I'd been wearing exactly the same dress, but then it contained a cushion and not a baby. Crying wolf or what? 'Shit,' I said aloud.

'Whaddya say, lady?' said one of the guys from the basketball court, towering over me, thinking it was a comment on his game.

'Nothing. Absolutely nothing,' I said weakly.

I stared, hiccuping with the occasional sob, at the dozens of pigeons pecking round the McDonalds' bags by the trash can. Then the pigeons started flying off, as though someone had blown a hairdryer through the middle of them. Agnes appeared in a slow shimmer in the space between the birds, and sat down on the bench, her hairy tweed suit seeming not to bother her in the 80-degree heat.

'Hi. I thought you'd abandoned me. Like everyone else.' The words caught in my throat.

'Don't be ridiculous,' she snapped, and then seemed embarrassed about being so brusque.

I noticed she was wearing the portcullis suffragette brooch she'd got for being in jail. I pointed to it. 'I think you were pretty brave doing that. Makes me kinda ashamed of the sort of things we do now.'

'Different strokes for different folks,' observed Agnes, superiorly. She saw my still-tearstained face and relented. 'I'm not saying what you do is a load of foolishness. I think what you're doing alone right now is brave. It's just that I had no choice: my decision was a simple one, and the injustice was obvious to anyone. Now, I think you've too many choices. Women can do anything, so you choose nothing. This painting business: well, maybe it has a point. They don't seem to march or protest about anything nowadays; it might be just the only thing you can do. I'll reserve judgement on that.'

Gee, thanks, I wanted to say. Your judgement is the last thing I need right now. What I need is the man who got me into this mess. She must have had similar thoughts herself, because she smiled a lean smile and said, 'Anyway, down to the business in hand. Now what did I tell you about that man, eh?' she said, gesturing towards the empty bus stop. 'You're well shot of him. They're a bad lot, most men. Look at it this way. Maybe you and the wean are better to start off life alone together at the beginning, so you know where you are, rather than what happened to me in a marriage with the wrong man.'

I looked despairing. She continued, 'I'll tell you one thing. When Duncan died, wee Isabel was only ten. I was frightened of bringing her up all on my own, even with Kirsty there, but she gave me a purpose, and feeling of worth, of being needed, something away from all the politics and protest. She made me alive.'

I was crying again. I shut my eyes, but hot tears kept bulging out. Agnes's hand fluttered near me, and then fell to her side. She looked frustrated. After a few minutes she said, 'I can't manage to stay here any more. You'll be fine. You just need to hold on another month,' and her face smeared through my tears into nothingness.

I sat there a while listening to the thud of the basketball, feeling like I'd been eviscerated. Then I went across the road to the deli, brought back a packet of lemon crunch cookies, and slowly ate every single one. Whatever Agnes said about Leonardo, a man of whom she, presumably, had no greater knowledge than I, I still wanted to find him. Just because he didn't get off the bus didn't mean he didn't want to see me. We weren't married, for Chrissake. The problem was, though, that I'd have no idea whether he'd left a message at my old address until Nosmo and Wanda returned from their two-week holiday and played back their machine.

Next, I thought laterally, and went over to the public phones at West 4th Street. I called Ianucci's Delicatessen in Brooklyn, but none of the family was in right then. I hung up. My mind became dark and closed and the arguments went round in circles. Perhaps he really doesn't want to see me, I thought. Perhaps I'm humiliating myself for nothing, like Agnes says, and he knows I'm crawling around trying to find him. Perhaps he's ignoring me. Because if he wanted to see me, he only needed to step off that bus.

Then I found myself doing something I later considered both dumb and embarrassing. By five o'clock I was on the subway to Brooklyn, and in my bag there was a note I'd written hastily on my sketchpad. I looked so flustered, gigantic and red-faced that two people rose up simultaneously to offer me their seats. I got out at Atlantic Avenue and walked down to Ianucci's, panting in the humidity. I saw that the windows hadn't changed in the last ten years: still lifes of olive-oil cans, Amaretto boxes and cartwheel-shaped pasta. Inside, there were queues at all the counters. I asked at the checkout whether Mr or Mrs Ianucci was in. 'She's right there on the meat counter,' said the cashier.

Mrs Ianucci looked like someone had rented her for the day from a play about Italian mammas. She was short, dumpy and wearing a wrapover apron and a hassled look. 'Yeah, next,' she bawled. 'Naah, you gotta get a number from the machine first. Next, seventy-six.' I took a ticket and nervously joined the queue. Unexpectedly, Mrs Ianucci smiled upon my pregnant form, more out of commercial instinct, I felt, than natural goodwill. I ordered a few slices of Parma ham, and tried to speak while Mrs Ianucci was slicing. 'Um, I'm a friend of your son Leonardo, and I wonder if you could possible pass my phone number and address on to him. I've been trying to get in touch now he's back from Uganda. Is he living in Manhattan right now? You don't have his phone number, do you?'

Mrs Ianucci's suspicions shot across her eyes. She looked down at my belly and then at my face, pink with blushing and heat, and snatched the note with a greasy hand. 'He's not got a permanent place yet. Sure, I'll pass it on.' She dismissed me with a glance. 'Next, eighty-one.'

Old cow, I thought, as I walked out of the door. (This later proved a not unfair analysis.) The woman suspected, of course, that although the note only contained my name, address and phone number, the subtext of it was: 'I am pregnant with your child, call me.' It was the sort of note no self-respecting Catholic mother would pass on to her son. I knew as I walked down the subway steps that my note was already in the garbage among festering rinds of salami.

Chapter Twenty-Six

PLEASE POST TO: KIRSTY MCPHAIL,
38 NELSON STREET, LARGS, SCOTLAND

HM Prison Holloway

18 March 1912

Dear Kirsty,

My love, you must not worry about me because I am in perfectly good health and fairly good spirits, although I have only scratched out 18 days with a hairpin on my wall, and there are 24 more lines to cross out before I see you both. Time has almost stopped for me; the hours grind past in this cell, which manages to be damp and musty at once – I am so thankful that I was arrested in that ugly tweed walking suit which you loathe so much, else I would freeze with the excuse for a blanket they give you. Oh, but six weeks here are so different from one. Looking back on it, one week seems a lark, playing prison like playing house, whereas this is real, far too real for my liking, and a long time to be away from your family at His Majesty's pleasure. Worse still, they have tightened up the rules since I was in here last year, and the suffragettes are no longer treated like political prisoners and we have no chance to associate. Instead we are locked up almost all day but for exercise, thanks to that Mr Churchill poking his nose in. They say at least 200 of us were arrested over four days, so there is a great deal of shouting out of windows and banging on pipes and even singing, which keeps us going. (If I was the sort of person who had learned Morse code, which I am not, I would even understand the messages that are being tapped out on the piping.) I have asked without success for official permission to write, so I hope this letter will reach you by illegal means via one of the Scots girls who is leaving this week. Apparently, letter-writing has become a privilege that must be earned. The paper is exactly what you think it is, the only sort we have access to, but it folds small and is convenient for hiding in hems!

I know the union has contacted you with my whereabouts and sentence, but I must tell you the details of my arrest and the successes of our mass raid, which I hear about daily in the exercise yard. On the train from Glasgow I met up with all the usual crowd: Mrs Swann, you know the one who keeps the Reformer's Bookstall in Bothwell Street, Margaret and Frances McPhun, Mrs John, Helen Crawfurd, Miss Janet Barrowman and Mrs Wilson, and every one of them is now in the clanger here. We all had our stones, some with messages attached demanding the vote, and each her assigned target. We were excited and nervous like a bunch of giggling schoolgirls – well, it is not the sort of thing grown, sensible women normally do. Mrs Crawfurd was assigned to break the windows of the house owned by the minister for education, Mr Pease, in Harvard Street off Piccadilly, and disappeared first on Friday morning in a taxi with two stones in her handbag.

I was next with a group who were to attack
commercial property: the Lyons Tea Rooms, Swann
and Edgar, Marshall and Snelgrove, Hope Brothers and
all the rest. Three of us also took a taxi (oh, the
extravagance) over to Liberty's on Regent Street, and
stepped down, looking for all the world like ladies
doing a bit of window shopping. Then I opened my
bag and launched my stones, the two Isabel picked off
the beach, straight at the window. One bounced back,
plate glass being surprisingly hard and the other ladies
armed with hammers did more damage in a shorter time
(and got longer sentences for their pains), but I was
through with a second lob right in the middle of what I
must admit was a very nice Oriental carpet display.
Two London policemen, conveniently round the corner,
came running up, more surprised than anything else at
us in our gloves and hats. They arrested us, and we
strolled – there can be no other word for it – round to
Vine Street Police Office, where we waited and were
given tea until we were moved to Bow Street
Magistrates. By the time we got there, half the
suffragettes in London were packing the cells, and half
the shops and ministries in the city were missing their
windows, well, you will have read about that in the
papers and about Mrs Pankhurst and two others
breaking windows at Downing Street. Did they quote
what Mrs P said before we began? 'The argument of the
stone, that time-honoured political weapon, is the
argument I am going to use!' The glaziers must be
thanking her fervently. My cheerful, victorious mood
collapsed when I heard the length of my sentence
although I had no idea how lucky I was: the women

arrested on Monday were given far longer terms, some as much as six months as the magistrates became increasingly vexed with the numbers and tales of destruction. Damage over 5 pounds resulted in horribly long sentences. (Or perhaps the stiffer punishments were a political decision from higher up, who can say, since I hear they also stationed nine thousand police in Trafalgar Square on the 4th.)

We may not have newspapers, but the gossip in the exercise yard is of a fine quality, and more information comes in each day with more prisoners pouring out of the Black Maria. The hour marching round under those great grey walls seems to pass in a flash. Of course, we are not allowed to talk, according to the rules, but the wardresses are on the whole a fairly doltish lot and I think they are intimidated a wee bit by all these well-spoken ladies who do not hesitate to speak their minds. Secretly, I think some are also entertained by us and our antics, although others give some of the grand ladies an unnecessarily hard time, whereas my Glasgow accent protects me from the worst of their bigotry – and they do not understand half of what I say. The ordinary prisoners have been shuffled off to some other wing of the prison because the behaviour of the suffragettes was deemed to be 'demoralizing' for them.

Oh, Kirsty, I do miss you. After all, we have not been apart this long for two years. Look after yourself and eat properly, and try not to work obsessively night and day, because I want to see you in the best of health when I come home and we can all be together. Well, the menu here has changed little from last time, although I have seen both an onion and a carrot floating within a cup of something dire, which I suppose is better than no vegetables at all. The soup – or is it stew, nobody is quite sure – is almost as cold as the prison walls by the time it reaches our floor. Sometimes I find it hard to get down, but I do my best, and my skirt which was a bit tight round the waist, fits properly now. (A change of clothing would be most welcome, because we are all beginning to smell a wee bit unlady-like.) There is talk among some of the women about going on hunger strike next week, not because the food is so bad – it is hardly worth eating anyway in my opinion – but because we are now being denied the privileges we fought for to be treated as political prisoners under rule 243a (Mr Churchill's hand in this again). Well, I am all for that, and less terrified than some about the prospect, because my sentence is shorter. It is not the fasting that worries me (I shall certainly not be going on a thirst strike as some have done, not after you explained how medically dangerous it was, and I have been trying to encourage the others not to risk it either). No, it is the forcible feeding that sounds like the worst form of torture, and one of the more malignant wardresses said that they will bring over medical officers from the criminal lunatic department 'who are practised in the methods' to do it. Still, what will be will be, and none of this, however unpleasant, does anything but good for the Cause, which is all that matters. (Please keep this to yourself.)

By the time you get this, I shall be coming home in two weeks, and I can think of little else but getting off the train at Largs and seeing you and Isabel on the platform. Knowing you are there looking after Isabel (and no doubt her looking after you) gives me great courage. Dearest Kirsty, how I miss you.

　　All my love,
　　　Agnes

Chapter Twenty-Seven

8 July 2000

I woke at six in the morning for the third time that week. I'd been dreaming I was trapped in a dank, dark prison cell with a six-foot-tall baby wearing a diaper the size of a tablecloth. I was jittering with stress and hormones. Impending birth was bad enough – at least you could take drugs for that – but impending artistic birth at a downtown gallery was much more unpredictable. I was nervous, I was excited, I was nine months pregnant and I wanted a cigarette like nothing on earth. Instead I ate two Pop-Tarts in around ten seconds, which immediately gave me heartburn, so I glugged down half a bottle of Maalox as well. Thus fortified, I picked up the telephone. Wanda answered straight away.

'Hi, sorry to ring so early when you're just off the overnight plane, but I reckoned you wouldn't go back to bed.' I hedged. 'Good holiday? Shop opening go OK? Um, have you checked the answering-machine yet? I thought there might—'

'Be two messages for you from Leonardo Ianucci?' Wanda sighed. Lianne was wailing in the background. 'You want the number he left? He was asking where the hell you were.'

Trying not to scream with impatience, I took down Leonardo's new number in Brooklyn, checked it twice, and arranged to see Wanda, Nosmo and their entourage at my opening party at the SoHo Gallery the next night. I decently waited until nine o'clock to call Leonardo, but there was another man's voice on the machine and I felt a stab of disappointment. I left my own number, and an invitation to the opening.

My heartburn re-erupted, and I looked down malevolently at Thing. I didn't have to look far, since I could almost touch my nose on my enormous belly. Not only had Thing created a whole series of gastronomic and emotional problems, but it turned out there was a conspiracy to pretend pregnancy lasted nine months, when in fact it lasted ten. Forty whole godforsaken weeks was Thing's expected residency, if not longer. I wanted Thing out right then. I'd had it right up to here with strangers and friends treating me like a bouncy castle in public, and if my leg half dislocated again with the weight and mysterious 'pelvic expansion', I planned to limp directly to St Vincent's and demand an elective Caesarean.

As I was considering this option, the buzzer rang. It was my grandmother. 'Hold it there, Rose. I'm coming straight down,' I said, in the intercom. 'Let's go get some breakfast first. There's nothing whatsoever to eat up here.'

Rose was wearing her pink Reeboks again and a sleeveless sundress which displayed industrial-strength bra straps. It was 90 degrees, but even I thought this outfit was a bit excessive. On the other hand, Rose did seem light and youthful compared to my shuddering, exhausted bulk. All the way to the Moondance diner on Sixth, Rose lectured me about having an empty fridge and by implication an empty head and an empty life, and said she could not emphasize enough the importance of keeping the kitchen stocked and eating properly once I had a baby. I pointed out there were things so old in the fridge that they might eat me, and Rose didn't laugh.

In the cool diner, I had a whoosh of appetite, and ordered a triple stack of buttermilk pancakes with fresh strawberries and maple syrup, while Rose had a bagel and coffee. She'd arrived in town for the exhibition opening and 'to set things to rights', as she put it. She had plans to inspect Thing's equipment and clothing and, I hoped, to clean up the apartment, a task which was increasingly beyond me. I owed Rose. She was good to me and had offered to come by every day after I had the baby, to show me which end the food went in, etc. She was showing a great deal more interest than my mother, who was staying firmly and huffily in Florida, much to my relief.

'You know what I meant to ask you more about when we were in Macy's a few months ago?' I said. 'Meant to ask you about Agnes and Kirsty. I know that they shared a bed and everything in Largs, but I didn't definitely put it together until I got to that one-off letter written to Kirsty from prison that they were so, well, intimate. D'you think they were lesbians?'

Rose looked displeased by the last word. I can't see why, because she watches that 'I slept with my poodle before his sex-change' stuff on *Oprah* all day. She shook some Nutrasweet into her coffee and stirred it, playing for time. 'Well, not just because they shared a bed. Lots of women did that then, you know, and nothing shocking about it. Those flats weren't awfully big – you'd often get two or three weans sharing the bed recess in the kitchen.' Rose went off into hard-times reminiscence. I brought her back sharply to the point.

'Do you think it was the sort of romantic friendship that lots of women had back then, or something physical too? But they didn't seem to need to hide it. She's always writing about it.'

'Well, I've never really thought about it, dear. Now you mention it, my mother sometimes took me down to Largs on a Saturday, but my father was never keen to come. He went to the football instead usually. Gave men quite short shrift, so they did, gave all their time to doing stuff for other women, Auntie Kirsty out all the time nursing, Granny running her campaigns. Well, I'm no' sure, really.' The waitress came over with more coffee. I made Stonehenge with the sugar cubes and waited for Rose to roll on.

'I remember going to visit them a lot as a wee girl in the thirties, they both had bobbed hair and they were about fifty I would think. Granny wore these fusty long suits that looked as if they'd been left out in the rain, but Auntie Kirsty was dark and still elegant, a wee bit forbidding. They both smelled a bit of old dog. They'd a series of Labradors, nice black Labradors, which I used to love taking on the beach. At the end of the day, Granny would put her hand down the back of the settee and fish out a half-crown. 'For books, not sweeties,' she'd say, and I'd be too scared to disobey her. Place was full of books, awfully untidy. My mum's old room still had all that Votes for Women stuff on the wall, and it was her, my mum, who kept everything, all those funny bits of clothing to dress up in, and those letters she got off her cousin. Gave it all to me when she moved into that wee flat in Pollock.'

'But what do you *really* think about the two of them?' I said, down to my last pancake in the stack.

'I think,' said Rose, looking around as though she might be overheard, 'that they were very happy together, quite in love.' She stared at me as though something had dawned on her. 'You're very interested in them. You haven't . . .' She faded out.

'Seen her?'

'Ay, well, I didn't like to ask. So Agnes appeared again, did she?'

'What do you mean "again"?' I said, pouncing.

'Well, I saw her just after the war, a few years after she'd been killed in the Clydebank Blitz.' I was shocked. I hadn't thought about her being killed by a bomb. Like everyone else, I've eight great-great-grandmothers, and I didn't really know how any one of them had died. Rose was running on . . .

'I'd met your grandfather towards the end of the war. Chuck was posted to Glasgow with his regiment from America. We'd go dancing up Sauchiehall Street, and he looked . . . well, he looked brilliant, sharp, like all men do in uniform, and he had dollars coming out of his ears. It was only later I discovered he was a slob.' (Rose took my grandfather's death four years ago exceptionally well, considering, and had recovered herself very quickly.) 'Anyway, I was only twenty, and one night I got drunk, my first cocktails, they were, in a hotel, and we ended up at midnight in the Botanic Gardens, and the upshot of it all was I was in a family way. No' the done thing then.'

She sighed, and took off her bifocals.

'You don't mention a word of this to anyone, especially your mother.'

I nodded.

'Well, I liked Chuck, but I wasn't sure of him. Och, he was handsome, but I wasn't convinced he was that smart, and he'd gone off on exercises – maybe he'd gone off for ever, because the post was bad in the war – so I had time to think about what to do. Besides, I had a good job in the library. So I thought the best thing would be to get rid of the baby.'

I looked surprised. 'Oh, aye, you could have abortions then. There was a good, safe woman doctor just off the back of Byres Road, and she'd helped a few of my acquaintance. I was on my way to talk to the doctor, but I was early, so I went to sit in the Botanic Gardens. I was on a bench by the Kibble Palace, and I realized I recognized the woman sitting next to me. It was Agnes, looking as calm and ordinary as the day.'

'Weren't you terrified?'

'No, and I don't know why not. I suppose it was a relief to see her whole and normal, after she'd died in the bombing a few years before. And she just started, very quietly, to ask me questions about what I was doing, what I was about to do, and it pulled me up short. I never walked down the road to the doctor's. I ended up with a baby – and you,' she said, smiling at me, 'but I also ended up with, I think, the wrong man. Maybe we all did. Still . . .'

'This is familiar territory,' I said. 'Did she appear a lot?'

'No, just the once, and she sort of faded away after a few minutes. I was so amazed I wasn't sure what I was seeing, but it was the war and strange things happened to a lot of people. I wasn't the only one imagining a dead relative. It was after that I got her letters off my mother and read them.'

'Why did you dump them, and her, on me?'

'I couldn't say. Just a feeling that it was the right time, that the turn of the century is an odd, open moment, like a war, and that you needed something, someone, who wasn't part of this city and its craziness.'

Then Rose folded her arms and stared at me expectantly. I told her of Agnes's prolonged and persistent interference in my life, which had gone from being an irritation to a comfort.

'I admire her,' I said, ordering a third tea. 'I admire her bravery, her conviction, but I don't think she's always in the right.'

'*She* does, though, doesn't she?' said Rose, laughing.

'But what's she up to? I once asked her if she was the ghost of feminism past and she just laughed. But it strikes me now that she's more in the business of protecting her own DNA through the generations, while finding abortion perfectly acceptable in theory, but not in practice. There's no logic in it.'

'Why should there be? She's no oracle. She's flawed like you and me. I don't know, Albertine, but if it wasn't for her, you wouldn't be here, so just accept it. I suspect that wee thing in your stomach owes her one too.'

'Sort of,' I grunted.

The conversation had left me feeling kind of wobbly, and Rose evidently elated, perhaps pleased she wasn't the only nutcase that had been haunted. I got the check and we walked back across to Broome Street in silence. I had funny indigestion pains all across my stomach.

Back in the apartment, Rose started bustling around, opening drawers and cupboards, poking her nose into everything, astounded by my lack of sensible furniture and useful crockery. Insulted, I pointed out that I not only had a sofa now, but a Moses basket, and Lianne's big pram, since Wanda was using a collapsible stroller. In the bedroom area, I emptied a black sack of borrowed baby-clothes onto the bed, and Rose began to go through them. 'Too small, too large, too vulgar,' she declared (as if Rose would know vulgar if it bit her), and made mysterious piles.

'Hey, Thing'll wear anything, don't worry. No way is he going to be the sort of baby that gets a mint on his crib pillow every night.'

Rose shooed me away and I went to put my feet up in the armchair as instructed. A light was blinking on the answering-machine. It was a message from Leonardo, cheerfully, matter-of-factly, saying he'd be along tomorrow night. I was unnerved, suddenly, because I was going to see him. He still existed. And I was irritated that I'd missed speaking to him. I wanted to play the message again, just to hear his Brooklyn accent, his tone, but Rose's vigilant presence and the sound of sweeping forbade that. Instead I sat by the window and stared out through the heat haze over the greasy Hudson and down to the Statue of Liberty and pondered on the dog with the eyepatch and its owner with the eyepatch who had offered to help carry my laundry on a day as hot and stagnant as this one just about a year ago.

A series of violent punches inside, coupled with Thing bouncing cheerfully on his head woke me early again the next morning, 9 July, the day of the opening, and exactly one week until I was officially due to give birth. I crept out even before Rose had stirred on the sofabed. Picking up copies of all the newspapers and the three magazines published that day, I went into the diner. There had already been a preview for the gallery's private clients and the press, so the reviews were just starting to come out, and thankfully there weren't many openings mid-summer. The one in *Newsday* the day before had been pretty OK; nothing to write home about. I took a sip of coffee to increase my already racing heartbeat and opened *New York* magazine. I saw the word 'Confinement' in bold type near the end of the art column. 'Andrews renders the lividness of mid-Western flesh, with a touch of both Freuds. The triptych "9 months" is a meaty corrective to the usual ethereal images of pregnancy: here there are stomachs bursting with life and stretchmarks, legs patterned with varicose veins like Stilton. The work is brazen.' I grinned at my reflection in the window when I reached the end of the paragraph. I was mighty pleased. Everyone appeared to be taking me seriously, but I still wasn't sure if it was all just a joke.

The *Talk of the Town* magazine, who'd interviewed me on the telephone, trashed me. I was in their gossip section rather than the reviews: 'Miss Andrews, presently nine months pregnant herself, has taken self-indulgence and feminist cliché to new depths.' All the faintly intelligent remarks I'd made about the exhibition weren't used. The item ended with my (low) expectations of the viewer. 'All I want to say is: Have a look at this. What do you feel, what do you think? If people go "yuk" it's enough.' I groaned to myself. I should've known.

The tabloids were kinder. They were most entertained by the breast-milk fountain, and the perspex and chocolate women. Under a headline: 'Mama in Meltdown' one said: 'The sculpture's tactile, sickly sweet smelling, and you just want to take a bite. The whole crazy show brings on a mixture of greedy guilt and relish . . . This artist's future course is totally and wondrously unpredictable.'

'You said it,' I muttered happily, feeling a rush of confidence in myself as I gathered up my spoils and headed back to the apartment.

I spent the rest of the day rushing round tidying stuff, since being upright kept my growing collection of stomach disorders at bay. I put my paints and sketches in order for the first time in years, cleaned all my brushes, knives and palettes, and packed a bag for the hospital. At intervals I called Jim, the installation man at the gallery and my new friend, who with his act of kindness in moving my pictures to the forefront last January had changed my life. Jim said there'd been a problem with clogging in the tubes of the Dairy Queen twenty-four-hour breast fountain, which had been solved by thinning the yellowish milk with water. Jim wouldn't let me come down to the gallery. 'Everything's fine. I don't want you round here interfering. See you later.'

I dressed that evening with care in a green taffeta Empire-line dress with spaghetti straps, which made me look glamorous from the bust up, and like a fat fairy from below. Reckoning that my physical size precluded any attempt at dignity, I added orange high-heeled sandals and tied my hair up so I wouldn't look like a spag bol gone wild. Rose appeared, after a marathon session in the bathroom, in a sequinned outfit, which could only be described as *haute Dallas*. Then Garrett came upstairs in a linen suit and a tie. I'd no idea he possessed a tie. 'I wanted to look my best for the finest art fraud ever perpetuated,' he said, gallantly holding open the taxi door for me.

Over the door of the SoHo Gallery was a moving neon sign, which remained on all night. Shamelessly stealing from the Wicked Women exhibition, I too had installed an endless loop of words. In red there was, HOOTERS >>> GAZUNKAS >>> SNACK TRAYS >>> BOSOMS >>> BAZOOMS, followed in green by, CONFINEMENT >>> UP THE JUNCTION >>> IN A FAMILY WAY >>> PREGGERS >>> UP THE SPOUT >>> BUN IN THE OVEN >>>

'My advertisement,' I said, pointing up. Rose looked horrified. We were half an hour early. Inside, the gallery was empty but for Jim, the PR woman, and two gallery assistants in little black dresses who poured the wine. The PR handed me the discreet laminated price list, and I gasped, both at the numbers of zeros, and the red dots already against four items. Three were paintings and the fourth sale was '18. Cravings. Body sculpture in white chocolate, $15,000.' An advertising executive had bought it at the private viewing, with who knows what purpose in mind – dessert? I felt the whole evening was becoming suspiciously unreal. Jim led me over to the sculpture, which was lying in state as the centerpiece of the front room.

'This advertising guy didn't just buy it. He bought it damaged,' Jim whispered. 'Look.' Indeed, my big toe was missing, and there were bite marks in the chocolate where it had been. 'Somebody brought their kids early on the other night. I didn't notice till afterwards,' Jim shrugged. I giggled.

The cloying smell of chocolate and slightly sweet-tasting white wine made me want to gag. I hoped that only the pregnant would be affected in this way. I sat down on the edge of one of my exhibits – the upholstered chintz armchair with an integral nine-month belly covered in rust and blue roses – and came eye to eye with my painting: 'The Right to Choose'. This showed the Virgin Mary in conversation with a witchy woman offering herbal remedies for all ills. Its sister picture was the aforementioned 'Virgin Birth Without Epidural'. This showed the scene missing from classical art, that of the Virgin Mary actually giving birth, her blue robe flung back over her heaving stomach as she pushed and screamed on a pile of grubby bloodied straw, with Joseph nowhere to be seen. In an arch above I'd written: 'I am the Lord's servant,' said Mary, 'as you have spoken, so be it.' Luke 1: 26–28. You could wear headphones attached to the wall for an accompaniment of genuine birthing screams.

People had started to arrive: my old classmates from Parsons; Wanda and Nosmo with Lianne in a minimalist black dress and a fake-leopard stroller; Nancy and Joanie;

some art critics everyone recognized except me; three fashion designers and two gossip columnists. I kept looking round hoping for Leonardo, too. There were lot of screams of 'darling' and 'sweetheart', much kissing of both flesh and air, and I felt right in the center of things for perhaps the first time in my life. Everyone wanted to talk to me, meet me, congratulate me, and I didn't mind one bit if their praise was not entirely sincere. Ray Washing's wife Stella arrived with a white chocolate cake on two tiers with pillars, and I nearly cried. 'Actually, this *is* what you feel like on your wedding day,' said Nancy, looking at me glowing, drunk with it all. 'You are the focus of all attention, your jaw aches from smiling, you're wearing a silly costume, and you seem to float above it all. I guarantee you won't remember a thing tomorrow.'

'I feel,' I said, smiling, 'like a hot celebrity whale.'

Rose, horrified by the gruesome cast of trendies in the gallery, announced she was taking a taxi home. I saw her out. Then I wandered into the second room where the Perspex version of my body filled with pink baby junk was reclining on a platform, just as the chocolate version dominated the first. Nosmo was staring at 'Mom and Pop', a demure white nightgown with a few blond hairs on its chest (acquired from his very own curly head), which hung from a hanger from the ceiling and turned in the air.

'I could not be more proud, either of my contribution or of you,' he said, hugging me and gesturing over to the wall which displayed the only item with a double name credit: Nosmo King. There were his two butterfly cases filled with crack vials and Metropolitan museum badges, but above them I'd stuck another case full of plastic pacifiers and a sticker which said, 'Growing Up. (Not for Sale)'. We wandered back out into the crowd to find Ned, who was holding Lianne.

Then the small but perfectly formed critic from *ArtAche* magazine broke into the circle of people round me. He was wearing green-framed spectacles. 'Delighted, delighted to meet you. I noticed you first in the Wicked Women Show, but here I can really see how those images have been nourished by the intensity of your reaction, yet you have counterbalanced that by playing with the possibilities in a teasing manner.'

'Um, thanks,' I said, struggling for a straight face.

'Your work invites us to scrutinize an extreme form. Of course, it raises questions of whether artists today are to be judged primarily by what they do or what they say about what they are doing.'

At that moment, time stopped. The critic's face blurred into the sidelines, although his mouth continued moving, and the roar of the party became muted. There was suddenly a tunnel of empty air across the crowd, at the other end of which was a tanned man with sunglasses and a sinewy neck. He stood framed in the doorway, like some movie cowboy entering a bar. The blood thundered into my head. I stopped breathing. But he was *with* someone. With a pretty, Italian-looking plumpish woman. For a moment I thought I was seeing the ghost of Leonardo's wife, but more likely it was his new girlfriend. She, whoever she was, had the piebald dog on a lead.

'Oh, God,' I said aloud, and then I noticed the critic

staring at me. 'Sorry. What were you saying? I'm feeling a bit dizzy with the heat in here.'

'That your paintings demand a formidable commitment from the viewer because they push . . .' I could hear the critic speaking, but it made no sense. Leonardo was coming across the crowd with the woman.

'Hi. How *are* you? Where were you? It has been the longest time,' he said smiling, and reached over my enormous frontage to kiss me. He seemed thinner, more weathered. He looked down suddenly at the belly he'd been squashed against. I reckoned it felt more like a rock than a cushion. He seemed disconcerted by its hardness.

'And, um, this is my sister Gaetana, who I'm staying with right now.'

Relieved, I regained what remained of my poise, and shook her hand. Gaetana slid tactfully away to look round. Leonardo took his sunglasses off, and the sight of his birthmark made me long to touch it again. He kept staring at my belly. He obviously hadn't got my letters. 'Is that . . .? I mean, part of the show? It's not real this time, is it?'

I found myself blushing. 'Yes. It's really real. Too real for my liking. I'm due in a week.' I smiled, helpless.

His brow furrowed. I could see he was doing those simple subtractions in his head that men have done for centuries.

'Who . . .? It's not . . .?'

'Darling!' Zindsi Hawkes appeared, her purple lipstick bearing down on my cheek, her elbow pushing Leonardo to one side. 'I'm so pleased for you, honey. I always knew. Didn't I always say when I discovered her,

Jerry?' she said, turning to Jerry Argent, towering at her side in a fetching silver dress.

'Well, thank you both so much for coming,' I said, scrabbling for composure. 'I'll be back in a minute. I must just have a word with someone before he goes.'

I took Leonardo over to the bar table and got him some warm white wine.

'This isn't the place or the moment for it, I'm sorry, but yes, it's yours,' I said. He was completely silent, and all color and expression drained from his face. I kept going: 'I just couldn't get hold of you. I wasn't sure if . . . and I wrote to the wrong address. Um, oh God, shall I meet you afterwards in about an hour and we can talk?'

His eyes grew black and wide open. His hands went to his head. 'Oh, Jesus, Albertine. You sure? You sure you're sure?' I nodded. 'I haven't had sex with anyone for nine months.' Flippancy was the wrong move in the situation.

'Why the fuck didn't you tell me before? Why the hell . . .?'

I was ready to cry. I started to overheat, and the walls lurched, as though I were on a boat. Nancy, appearing suddenly, took one look at the angry Leonardo, another at me and dragged me off to the washroom. She shut the door and made me sit down on a chair.

'That was Him, wasn't it?' said Nancy. 'You told him. Ohmigod. You went completely pale. Drink some water. Here. Breathe slowly.'

Moments later, I had an enormous urge to pee. I rushed into the cubicle. Warm liquid started pouring down my bare legs and onto my shoes before I even sat down. I started to panic and then began to howl. Nancy took in the situation and calmly handed me a towel and started mopping up with another. 'I reckon your waters have broken. This is not normal, this. Just sit where you are and I'll sort you out and then I'll get Wanda.'

I gripped my knees against the pain, as the contractions hammered in a minute later, and sobbed staring at the dirty grouting between the white tiles on the floor.

Outside, she told me later, Wanda had propped up the other casualty who was gibbering, 'But why didn't she tell me? She could have got hold of me. She could have written or called the fucking TV company or someone. I was only editing in Atlanta for Chrissake. I mean, we only . . . How was I to know? Didn't she want me to . . .?'

Wanda had taken the glass from Leonardo's shaking hand and refilled it with wine.

'Now, calm down. This is not a disaster, whichever way you look at it.'

'Yeah, but I'm still in shock. You're sure—'

'Wasn't anyone else, unless it's a virgin birth,' Wanda had said, beginning to enjoy the drama. Then Nancy had pulled her away, leaving Leonardo half-way through another question. He'd drunk a third glass of wine in one gulp and had wondered aloud if he was hallucinating the giant white chocolate Albertine lying before him on a pedestal, heavily pregnant.

He was apparently on his fourth drink five minutes later when Wanda had returned. 'Nancy and Albertine are leaving by the back door to get a taxi to the hospital.'

'What hospital? Why?'

'Her waters just broke in the bathroom. She's started

having contractions. You want to speak to her back there before they go?'

Leonardo's hand had come up ready to cross himself, a gesture he hadn't employed since he was twelve.

'Oh, Holy Mother of God,' he'd said, and followed Wanda out.

Chapter Twenty-Eight

Nelson Street, Largs

5 May 1912

Dear Ishbel,

How happy I am that you will be coming home for ever in September. Delhi is not the place to bring up weans and I can hardly wait to talk to you face to face after all these years. Your letter was one delight on my return from prison. The other was stepping off the train on the platform at Largs and seeing two figures at the gate – Kirsty tall and dark in her new pale grey coat, and Isabel beside her in her school uniform. They were holding hands and had matching frowns, and they did not recognize me until I was almost upon them, and then I was engulfed in smiles and hugs. I had lost my hat somehow during the arrest, and had lost a good few pounds too, so in a way they were expecting someone else.

I do feel I am someone else now, or at least changed utterly by all I have been through – several of the other suffragettes who had long sentences and were forcibly fed say the same thing. I have had a lot of time to think, Ishbel, six weeks of it, the last two in solitary confinement in a hospital cell. At one point, bored to near madness, I wrote my autobiography in my head, as though I were some politician or great man or woman.

I went right through my life, from my first memories of falling out of my pram up until the present day, every happiness, every sadness, every mistake. Now I know that the greatest error I ever made, for him and me, was marrying Duncan, but then I would be without Isabel, who is dearest to me in the world. Yet I wish I had been the woman Duncan thought he was marrying at the time, and not the woman I turned out to be. Duncan was such a good, kind man, and he tried his best to be tolerant of my politics and generally unlady-like behaviour, and I only repaid him with more troubles. It must have been like bringing up an extra wayward daughter for him. How I wish I had paid more attention to his health, for things might not be as they are now, and a burden of guilt lies with me for ever for that. I cannot turn to God now for forgiveness; He is another loss for me along the way.

Still, marriage stunted me with its conventions, and I am glad to have it behind me. I know now I am doing the right thing, but there were times in Holloway after the wardress turned off the gaslight from outside the cell, and left me in darkness for many hours before sleep, that I thought I could not hold on any more.

I stopped eating two weeks before the end of my sentence (I was less courageous than those who had months to go). I thought this would be no great hardship, since the greasy, lumpy food was disagreeing with me anyway, but I had not reckoned on the prison authorities suddenly finding fruit and freshly baked rolls in the building. These were placed in my cell, and for the first day or so, I had to imagine the basket was made of plaster to keep my hands off it. Yet being hungry is not painful, merely irritating, my stomach gurgling and constantly interrupting my thoughts. By the second day, I began to feel light-headed, and by the third, everything had become rather dream-like. I was cold and shivery and I felt no desire ever to eat again.

The prison doctor arrived and took my pulse and examined me, and told me I must start eating, or they would commence forcible feeding on the morrow. I refused, and spent half the night pacing my cell, five steps up, turn, five steps down, faint and terrified out of my wits. It is one thing making a political commitment, but quite another to physically, very physically, carry it through. I looked at the apple in the basket in the cell the way Eve must have looked at hers: one bite and everything would change. By morning I was in such a paddy that it was almost a relief when four galumphing wardresses and another doctor arrived, carrying various clamps, a tin funnel, what looked like a pail of milk, and two yards of red rubber tubing.

I never thought I would put up much of a fight, but somehow the banality of the equipment frightened me so that I shot into the corner of the cell and lashed out at anyone who touched me. Two of the muscled wardresses dragged me over to the bed – I was not exactly in fighting condition – and one sat on my feet, while the other held down my shoulders. Then they did a curious thing, they wrapped me in a white sheet, like swaddling, like a shroud, so I could not move. I shut my eyes, but the doctor was trying to shove a sharp metal clamp in my mouth. I tasted blood as it cut into my gums as he tried to get a grip and gagged on my own saliva. Then more horribly, the clamp began to push my jaws slowly apart, so they were held in a frozen scream. The pain was unbearable, and all through my back and chest from the tension and the fear. I thought I heard one of the wardresses laugh, and the humiliation, the helplessness was awful. With me coughing and spluttering, they shoved inches and inches of the rubber tube into my throat. I gagged and gagged. I shut my eyes again but I could feel it ripping down the passage to my stomach, and suddenly there was something cold down there, the milk or whatever. I could not taste it, only feel its cold against the pain, which seemed to last for ever. Then they unscrewed the vile contraption from my mouth and it was over. They left, and I lay shivering and crying on the hospital mattress, holding my pillow, curled up like a miserable child.

It did not get any better, but I learned not to fight the actual putting in of the clamp, and managed to keep my mouth from becoming completely cut and ragged. I still have yellowing bruises on my back from being held down, and I cannot forget the two weeks of constant, unreasonable chest pain. But in the end what was worst, I decided, was not the forcible feeding itself, but waiting for them to arrive, not knowing whether it would be morning or afternoon, and hearing the screams and struggles of others in cells along the corridor, getting nearer each time. Some women tried to barricade their cells up, so terrified were they. Soon, I learned to shut off my mind, to concentrate hard on something else while the indignities were happening to my body. Often, I thought of the salmon trying to leap the beautiful falls at New Lanark, where Kirsty and I had gone last year, thinking about them trying and trying again until they succeeded. What brought this to mind was a remark Mrs Crawfurd, another suffragette, made in a speech about the struggle for emancipation.

'When I think about us, us pioneers, I think too of those virile fish,' she said. 'The salmon that fight their way against the current of the river, taking the leap up over the falls, their bodies bristling with life, their scales shining, while the spray falls from their backs like showers of diamonds glittering in the sunshine. They make this supreme effort again and again after their long and laborious fight against the stream, to reach the spawning bed and fulfil their destiny. What we do is no different.'

So there you have it. No surrender. I am as well as can be and rested now, although still being treated like a queen by Isabel and Kirsty. I look forward, more than anything, to the end of talking to you on paper, and the beginning of talking to you in real life,

With all my love,
    Your affectionate sister,
    Agnes

Chapter Twenty-Nine

9 July 2000

'OK guys, we gotta woman in labor coming in. Main camera on the entrance, auxiliary cover the corridor down to maternity. Roll.'

Nancy and I emerged from the taxi into a blaze of arc lights. Immediately I had a contraction and gripped the cab door for support. The crew filmed me leaning over from behind (the orange high-heels and green dress won a thumbs-up afterwards from the director to the cameraman). I was dying from pain and humiliation. Leonardo was paying the driver.

'What the hell's this?' he said, as he got out.

'Let's just get in there,' said Nancy.

The TV camera zoomed in for a close-up on my mascara, which had run around my eyes. My hair had escaped and this, coupled with regular grunts, gave me the demeanor of a cave woman. Another cameraman ran backwards along the corridor filming the three of us walking. At the elevator, a woman with a clipboard came up. Nancy started trying to register me for birth at St Vincent's, but the woman stopped her.

'No, no, I don't work for the hospital. I'm Cindy, the producer for *Emergency Live*, and we're filming at St Vincent's tonight.' She turned her smile upon Leonardo, while I began another contraction holding the wall. 'Are you the lucky father, sir?'

'Um, I think so.'

The producer looked a little puzzled. Leonardo looked like he might punch her. She continued, oblivious, 'Well, if you would like to be part of this week's series, we can have you sign a release, and we'd really love to follow this wonderful event the whole way to the birth. Obviously, there's a fee for you and your wife. Can I take your name?'

'No. Just get outta my sight.'

Like a pointer dog on a fresh scent, the crew immediately turned away from me to film a whimpering man rolling into Emergency on a gurney. 'Riddled,' the paramedic was saying dramatically to the nurse on reception, knowing he was on film. 'At least four holes in him. Gonna need a lotta blood.' He parked the gurney cheerfully in a corner and went over to the coffee machine. The injured man continued to groan.

Leonardo pushed Nancy and me into the elevator, and we emerged into a scene no less disturbing eight floors up. Gross, grumpy women in blue paper shifts and furry slippers were marching the long corridor, pausing now and then to lean against a wall or a husband and moan horribly. In their uniform blue, their faces worn to gray, their hair sweaty and bedraggled, they looked just like prisoners walking round an exercise yard, I thought, in a calm moment between contractions. Then I dug my nails into Leonardo's arm, which I found I was holding. Extreme pain wipes away any sense of embarrassment. Someone had filled my belly up with bricks and now they were slowly tightening an enormous belt round my middle. Each contraction rippled like steady blows from a jackhammer inside. I clenched my teeth and made a noise more usually heard in wildlife documentaries. 'Sounds worse,' said Nancy, staring at the red claw marks appearing on Leonardo's tan skin. 'Looks worse. Let's find a nurse.'

There was no nurse. Instead a woman who was half midwife, half werewolf appeared. She had huge teeth and hairy arms. She took me off, staggering on my stilettos, for a preliminary examination and told Nancy and Leonardo to sit in the waiting room next door.

'Now let's have you out of that ridiculous dress and up on the bed. Where's your overnight bag?' I gasped helplessly in mid-contraction. 'Well, put on one of these,' said the midwife, handing me a blue paper gown. 'I'll be back in a minute.' She went out of the other door. I lay lowing on the bed. I could see Nancy and Leonardo moving and talking through the half-open door, but I don't think they knew I was listening between contractions.

It was ten thirty p.m. The waiting room was lit like midday with fluorescent lights over the orange plastic chairs. Leonardo opened a window and hung his head out into the hot darkness so he could smoke a cigarette without setting off the alarm. He exhaled in long sighs. Nancy pretended to read an ancient copy of *Parent* magazine. Leonardo stubbed out his cigarette and ducked in the window. He sat down with his head in his hands and then looked up at Nancy. His eyes seemed watery and he looked green under his tan.

'D'you think she's all right? Do you think she knows what she's doing? Has she gone to those classes or whatever you have to do? I mean, I have no idea what's supposed to go on. This has never happened to me before. What do you think I, we . . .'

'She'll be fine. She's read all the books and, well, she walked out of the pre-natal class because it was too touchy-feely, and everyone else had a partner.' Nancy realized what she'd said. 'Um, still, people do this naturally all the time you know.'

Next door, I thought about shouting out to them, but I was poleaxed by another contraction. I reckoned they were coming every three or four minutes.

Meanwhile Leonardo was pursuing the question of why I'd left it so late to inform him of his impending fatherhood. I wanted to shout out 'incompetence', but I wasn't convinced that was true.

'Maybe she wasn't sure you wanted to know,' said Nancy, shrugging. 'I dunno. Ask her, but perhaps not tonight.' She sounded irritated by his frowns and pained expression. 'Look, it's not you that's in labor, and there are a lot of people out there who don't ever manage to conceive. You've been lucky. It's not a problem. You should be ecstatic, supportive, or something.'

He was silent, and then his head vanished out of the window for another cigarette. Three minutes and one bloodcurdling contraction later, he reappeared, muttering, 'You're right. I can't go away now, but you know I'm panicking, I'm half in shock.' He paused and said, 'I suppose it would be even worse *not* being here.'

Obviously, by this point I was feeling truly crapulous, because the-father-of-the-child wasn't even sure he wanted to be here for its birth, or whether he wanted the baby at all. Meanwhile I was gripped with terror and uncivilized amounts of pain, and added emotional drama was the last thing I needed.

The wolfish midwife returned and started examining me. 'Wonderful. You're fully effaced and four centimeters dilated. You've probably been in latent labor all day and not noticed it. Now, let's get you into the labor ward.' She went out and called Leonardo.

'Mr Andrews?'

'Mr Ianucci,' he said, stonily.

'Whatever,' said the midwife. 'If you could take your *partner* along to labor room G down there and get comfortable, I'll be down in a minute.' I suddenly roared like an injured bull elephant. The midwife looked irritated. 'Now, we save that sort of sound for when we're pushing, er, Albertine,' she said, looking at her notes. 'Just breathe over the sensation. The pain will go away if you relax.'

'When do I get an epidural?' I grunted.

'Now, honey, you're so far along I think we could get you through a drug-free birth, a natural birth, and then you'd be really proud. It's only a few hours more.' She slapped me on the back, bared her snaggly teeth, and walked briskly off. I couldn't believe it.

The three of us regrouped in the labor room, which contained a high bed, a beanbag on the floor, and lots of flickering screens and machines. Nancy and Leonardo sat on either side, impotently watching me coil up every few minutes in pain. He put off some of the lights, so we didn't feel like we were under interrogation.

'Bag,' I panted. 'It's got my big T-shirt and juice and the birth book and the baby clothes in it at home.' Leonardo offered to fetch it, but I glued him to the floor with a stare. Nancy looked relieved and sloped off with my keys.

For the first time that evening, we were alone. I looked hungrily at his face blurred by time, remapping it: the sharp bones, the Roman nose. His hair was longer, unkempt, and he kept pushing back a black lock that hung over his eyes. His blue cotton shirt was rumpled and his skin smelled hot and dusty. I still wanted him. Nothing had changed. Whether he wanted me – a great, white, birthing, screaming hippo – was a question I did not wish to address at that moment. I felt embarrassed, as though a complete stranger, which is almost what he was, had invaded my life at the most inopportune moment. It was somehow incidental that he was the father. Leonardo took my hand in long fingers, and stared, saying nothing. In the silence, I watched three minutes pass on the red digital clock of one of the machines. He felt the next contraction grow as I crushed his fingers. Then I became almost normal again.

I blabbered into the silence, 'Funny thing is, there's no pain between them. I feel perfectly all right and then suddenly it's like Jekyll and Hyde, I turn into this yelling monster. Weird.'

Leonardo, never a man of many words, was watching my belly, which had escaped out of the paper gown I had on back to front. His other hand went out, seeming of its own volition, and rested on it just as the muscles tightened up for another contraction and became rock hard as I ululated unpleasantly, and then slowly soft again. He put both hands on, and underneath the skin he felt a bump suddenly pushing him.

'That's a foot, I think,' I said, half smiling. Leonardo crumpled on the bed beside me.

'Shit,' he said, amazed and probably horrified.

Stiffly he wrapped his arms round me: because he ought to, or because he wanted to? I wasn't sure then. We lay together uncomfortably on the narrow bed staring at the ceiling. 'I can't believe it,' he whispered, mostly to himself. 'I can't believe this has happened to me.'

'What about me?' I felt like saying. 'I'm going to have to look after it,' but instead I inadvertently shouted, 'FUCK. FUCK-FUCK-FUCK,' ripping the calm apart and doubling up with the agony. 'It's getting worse. My back hurts. I can't do this any more. CAN'T DO IT. CAN'T FUCKING DO IT.'

In the next few minutes of sanity, we agreed I should get an epidural before my vocabulary of swear-words ran out. Leonardo went to look for the midwife-from-hell. Turned out she was busy watching *Cooking with the Saints* in the glass-walled nurses' station. She came in and her hairy hands started strapping a belt round my stomach attached to an electronic monitor, which showed the baby's heartbeat, steady in between contractions, then rocketing up in enormous zigzags as I screamed. She took a look inside. Leonardo looked away. 'Still four centimeters. You're doing well. Keep going.'

'I need to have an epidural immediately,' I groaned, grinding my teeth. 'I can't stand this shit any more.'

'Did you put down for an epidural on your birth plan, and check with your insurance?' asked the midwife.

'No. What fucking birth plan?'

'Language, please,' she said, looking all pious. 'The one you made at your last childbirth class and sent here.'

'Never did that. Oh God, it's coming again.' I started crying. 'I WISH I WAS DEAD, I WOULD RATHER BE DEAD.'

Meanwhile, the midwife was observing to Leonardo that really she thought an epidural was not required here, and the hospital had to be careful because my limited medical insurance did not cover unnecessary expenses. Would I like some aromatherapy to help me feel more calm and peaceful?

I snarled, 'Do you offer aromafuckingtherapy to some prisoner in Iran who's having his hand chopped off by the state? Do they say, "Hey, smell a little lavender oil, it's really healing," as he stands there with his stump? Well, that's what it feels like. I need drugs, any drugs, now.'

The midwife looked pretty pissed. 'I've got ten other patients to see to, and I think you can manage perfectly well.' She suggested in a deadly calm voice that I coped with the 'increasingly strong sensations' by walking round the room or leaning over the beanbag. It was then that I lost control and rolled on the bed weeping. Leonardo followed the midwife to the door and pushed his face close into hers. She jumped back, scared by his birthmarked eye. 'Get this,' he said. 'If there isn't an anesthetist here with an epidural within a quarter of an hour, I will go get the *Emergency Live* crew from downstairs and have them film every word of this shit. She does not want your natural birth. She asked for an epidural, and you better get one or there will be a camera right in your face. I want to talk to the doctor on duty here, now.'

'Just you do that, then,' snapped the midwife, and stormed off down the corridor. Leonardo went after her. 'I'll see what I can do. I'll be back soon.'

I was suddenly terrified at being alone with the flickering, death-registering machines, and the mind-blacking pain. It was at that U-bend moment that Agnes made her final and most useful appearance, marching in the swing door all brisk, efficient and nurselike, her white blouse sleeves rolled up to reveal arms like sticks.

'No need for such a paddy. Now let's get you sorted. Here, sit up and put these pillows behind you. I'll just rub your back here, and you push down.'

Her hands were cool and calming, and only then I realized she was actually touching me. The ghost had become flesh in the madness of childbirth. I had barely time to think about that because it felt like the baby was tunneling out the back of my spine, headbutting its way through the bone. But Agnes repelled some of the agony by her very presence: she seemed so competent, and her bossiness was for once reassuring. Without blind panic, the pain didn't seem so bad. 'Remember, it goes away. You just have to make it through the peak of each one, and you can relax. I didn't live with a midwife for all those years without learning something.'

Between contractions I tried to talk to her about her life, and her interference in mine. I asked Agnes why she appeared in the first place to Rose and me. She was, as usual, enigmatic and unhelpful. 'Well, it's obvious, isn't it? You needed me. And when you don't, I'll be gone. It's that simple, dear. There's got to be room in people's lives, time, an open space, before the likes of me are drawn in.'

Another contraction walloped and my face screwed up with the effort of not screaming. Agnes looked thoughtful. 'Imagine each time that you're a salmon trying to leap up a waterfall, struggling again and again, more and more exhausted until suddenly you're over the top, you're there, you've done it.'

'I'm not a fucking fish,' I said, exasperated.

'Hmmn,' said Agnes. 'I take your point.'

Then she gave up talking and for about ten minutes she just held me, the body that held her great-great-great-grandchild, and rocked me through each contraction.

I heard sounds in the corridor. 'Someone's coming.'

'I know. You're all right now. The baby'll come out fine.'

She paused, a little uncomfortable for once. 'I just want you to know that I have, against all expectations, grown quite fond of you, and what you do.'

'Me too.' I knew she was saying goodbye. I held onto her hand, pleading with my eyes, but she pulled away. As she turned, I saw she was still smiling. Then she walked out of the door as Leonardo came in to replace her, in many senses.

I was still crying, not from pain now but from loss. I suppose it looked the same to him. He stroked my forehead.

'Oh, honey,' he said, looking at my pain-squashed face. 'I'm sorry I took so long. Had to track down the anesthetist. You're next in line.'

I felt drugged already with relief.

Leonardo stared at me. 'Who were you talking to just then?'

'Nobody. Nobody's come in.'

'Hallucinating, then?'

'Probably.'

He persisted, 'You know, we filmed these tribal women giving birth in Uganda. They dream, and hallucinate, and take weird medicines during birth, and scream and shout at all their ancestors.'

'Yeah, well, it was something like that.'

Just then Nancy walked in with the overnight bag, nodded to Leonardo, and gave me a carton of orange juice with a straw. It was midnight. I changed into my long EXISTMYFUTURE398MODERN T-shirt, and felt better. Nancy got out *Childbirth the Easy Way*, and flicked to the relevant section. 'Coping with Labor'.

She read out: 'Although the curse of Eve in Genesis 3:16 says, "I will greatly increase your pains in childbirth; with pain you will give birth to children," we have found that with total relaxation, pain diminishes to mere sensation. The uterine muscles in fact have few pain receptors, and if the mother gives herself up fully to the—'

'SHUT UP,' I bellowed, now on all four over the beanbag. Leonardo came over and held my shoulders. 'Don't touch me. I HATE YOU. THIS IS ALL YOUR FAULT.'

Leonardo stood looking shocked. As the pain subsided I became perfectly cheerful and amnesiac. 'Phew,' I said. 'Why're you looking at me like that?' Nancy read from the birth book: ' "As the contractions become more intense, the mother may abuse her partner, attribute blame to him, and perhaps even swear. This should be expected, and should not be a cause for worry." There. You're a textbook case.'

Leonardo and I both turned round and stared at Nancy as though she were a cockroach.

'I'm sorry,' she said. 'I don't know what to do in these situations. I only do irony. I'm not so good on comfort.' She slid quietly out of the door and said she'd be having a nap on the sofa in the waiting room if anyone needed her.

Leonardo got down on the floor to hold me. I went on rocking on my hands and knees, while the industrial chainsaw cut through my middle. I pointed out from time to time that dying in childbirth was not a bad idea. Then came a messenger from God. A small, red-haired woman appeared at the door. 'Shift change,' she said, in an Irish accent. 'I'm Kathy. You're wanting an epidural? I'll just take your blood pressure and they'll be in in a minute.' She examined me, and said cheerfully, 'Oh, you haven't dilated at all. You're still four centimeters. It's a back labor. Your baby's head is hitting your spine instead of going down. No wonder you've been complaining. You'll need the epidural to relax it.'

I wanted to kiss the replacement midwife. She ordered Leonardo out for a coffee – he looked like he needed an epidural too – and turned me on my side and plunged a drip into my hand. Then a man came in and stuck a large needle followed by a thin tube in my back, a painful sensation which at last I experienced as pleasure, waiting for the drug to kick in.

Leonardo returned with two pastrami on rye, grapes, designer water and various muffins from an all-night deli. The very thought of food made me shudder. But then the curves of pain flattened out, until I could see but no longer feel the contractions. My madness went and I breathed calmly, luxuriating in the feeling of nothingness below my waist. The midwife turned the lights down, and left us alone for a good while.

Leonardo drank his coffee and poured me water, the relief showing on his face. 'I couldn't stand it when you were screaming. I felt so helpless. I didn't know what to do.'

In the lull and the half darkness, we tried to fill in the missing parts of the last nine months, the comedy of errors. My letters were, no doubt, still sitting poste restante at the wrong address in Uganda. Leonardo asked me why I didn't think of contacting National Geographic TV or his family.

'Well, I faxed them, but nothing happened. And I did go to the deli in Brooklyn and leave my address with your mother.'

'But she never . . . Typical. When I see her I'll—'

'Never mind,' I said. 'You would've known what was going on if you'd got off that bus on Sixth Avenue. But you didn't. Did you?' I sounded bitter.

Leonardo pointed out at that stage that as far as he knew I'd neither answered his cards nor his phone call. What was more, I was obviously going off the rails, still wandering around Manhattan with a cushion stuffed up my dress. It turned out he'd been on the bus going to an interview at CBS television for a job directing a series on the life of the world's largest garbage dump on Staten Island. He'd got the job. 'They took one look and they just knew I was the kind of guy who'd want to spend all July and August surrounded by rotting junk.'

'So you'll be around for a while,' I ventured.

'I'll be around for as long as you need me. If you want me.' He raised his eyebrows, questioning.

I felt a huge rush of relief, a melting. I looked at him, into the shadows of his eyes, and we connected up. I didn't need to answer. My skin was paper thin, all the emotions showing through like veins. He held me, weaving his fingers in my hair, and for minutes the room was silent but for the beeps from the fetal monitor.

'What I can't imagine,' started Leonardo, hesitantly, 'is *not* being there for my child, not being there while he or she grows up. And that's as far as I've thought.' He looked me in the eye and quickly looked down again. 'I've been thinking a lot about such things, not intentionally but generally. I sort of gestated in a different way, that's all. I had a hundred insomniac nights alone in strange houses and tents, listening to the sounds in darkness of the bush and wondering what the hell I was doing with my life. But you've simplified that . . .'

'Maybe.'

The steady bleep of the fetal monitor burst into one long beep, and a flat, dead line emerged from the print-out. 'Get the midwife,' I said, panicking. Leonardo ran out.

The midwife appeared in seconds and felt my belly. 'Nothing to worry about. Belt's slipped and lost contact. The baby's just fine.'

Leonardo ostentatiously read the birth book while the midwife examined me and said I was almost fully dilated. 'We'll let the epidural wear off a tiny bit so you can feel to push.'

I was horrified. 'Don't worry, it won't be anything like the pains you had before,' said the midwife.

For distraction, Leonardo started reading aloud from the more ridiculous pages. 'Here. This you'll like: a quotation from some nineteen-twenties obstetrician, Dr Joseph DeLee: "I have often wondered," he says, "whether nature did not deliberately intend women to be used up in the process of reproduction, in a manner analogous to that of the salmon, which dies after spawning." Nice man.'

I hoped Agnes was listening. Leonardo nervously started to eat his pastrami sandwich, and then mine. He also opened a beer. 'Not sure if I can deal with the F-word stone cold sober at two in the morning.'

'F-word?'

'Father.'

I grinned. 'What, as a father-to-be, would you like to call your child?'

'Oh. I've always thought I'd call 'em after a president – Jackson, Franklin or Nixon if it's a boy, Madison, if it's a girl. I'm kind of serious apart from the Nixon.'

'Jackson,' I said, only half surprised. 'Funny. I thought about that too. I dreamed it. Months ago.'

I started to feel a tiny pocket of pain on my left side, sample-sized pain compared to the full-scale model earlier. The midwife made me push every time the pain peaked.

'I hardly know you,' I said abruptly to Leonardo. The midwife's eyes bulged with astonishment.

'I hardly know *you*.' He shrugged. 'It doesn't matter.'

The pain worsened again. A vice was being opened inside me. 'But I'm about to give birth to a thing that stays up all night, has disgusting things pour out of either end, and in general is known to make people's lives hideous.'

'I know. I'm very pleased about that. Hold on, not long now.'

I went red in the face with the effort of pushing. My hair turned into ringlets of sweat. Leonardo held me tight. I growled and pushed again.

The midwife pulled my hand down and told me to feel. There was something warm, wet and oddly soft barely bulging out. 'It's the top of the baby's head. It's there. Now push.'

At the peak of the next contraction, I felt a strange pop and release. I pushed once more and felt a rush as something flowed out. There was a small shout, which grew more abusive by the second. The midwife held up a furious red being with a scrunched face, its knees pulled up, its skin covered in mozzarella, the purple and white cord like spaghetti. An Italian baby, with dark hair. The baby held its arms wide open in a gesture somewhere between freefall and welcome.

The midwife slid the hot, slippery little body up onto my skin, and it rested its head on my breast. The baby stopped crying in order to size me up. We stared at each other, wide-eyed. Its breath smelled like cream.

'Hello,' I said softly, too surprised to cry myself.

We'd forgotten something. I lifted the baby up. It fitted neatly into my palms.

'It seems to be a boy.'

In fact he looked like a little wizened politician with

too many years on the road. He'd wet hair and a squashed nose. Round his eye there was a tiny patch of raised purply-red skin.

I kissed him there, on his birthmark.

I handed the baby to his father. The baby studied him seriously. Leonardo smiled back in astonishment.

'Mine,' he said.

'Yours.'

Epilogue

Albertine Andrews married Leonardo Ianucci on 1 May 2001. They have two children, Jackson and Madison, and divide their time between a duplex on the Upper West Side and a house in the Berkshires. Albertine is the art director of *Brides and Setting Up Home* magazine. Leonardo is an executive at CBS television.

Agnes McPhail was imprisoned three further times in support of the suffrage cause. She campaigned until the WSPU suspended political action at the start of the First World War, and then became a manager in a Glasgow munitions factory. Kirsty McPhail worked as nurse in mobile military hospitals in Calais and later Serbia. After the war, they returned to live together in Largs. In 1922, four years after women were given the vote, Agnes became the first woman councillor for Largs. She was killed during the Clydebank blitz in 1941, when a bomb hit the Scottish Women's Trade Union branch as she was attending a meeting. Kirsty died nine days later of a heart-attack while walking her dog on the beach at Largs.

Notes and Acknowledgements

The character of Agnes McPhail is based in part on the Scottish suffragette Helen Crawfurd, whose unpublished memoirs were kindly made available by the Marx Memorial Library in London. I would also like to thank the librarians of the Glasgow Room at the Mitchell Library in Scotland for their help in research, my parents in Glasgow, and my late father-in-law, Angus Macintyre, for writing a brilliant suffragette history reading list over bagels on the Greenport–Connecticut ferry.

Gill Coleridge, my agent, bravely took on an author with half a half-cocked manuscript, and worked tirelessly to make it whole. At Macmillan, Suzanne Baboneau's sensitive editing has been a pleasure. My husband, Ben Macintyre, went above and beyond the call of duty in his courageous edits of this book. I thank him for that, and everything else.